Praise for
GRASSHAN

"*Grasshands* fulfills the promise of the term 'mindbending' in ways drugs never could. Prose and dialog that are effortlessly engaging, horror that builds in an almost absurdist fashion making the dread that much more effective when it drops. And oh, how it drops. More than the sum of its parts—and damn, those parts are impressive on their own—*Grasshands* is a vehicle for experiencing the human condition, the ultimate drive for horror. I'll be thinking about it for a long, long time." — Laurel Hightower, author of *Below* and *Crossroads*

"In his novel *Grasshands*, Kyle Winkler once again renders the deeply familiar pervasively uncomfortable. I find no place to rest in his work, where time keeps shifting, good and evil constantly switch positions like mobile surfaces on a semantic Rubik's cube, and the nostalgia of beloved fairy tales clashes with the modern reality of bills, eviction, imperfect love, and existential uncertainty. *Grasshands* is both mournful and hopeful, passionate and disappointed; a gorgeous romp through the conflicted folklore of our everyday lives." — Joe Koch, author of *The Wingspan of Severed Hands* and *Convulsive*

"*Grasshands* is an enchanting and lovely dark fantasy novel, with echoes of Bradbury, Jackson, and Gaiman—yet its own, startlingly original creation. Kyle Winkler is a distinctive and inventive young writer with an exciting future ahead of him." — Dan Chaon, author of *Sleepwalk*

"*Grasshands* is a fairy tale for a time too jaded for fairy tales. Where the twin serpents of content and consumption coil and wait in the dark, followed to their terrifying logical conclusions. Our heroes' reluctance resides in our collective traumatic detachment, and the real horror is how far we must descend into the abyss to finally feel something. It is a book perfectly suited to an era when we are on the threshold of machines digesting our stories and spitting them back to us as meaningless pablum. A warning nestled in the quiet tragedy of knowing it will go unheeded." — Michael Tichy, author of *Behind Every Tree, Beneath Every Rock* and *Wound of the West*

"What I like best about *Grasshands*, and Kyle Winkler's work in general, is that he allows mystery to remain, stitched into the story laid out for us like a carpet of treacherous moss. How confusing is the world, is nature? How tenuous. What are our lives made up of if not what we know, remember, and hold close? *Grasshands* combines sharp, direct writing, with strangeness and adventure, satisfying scares and weird turns; but what remains with me are the wonderful people: Sylvia, Albert, Clara. A novel of horror, friendship, and swashbuckling, laced with a mourning for the childhood of the world." — Richard Mirabella, author of *Brother and Sister Enter the Forest*

"By turns cosmic and intimate, horrifying and hilarious, *Grasshands* is weirdly and wonderfully unlike anything else I've ever read. With a perpetual motion plot, corkscrew turns of phrase, and almost alien imagination, Winkler's novel steadily grows beyond the confines of any genres or expectations." — Gordon B. White, Shirley Jackson Award-nominated author of *Rookfield* and *Gordon B. White is Creating Haunting Weird Horror(s)*

GRASSHANDS
a novel

KYLE WINKLER

JOURNALSTONE
YOUR LINK TO ARTIST TALENT

Copyright 2024 © Kyle Winkler

All rights reserved. No part of this book may be used or reproduced by any means, graphic, electronic, or mechanical, including photocopying, recording, taping or by any information storage retrieval system without the written permission of the publisher except in the case of brief quotations embodied in critical articles and reviews.

This is a work of fiction. All of the characters, names, incidents, organizations, and dialogue in this novel are either the products of the author's imagination or are used fictitiously.

The views expressed in this work are solely those of the authors and do not necessarily reflect the views of the publisher, and the publisher hereby disclaims any responsibility for them.

ISBN: 978-1-68510-117-6 (sc)
ISBN: 978-1-68510-118-3 (ebook)
Library of Congress Catalog Number: 2023950498

First printing edition: January 19, 2024
Printed by JournalStone Publishing in the United States of America.
Cover Artwork Design: Don Noble
Edited by Sean Leonard
Proofreading, Interior Layout, & Cover Layout by Scarlett R. Algee

JournalStone Publishing
3205 Sassafras Trail
Carbondale, Illinois 62901

JournalStone books may be ordered through booksellers or by contacting:
or
JournalStone | www.journalstone.com

*For Kit, Dorian, and Tilly
& every librarian who ever helped a child find a book*

SYLVIA ATE THE spider on accident. It was tiny, small as a chocolate chip. It fell from a branch in the woods and landed on her arm and didn't move. Unafraid of spiders, she leaned in to inspect it. The hairs on its legs. The rounded abdomen. The cluster of eyes. She meant to whisper something to it, to vibrate its spindles, to say hello to this small velvet traveler.

But when she opened her mouth, it leapt in. She coughed and swallowed. She waited. Nothing. She couldn't feel it in her throat or in her stomach. A small tragedy for the spider, of course, but no harm done to Sylvia.

Someone once said that history repeats itself—first as tragedy, then as farce. But no one told Sylvia that it is often the other way around. Farce lands first. Tragedy knocks later.

And no one told her the worst monsters first appear as friends. Years later—many, *many* years later—Sylvia thought back to that spider, that accident. She wondered if that was the start. Or was it that perhaps she had wanted it to happen, that she had wanted to experience eating a spider on accident? Maybe she'd welcomed these oddities, these devastations, into her life.

Sylvia had always wanted to walk a path worn down by her own steps and meet a cunning wolf. Or she wanted to tumble down a hill and find a tiny dwarf's hut with smoke curling from the chimney. But most of all, she wanted something she couldn't understand. Something that scared her. She wanted to open a window into a far-flung future.

She never saw a wolf except in a zoo. She never smelled smoke that wasn't from her own family's firepit. And, in her youth, she definitely didn't find anything that scared her. But Sylvia was patient. As a young woman, Sylvia spent all her time in the woods behind her house, camping and listening to the violent clicking of insects and the sad songs of birds and mammals. She weaved through stands of oaks and maples, running, pretending to fight faeries and demons with twigs or sticks fallen from trees. She sat in piles of curled dry leaves under naked canopies writing stories with stubby pencils. She smelled deeply in her jeans and shirts of petrichor then soil then rot.

Maybe, she wondered some days later, *I didn't eat the spider. Maybe it wanted to live in my stomach.*

The woods made Sylvia live by grasshands. That was Sylvia's name for it. Grasshands was the clock that nature or the universe obeyed, one which was surely slower than any clock that ticked or tock'd in Sylvia's house. Distant stars and galaxies lived by grasshands. The spiral arm of the Milky Way lived this way. So, if every person had a subjective clock that they lived by, and they did, it was something like the-speed-of-the-phone, or the-speed-of-the-car. Some, like her mother, lived by the-speed-of-the-book. And that could've been literal, since she was rarely seen without a book in one, or both, of her hands.

While her mother spatchcocked a chicken for supper, Sylvia decided to wander in the woods one morning. The insects sounded like jewelry in the trees. The birds sang the air. One song in particular stretched out over a series of long twisty notes. Sylvia leaned against an ash tree. She felt snug. Her stubby pencil was almost finished. Today would be the end of the pencil's life.

She didn't write anything, though. She just stared off into the distance, listening to the winding notes of the birds. The hush-hush of the canopy joined in. Sylvia's gaze was fixated on a sandstone escarpment fifty yards away. The birds' dolorous songs replayed in her mind. The escarpment jutted out, covered in vines and small white flowers.

It's hard to say how long she sat at the base of that ash tree staring into the distance. But eventually she noticed that a small, humped bit of green appeared. Right in front of the escarpment. It had to have been a gradual thing because she'd not seen it happen all of a sudden. Now she stared at the green hump in the middle distance. For an hour, she stared. Relentlessly. And before the hour was up—she knew.

She knew what it was the way you sometimes knew who was on the other end of your phone when it rang. This happened a lot to Sylvia. Her mother joked that she should buy lottery tickets.

The hour ended and the hump had grown sharper at the peak, as if something underneath the moss carpet wanted to break out. Like a finger poking up under a bedsheet.

"Grasshands," she said aloud. It was an answer to a question no one wanted asked in the first place.

Sylvia's patience was being tested. She told herself that something marvelous was trying to break through the thick moss carpet. She knew this in her belly. She didn't dare move her hands or legs. Her neck and back started to cramp. And her hollow-hungry stomach gurgled. But she persisted.

Lunch came, went. The sun steered across the forest.

She considered how small microbes had fought and died over millions of years to create the thin layer of soil in which life on earth had sprung. She looked up and admired the moon for being the secret cultivator of existence: controlling the pull of tides and tidal pools where life started. Without the moon, we have nothing. Maybe the moon started Grasshands. Maybe the moon was her mother. The real mother she never met behind her human mother.

Grasshands wasn't the slow growth of a lawn. She knew that. It wasn't the typical time it took for paint to dry. Or a corpse to decompose in a ditch.

A fuller shape was emerging in the greenery by the rock. By evening, Sylvia's legs were all pins and needles. The shape was now a tall lump. It resembled nothing less than a tall tree stump with all the limbs cut off. A sharp smell came on the wind. It reminded her of metal swing set chains, the way they rusted and the odor clung to her hands. She rather liked the smell of old metal before that.

Nearing dark, she tried to stand but couldn't. She'd sat cross-legged for too long. Her legs were fully numb. Totally weak, totally senseless. Without taking her eyes off Grasshands, she hand-walked her way up the ash tree. The blinding half-light of dusk made it hard to pinpoint Grasshands. Part of her wanted to call out, but she knew that was idiotic. That was asking for trouble.

From the corner of her left eye, between her and the moss carpet, a large dark humanoid-shape shambled into view. It stopped. Instinct told her it was another moss-carpet shape. Another manifestation of Grasshands. Sylvia's breath fluttered. Her heart squeezed in her chest. Sweat stung her eyes. She dared not move.

Slowly, Grasshands turned toward her.

Sylvia regained her body and ran. Or she tried to run. She fell forward into a pile of leaves and dropped her pencil and paper. Her legs felt like Styrofoam wrapped in gunmetal, light and heavy at the same time. The forest was quiet except for her struggling. And while she wanted—needed—to look behind and see where Grasshands was, if it still *looked at her,* she couldn't bring herself to do it. But a rhythmic stomping rose up behind her and she cried out.

She fled. She pumped her arms. She leapt over logs. Leaves crunched under her shoes. Twigs snapped. She dodged saplings and ferns. All the while, Sylvia tried to listen for that large thumping step on the forest floor behind her. But every noise at that moment was apocalyptic.

Only when she reached her porch did she turn around to find nothing. Nothing but a leaf-scattered front yard. Her mouth tasted full of salt. Which reminded her. She grabbed a saltshaker off the kitchen table and, giving in to one of her mother's superstitions, sprinkled salt on the floor outside her bedroom. Her mother said she used to do it as a little girl to ward off evil. Salt was a preservative, her mother said, cryptically. What it was keeping in or keeping out was another story. Did the salt preserve the monsters or preserve the humans? Sylvia didn't believe any of this but did it anyway. Later, in the safety of her own bed, sleep arrived only through sheer exhaustion. Then:

Tap tap

She woke and looked at the door.

Tap tap

"Mom, please go away!" she said. "I'm fine." She kept her nightstand lamp on all night.

The next morning, Sylvia pulled her mother with her into the forest to see if everything the day before was a dream, to see if Grasshands was a hallucination. Ever the supporter, her mother eventually marched along into the forest. Like her own daughter, she entertained the wildest fantasies. It was enough to grow up from age six without a father (Jeep slid on ice, broken neck)—she didn't want her daughter's imagination depleted like a sick balloon.

They sat at the base of the ash tree together for hours. The original lump of moss-carpet was there. The second one, the walking one, was missing. So they waited and waited, and when the afternoon was furious with insects clicking and biting, her mother apologized for not seeing anything. "Must be scaring them off." Dinner needed cooking anyway. She stood up and brushed off her jeans and hands and left Sylvia.

Sylvia didn't need her. She concentrated on the moss carpet. She willed it to move. Dared it. Cursed it. She even yelled at it. But nothing happened.

The next morning, Sylvia begged her mother to come along again. She pulled on her. When her mother finally nodded and shrugged, as if to say, *What could it hurt? Childish fantasy is the parent's burden*, it was obvious to Sylvia that she just played along. They leaned against the ash tree. Her mother asked questions about what they were seeking out. Sylvia pointed to the moss carpet. She smiled, knowingly. "Oh. There." An hour passed. Mother nudged daughter. "You see? It moved."

"Really?" Sylvia said. But immediately she felt green stupidity. Grasshands wasn't fast. "Fast" wasn't even a concept in the vast world vocabulary that Grasshands would, or could, communicate through. It was absurd. Sylvia was losing patience, with herself, with her mother, with Grasshands. That was bad. It would never show itself again if she lost patience. (Later, much later, she would learn that the word "patience" came from a Latin word that means *suffering*. That struck home for her.)

Again, her mother nodded sagely. Like a broken doll. Part of Sylvia cracked inside, watching her fib and fake her way through earnestness. At that moment, she knew she couldn't *truly* trust her with anything. From here on out, anything vital would have to be vaulted inside her. Never shared. Never released.

Grasshands would understand. In fact, this was fundamental to understanding something like Grasshands. All those normal people feared boredom. They feared silence. They feared, more than anything, themselves.

Her mother pretended the moss carpet moved only to make Sylvia feel better. She'd rather have her mother call her a liar to her face. Anything but patronize her. And like last time, her mother got up to eat. Except her mother didn't even make it to dinner. She left at lunch. Just to be fair to species other than humans, Sylvia lured her dog, Mosby, but he barely got near the forest. He sank down at the property line and whimpered.

Deep in the wood, the bulge of moss carpet stood. Sylvia didn't know what was under it. Her imagination tossed out examples: a thousand skeletons; slimy aliens; grotesque ancient worms; her father, rotted; her father, normal, but with no eyes; a doppelgänger. Or maybe it was nothing. Could she cut it open and find out?

She knew she needed more patience. She'd been distracted by trying to prove her experience to others. What she needed was to lean against the ash tree and slow down. But leaning wouldn't cut it. She'd never gotten closer than thirty or forty yards. Sylvia wanted to touch it. She wanted to remind it that she was present.

A week before school started, she sat against the ash tree and waited. And when her patience burned, she waited more. The moss didn't move. It didn't grow and it didn't shrink. There had been an invisible boundary she felt repelled by, but now she would walk toward the escarpment and the moss carpet. (She wished she'd brought that stupid saltshaker with her.)

Not but a few steps over the boundary line, her arms and legs tingled. She was getting pins and needles. She was going numb in her limbs. Sylvia wasn't even halfway to the moss carpet and was partially paralyzed. Had she been sitting that long?

When she reached the moss monument, she couldn't feel her body. There was just enough feeling in her arm to briefly touch it. It stood three times taller than her. Its size was deceptive from faraway. Her finger was stuck on it, as if magnetized to the moss. She pulled. Grunted. Cried.

Her face started to lose feeling. She was falling into herself.

From around the back of the monument, she heard a *skritch*. Then a soft tapping of legs. A long, thin spindle of stick, segmented, emerged from around the moss. Then another spindle, and another. A tangle of vines and sticks in the shape of a spider crawled toward her. It was, perhaps, no bigger than her own fist. But it was still terrifying.

Sylvia couldn't scream, because she couldn't feel her face. She hated herself for coming this far. For giving in. For thinking that Grasshands had something positive to show her. All the same, she tried to scream. Her mouth, dry and pained. Nothing came out. Her vocal cords were wooden slats.

Unexpectedly, the twig spider squatted, seemingly scared and curious. She noticed that much of it wasn't twig but made of crumpled paper. Scraps that she recognized. Old tests. Report cards. Pictures of friends. Her stories written in stubby pencil. All of it was from her room. So much for the salt, she thought.

Then it did what she least expected. It tapped her hand. *Tap tap.* With a tiny spindle, *tap tap*. When it seemed satisfied with her hand, it crawled up her arm and into her shirt sleeve. More tapping. Of course, this *thing* was an extension of Grasshands—its mobile rover, sent to pick up information. But Sylvia was more terrified by the lack of feeling on her skin. There was no way to know what it was doing to her. Or where it was. It appeared in the corner of her eye. She shut them tight. And her mouth. The spindle pried into her ear. *Tap tap.* The twig spider tried to fit more than a spindle in. Three—maybe four. But it was too big. All Sylvia felt was pressure. Not pain, just pressure.

She didn't want to do it, but she cracked an eyelid, ever so slightly. The spider hooked a spindle underneath and yanked it open. She stared into the claptrap body of the thing. Paper, trash, memories. It was composed of herself, really. She hated that. It was bundled and pulsing. She heard a noise coming from it or from around it.

fa fa fa fa

Maybe it was in the moss monument. Or in the ground. Or in her own head.

fa fa fa fa

The spider tapped on her eyeball. It quickly dismissed her eyes. Sylvia let out a stressful breath from the side of her mouth. A spindle curved up her nose. It tapped her chin and neck, *tap tap*. For some reason, a part of her neck had feeling, and the soft walk of the spider tickled. She tried to pull away. The spider brushed the spot again. Against her will, she laughed.

The spider tensed. It tickled her again. Sylvia couldn't help it. She laughed. Her mouth opened wider. The thing shot two spindles into her mouth like a wedge. It tapped her hard teeth, *tap tap*. Her soft tongue, *tap tap*. It seemed pleased, so it pushed her mouth open more. The pressure she felt was immense. Then the spider squeezed its whole body into her mouth and settled.

Sylvia panicked. Should she cry, swallow, yell, resist? All of the spindles folded into her mouth. She saw them retract below her nose as if they were part of her, like she was a fastidious robot.

For some reason, she thought of Little Red Riding Hood. She thought of how that girl felt inside the Big Bad Wolf's stomach. Did she feel stupid? Trapped? Calm?

There would be no woodsman for Sylvia.

She had one hand stuck on the moss monument. She also had one hand free but unable to move for fear of the spider. She stood like that for hours. Again, the sun steered across the sky and sank. The dark reigned. Part of her thought maybe her mother would come looking for her, come calling her name. Grasshands and the spider wanted something from her, as if testing her. The spider had been checking her points of articulation, perhaps the better to take her apart? Or inhabit her? All she knew was that Grasshands desired something from her. Another part of her guessed that there were more twig spiders. And that they were already in her home, searching her dresser, her closet, under her bed. Her mother. Grasshands could move like a spider then, so fast and sudden.

Grasshands had a hold of time like an owner gripped a dumb dog's collar. Sylvia felt she had to temper herself. She had to think like Grasshands. She welcomed the slowness, the twig spider, the patience. What was a minute to the rest of the world turned into a timestretch. It was an hour put upon an axle and spun forever. She was being weighed. Judged. The spider held the heft of a gavel. But it wasn't death or a part of death. If anything, she knew Grasshands and the twig spider, together, belonged to the opposite—life run amok.

The spider stirred. Spindles emerged. It exited her mouth and leapt onto the monument. It paused, tensed, then fled around the curve. The last thing she saw was the hind portion of the spider, which was made of a picture of her parents. Taken before she was born.

Sylvia took this moment to grab her locked hand and pull. She pulled with everything she had, and a massive chunk of moss came off. Rushing out from the hole was the rusty metal smell and a sound.

fa fa fa fa

She could almost see the sounds pouring from the monument. Feeling returned to her slowly.

She fled.

That sense of time rushing by without caution or care was real. To Sylvia, she'd only been gone an hour or so. But outside the woods, she'd been missing for a whole day, maybe more. That night her mother read her the riot act. And a couple of lesser-known acts. The police had been contacted, and neighbors were out searching for her. She was sent to bed without supper. Sylvia thought that only happened in fairy tales.

Not so.

Instead, she was served a hot bowl of common sense. Quit spending so much time in the woods. Quit telling stories and dragging her mother out there. She was told to move on; stop wheedling other people into her games and delusions. School was coming up and a young woman couldn't be filled with distractions like sitting against trees all day. "And why is your mouth filthy?" her mother said. "Looks like you've been eating dirt. Grow up, already."

Soon she entered seventh grade. The public school system took over the work of flattening her out. Any possible interesting thought or memory of moss or twig spiders was shaved off by homework, extracurricular clubs, and new friends. It took a long time for Sylvia to think of anything other than Grasshands. To not see, write, or dream of the moss carpet turned moss monument turned twig spider.

It took years for her to agree to a dentist visit.

But the brain is savvy. And Sylvia's brain took that day and locked it away behind some mental furniture in the attic. Really big furniture. And there, one may leave the story of Sylvia Who Lived in a Wood by Grasshands in the American Midwest.

And yet.

Here's another story, this one somewhat similar to the first. It is a story whose ending has yet to be written.

Some time ago in the American Midwest, a young woman in high school lost her mother to a deteriorating version of multiple sclerosis. She went to live with her grandparents. When they died soon after, she lived in the city by herself. She never spent time in the woods, in any woods. She never camped and ignored the violent clicking of insects and the sad songs of birds and mammals. She had long stopped weaving through stands of oaks and maples. She quit running and pretending to fight faeries and demons with sticks fallen from trees. She never sat in piles of leaves under naked canopies writing stories with stubby pencils.

But most of all, she *never* walked, waited, or listened patiently. She *never* waited for something she couldn't understand, something that scared her. She forgot to walk along paths worn by her own steps to meet a wolf. It never crossed her mind to climb down a hill and find a small dwarves' hut with smoke curling from the chimney. There were no windows opening into the far-flung future.

Besides, if she found any of this, she'd have called the police. So, of course, she never found these. The wolf in the zoo died. The smell of smoke faded. And she found nothing that scared her. Why? Because she was living by the-speed-of-the-car, the-speed-of-the-phone, and the-speed-of-the-screen.

She still read books. No one could've stopped Sylvia from reading. Not in three hundred years. Although, often, books felt too slow for her. Books had become a sort of loving chore. The unhinged joy of books had worringly drained away.

Because of that, she forgot. She forgot all of it—the wolf, the trees, the smoke, the pencils, the twig spider so subservient to the moss that she called Grasshands, the numbing, the judging, the time-that-was-no-time. She forgot all about Grasshands.

But—Grasshands didn't forget her.

GRASSHANDS

CHAPTER ONE

1.

"EVERYTHING WRONG IN the world is wrong with books," Sylvia Hix said.

No one heard her say this, alone, in the back of the library, surrounded by incoming items. She beeped each item with a corded laser gun. Children's abecedaries beeped. Exercise videos beeped. Chopin's Nocturnes beeped. Political thrillers, Georgian romances, contemporary pastorals, simmering Amish steamers. All beeped. All brought home. All carefully examined as a jeweler the jewel.

It was unseasonably October.

Everything wrong in the world was wrong with books.

Their spines were broken and needed taped or glued or restitched or altogether rebound.

Their pages crimped and curled. They were, ostensibly, just plants repackaged into another form, books, and so it made sense to say that what was wrong with the world was wrong with books.

The assistant head librarian, Albert, edged his nose over the cubicle wall and asked if Sylvia would care for a diet soda.

Albert's glasses belonged, spiritually so, on an older, deceased laboratory director. His nose, to a long-dead face of a duke of Habsburg. In any case, Sylvia could only perceive portraiture when she saw him. A long thick black hair poked from a deep nose pore. He had some dark, greenish material under most of his fingernails, like he'd been scraping a garage floor.

"Tell me something about Aristotle," she said. "Checking in materials is murdering my soul."

Dead-faced, he stepped aside the wall and cleared his throat. Albert fit in the library the way skis fit into a garden shed. He paused.

Asking Albert about Aristotle embarrassed his knowledge. He overflowed with info. But he kindly paused before setting upon friends and patrons with stray facts like bullets. Even when prompted, he blushed.

Children's librarian Teresa Bardin popped her head in to say she adored Sylvia's cardigan. She wanted to thieve it for the upstairs. "Children's kept *coooold*," she said. She cartoonishly rubbed her arms.

Return to Albert: waiting. A patient, bloated, loving face.

"Okay, forget Aristotle. Tell me again about that woman," she said. "The follower."

She remembered, as he spoke, that some years ago a huggish woman put herself forward as claimant to All Things Albert. She was a leeching personality. A stalker, in so many words. This woman, this human flytrap, Deena, she petted Albert's hand and pursued his personal history. Which meant she researched the History of Albert. Deena perpetually appeared cheery, outfitted in a mackintosh. Sun, moon, wind, rain, plague.

When Deena discovered Albert had written a senior thesis decades ago on Aristotle (thank you, internet), some conclusive boulder rolled to the back of her mind. Nothing else should be spoken of but Aristotle.

Deena was so esoteric about her obsession that once she strutted into the library with a t-shirt for Albert that read *More Macedonian Metaphysics!*

Sylvia stopped the story. "Huh?"

Albert said that Aristotle was Macedonian actually. Deena had made this insane shirt for him. She'd scrawled on an old used white t-shirt with a Sharpie.

"Aww," Sylvia said. "I want that! I want intelligent stalkers."

Albert rejected this.

"Stalkers have wretched needs. They're petulant like rare flowers."

In fact, Deena's undiluted affection for his Albertness forced him to proclaim that Aristotle was wrong. Wrong about it all!

Well.

This set Deena off. She ended her infatuation right then and there. She declared Albert a prophet of doom. A troll. Sub-human. An incomparable and reckless minotaur in the labyrinth of sorrow that was the public library.

Sylvia couldn't help it. She was doubled-over, laughing at the desk.

"Okay, but was Aristotle wrong?" she asked.

Albert configured. He bit his thumbnail, remembered the gunk under it, then spat it out. He was thoughtful—and this was okay to indulge when it took a full minute, Sylvia thought, wherein most people considered it punishingly autistic.

"Wrong? Yes. But in ways we'll never be right."

2.

Delores the head librarian ironed back into a satisfying form these huge pages of encyclopedias right on her desk. The iron had an old frayed fabric electrical cord. Clearly a fire hazard.

She was brutally pragmatic. Which meant cutting out middlemen, middlewomen, middlechildren.

Most middlepeople were vermin to Delores.

Despite this—or because of this—most days she funneled Sylvia into her office because the older woman liked to speak out loud and Sylvia liked to listen inside. Delores moved files around on her computer and Sylvia sat on the naughehyde couch as if waiting outside a principal's office.

Today Sylvia was funneled in as she finished her morning ritual of Beeping Returned Items. Delores's office smelled like burnt hair and plastic left in the sun.

"Diet soda?" Delores offered.

"No. I prefer lots of sugar." Sylvia smiled.

Delores said it would rot the teeth.

"I plan on getting new ones," Sylvia said.

"Who has money for that?"

"I quit college. Remember?"

"My mother had all her own teeth till the end."

"No kidding? Dentures at forty for me."

"Why not thirty? Make it thirty."

"Poverty becomes me," Sylvia said.

Now Delores smiled. Then she didn't. The encyclopedia pages curled with age and investment value. How many thousands of dollars was Delores stroking away with each rub of the iron.

"Sylvia, why do you want to keep working for us?" she asked.

"Because I'm bright? Because I have a fruitful future?"

"Maybe. But fruit rots, dear. Like teeth. From sugar."

"Dentists love rot. They need it. No rot, no business."

"Wit is also like sugar, Sylvia."

Sylvia hid her teeth.

Albert walked in with two diet sodas anyway. It was joked around the library that Albert could read Delores's mind. Though not the other way around. Delores often admitted she *never* knew what Albert thought or could be capable of thinking. A tall fricking enigma, that guy.

No one moved for the diet sodas. They sweated on the desk's corner. Then the soda sweat rambled onto the berber carpet. A small waterfall going into a dark stain. Berber carpet was the devil.

"Tell me more," Delores said.

"About?" Sylvia said. "This morning's returns? There were no less than two children's books covered in a combination of Vaseline and snot."

Delores was the unmoved mover. "No. Tell me about the state of the contemporary library. The monument to supposed free learning. Free to all. Guarantee to none. We keep cataloguing, but what changes? We're a secular monastery in the wasteland of remembrance. What happened to forgetting, Sylvia? How is digital storage an affront to Darwinian evolutionary theory? Does it matter?—It doesn't matter. Species change because there's no space for all of them. Yet facts have all the space in the world. Or, not facts, I guess, but pure information. Information has individual rooms with daybeds." She picked at her teeth with a pen cap.

"Are you high, Delores?"

Her boss ignored this.

"There's no culling here. Sylvia, sweetie. If I could, I'd appoint you Official Culler. Imagine it: Pith helmet. Fake wooden machete. We'd make a spectacle of it and get patrons involved. Reality television would revert back to reality. No cameras involved. No middlemen."

"Sounds sweaty."

"Nothing we're not already used to," Delores said. She checked the hallway for passersby then smelled her armpits. "I have something particular in mind for you."

"A mission," Sylvia said.

"A charge," Delores said. "An investigation, of sorts."

"I'm game."

Delores curved around the desk and opened a diet soda and drank all of it in a throaty chug. Sylvia thought she heard the aluminum can sigh.

"Our stacks are melting."

The head librarian did not care to elaborate. She picked up a wadded Kleenex from the desk and inhaled. She put it down.

"Delores, are you high?"

"Do me a favor. Say the word *deliquesce*."

Sylvia did not.

"Well. It's when a solid becomes a liquid." The older woman leaned forward as if a high-powered stockbroker. Spread her arms wide. "Can you imagine the books as beings that are rotting on the shelves?"

Blood trickled from Delores's nostril. Sylvia pointed at her own nose. Delores fidgeted for something to stanch the drip. She signaled for Sylvia to skedaddle. The meeting would have to continue post-nosebleed. As she left, she heard Delores crack open the second diet soda.

The books weren't melting but they wore a beard of moss. At least, at that point, a few shelves in the basement did. Some looked enrobed by the hand of a creeping alien lifeform in a late-night horror film. Sylvia found out from Albert right after the Nosebleed Meeting that he'd been the original investigator of the moss. That was what he had under his nails. He'd been pulling it off over the past few weeks, actually. And, as an inveterate nail biter, who knows how much of it he'd already licked off his fingers on accident?

He'd found the moss when Deena requested a long-neglected work of Aristotle's, buried deep in the basement storage stacks. It was a thin book called *On the Soul*. "I don't know why Deena wanted it. I only remember it for a passage where he states something about how plants have part of a soul. Ironic, considering it was covered in that junk. She returned it all wet."

"Fun," Sylvia said. All she could imagine was Deena sitting at home licking Aristotle's *On the Soul*, moss and all, just because Albert had recently touched the book as well. Gross.

Albert also mentioned that the library had hired underlings. Kids with putty knives. Teens with no sense of delicacy for stitching, backing, folios, the holy silence of the stacks. These were adolescent boys who pretended to slice and stab one another with their tools. Greasy, loud, awkward boys. The library offered them temporary shit-pay.

"Where did they come from?" Sylvia asked.

Albert said Tina Hamsun in Children's said she had a nephew, and that he needed work. He played video games and jerked off too much. He probably had friends who needed pocket money. They jerked off a lot, too. So there was your workforce.

Sylvia heard them sniffle and fart around the aisles. She heard them curse in show-off fashion. Fuck, piss, cunt, they said.

Idiots.

God bless their mothers. Mothers who had to witness boy-youth spurt and leap and sag. Such a horrorshow. Sylvia couldn't allow these puckish dipwads to screw up stacks of precious books, even if they were stowed in the basement. So she assigned them menial tasks.

Sylvia doled out duties she could do but didn't want. Banal shelving orders. Re-labeling all the travel guides—just 'cause. Dusting the tops of the stacks. Dusting the bottoms of the stacks. Shifting 350 linear feet of books to add a few new titles. Then re-shifting those books back because—*ooooops*—Sylvia screwed up. Darn.

Albert said that, so far as it goes, these boys were her responsibility.

"Do I get a pay raise?" she asked.

"You get authority to tell others below you what to do. Insecurity trickles downward."

Behind him, Delores continued ironing those encyclopedia pages. Day three, now. The smell of cooked old paper wafted out into the cubicle farm. Hot dirt stench took over the hot plastic stench.

Sylvia's nostrils flared. Her shoulders sank. "Never mind. I'll write up my manifesto against unfair labor practices later."

"Attagirl," he said, patting her back. "Be the revolution you want to see in the management hierarchy." He strolled back to his cubicle.

This particular day was nooning. Sylvia felt it in her gut. It roiled. Patrons got cranky. Interlibrary loan orders disappeared from the system. No less than three babies puked on the carpet. Nothing dramatic, but nothing fun, either. Upstairs, the library bustled. The smoldering October heat lurched about on trunky thighs. The air conditioning was so bad in the library, excepting Children's. Sylvia swore off work, sweaty boys, and her eccentric boss for lunch in the basement, where it was drier, cooler, darker. It also didn't smell like steamed infant vomit down there.

She ate like a yeoman: hard cheese and homemade bread. She paced back and forth between the water fountain to moisten her food like some large beast. Soaked wads of bread left in a fountain basin were a sure sign Sylvia had just eaten.

She wanted to get eyes on this moss. Didn't take long to find it. The moss was dripping quite prominently over E332—the letter/number combo carved out for Thomas Jefferson. The downstairs was for overflow, storage, and discards. A makeshift breastfeeding closet was also down here and she heard often the soft whine of a breast pump doing diligent work.

The moss looked normal. Smelled normal. She poked it. It felt normal. What wasn't normal was *the moss itself*.

A putty knife, the kind given to the teenage boys, lay in a box with other utility items. Sylvia scraped a chunk of the greenish brown. It was softer than she originally imagined.

She nudged a toe at it. Pressed it with a sneaker heel. She scraped the rest off and flung it in the trash. She washed her hands in the water fountain like a prospector, leaving bits and niblets of mossy fibers all over. Not her best showing, but she wasn't making any extra on this gig as a supervisor to wayward teens, so she had zero compunction about making a minor mess.

She turned. E332 cried out for damage control, dampened from moss. The boards and cloth were umber from moisture. A phrase ballooned up in her: *life run amok*. Cellular division having a free-for-all.

"Tho*moss*," she said. She laughed. "Thomoss Jeffer*moss*. Ugh."

She felt a sense of completion from that small scraping. Like she'd saved all of the second president's reputation. And anyway, how much more moss could there be? When she returned upstairs, she felt slightly dazed, as if she'd pulled an all-nighter. Albert asked her why she missed the staff meeting. Baffled, Sylvia said she'd been in the basement working on "Project Moss."

Distracted, he said he got an aggressive phone call late at night from Deena.

"So this stalker thing is really real? Have you called the police?"

"Thought I could laugh it off. Become her friend and show her I'm not worth her time."

"I don't know if rational arguments work with stalkers."

"It's strange. More than the stalking, it's something in her voice. Like there's something in me she wants to worry out. Like a pit in a peach. She wants to chew through me to win the pit." Pause. "Still can't believe you missed the staff meeting."

"I was only down in the basement a half-hour," she protested.

Albert squinted. "You've been down there for two hours, dear."

3.

There was, inevitably, more moss. More moldish stuff on the books in the basement. There was also some of it now in the breastfeeding closet on a copy of *What to Expect When You're Expecting*. There was also a swathe of it here and there upstairs on the Large Print inspirationals and the YA romance. Some on the periodicals. Some on the opera CD cards.

The E332 shelf in the basement had the creeping hand of darkness back over it. Thom-moss Mosserjeff, more like.

Delores roamed her library and stood plaintively at each afflicted spot and thought hard. As if willing the moss to evaporate on her command through sheer cognition. And in retaliation—as if willing to cultivate more ulcers in Delores—the moss spread.

Delores told Albert, who told Sylvia, that they needed to have this moss crisis under control before the Library Board of Trustees held their Building Committee Meeting. Ms. Gamelin would be there and demand a sharp update from Delores. A Mutual Hatred Society existed between them. Sylvia once heard Delores say that she'd light Gamelin's hair on fire if she had the chance. Sylvia thought this too brutal and unforgiving. Didn't villains also deserve to feel pretty?

"Tomorrow morning, get scraping," Albert said. He moved away from her toward the exit like a frustrated boulder. Sylvia wondered if

Albert was cursed by a witch to slowly grow forever. He'd always been a big fella, but lately his sheer size was dumbfounding. He'd grow until he couldn't leave the library and the library would become a jacket to him. Then the jacket would explode, and he'd destroy everyone inside it.

Low syrupy light cut through a west window, and she found herself alone. The library closed at 5pm on Fridays. It was unusually empty that day.

"No rest for the poor," she declared to no one.

4

All this talk of Aristotle with Albert made her pull the *Nicomachean Ethics* off the shelf. Much of it was boring, but every so often a zinger popped out and kept her plugging along. That seemed to be philosophy's whole shtick. Rely on the zingers. Aristotle's *Nicomachean Ethics* was assigned to her in a college philosophy course. She didn't read the book back then. She dropped the course three weeks in. Dropped the whole routine, really. Quit school by mid-terms. Got a job shelving, then front-desking. Got an apartment with roommates and devoted her life to a solid misfit outlook. She only owned five or six books lined up against the baseboard like drug cartel hostages.

In the break room, she changed into black slacks and a white blousy dress shirt that smelled of asparagus and pork medallions. A faux bowtie completed the costume. Three nights a week her job was a catering waiter for weddings.

The public library held joint custody of the parking lot with a catering hall called Throckmorton's. Like a child of joint custody, the parking lot could never decide who to really put loyalty behind. So fights broke out constantly between drunk weddinggoers and pettifogging library patrons. Recently, someone had busted out the lights in Throckmorton's neon signage so it read *Fuck tons*. O, the joys of soft-core vandalism in a Midwestern city!

Sylvia scrounged free meals after each gig. Roasted red potatoes with thyme. Blackened asparagus spears. Chicken à la king. The hefty gratuities she received in her paycheck justified the baggy black slacks. The wedding drama also kept her aroused. She witnessed families disavow sons and daughters during speeches and dances. She cringed at food choices, flower arrangements, and bridal party colors. It was a total judgment zone.

The wedding was wall-to-wall soap opera body doubles. Low light, romantic strings, the delicate clinking of glass. Sylvia cruised the dresses and ties with plates of ham spirals and mini quiches. Tiny avocado toasts with heirloom tomato relish. The body doubles slyly shoved their gobs with it. Sylvia tucked Aristotle into her waistband.

Ms. Gamelin also navigated among wedding guests and lackeys. She moved like a track star in the skin of a Mary Kay saleswoman with the money of a mediocre lawyer. Was she really friendly with these people or was she testing out her sociability? Reading the *Nicomachean Ethics*, it was hard for Sylvia to ignore Aristotle's obsession with friendship. The philosopher claimed that one needed to "spill salt" with another, to share food with others before friendship was conceivable. Sylvia wondered: Did appetizers count?

Sylvia made a circuit near Ms. Gamelin to hear what she was whispering about. She'd met her a few times, but there was no way the older woman would recognize her face.

The bride wept in a corner because she spilled wine down the front of her dress. A small faction of bridesmaids surrounded her like antibodies attacking a virus. Dabbing, comforting, co-crying. No one in the crowd bothered to notice. The groom was unavailable. Sylvia couldn't unsee the tragedy of new marriages. This one was folding itself inward like an origami torture device.

"Sylvia?"

She was caught. *Fuuuck.*

"Ms. Gamelin? Oh, hello." Sylvia forgot she was catering. She lifted her platter a little too high. "Would you care for a bacon-wrapped prune?"

"I would not care, no."

"Very good. Enjoy the reception."

"Ms. Hix, does the library not pay you enough so as to keep you from waltzing about with that plate of canapés?"

Ms. Gamelin was rather fetching in a casual camisole and a shrug. She wore a patterned and dramatic headscarf and what appeared to be a real and very small carrot pinned to her lapel.

"The library pays me enough to cover my share of rent, sure. But then there're those pesky things like water, gas, electricity."

"You're a rather fresh monkey, Sylvia."

"Thank you?"

Someone reached between them and clutched a fist's-worth of prunebacon.

"Shall I tell Delores to increase your pay?" Ms. Gamelin asked.

"If you'd like. I don't want to ruffle feathers."

"Delores speaks well of you. She likes you. She says you're handling the issue in the basement. Although what it is, I'm still unaware. I've been told that the books are gathering some kind of..."

Sylvia began to speak, to say *moss* or *mold* or *alien spunk*, but Ms. Gamelin put a finger to her mouth.

"Don't. It's enough to know you're motivated and not complaining. I don't really care what it is. Just fix it. While I have you here, I'd like to offer you something."

Sylvia imagined Ms. Gamelin's offer as a broad box under a large plush blanket. A demonic game show prize.

"How long have you known Albert?"

"Since I've worked at the library. So, five years, I think."

"And do you find that he does a good job?"

Sylvia recalled Albert hunched over like a clerical giant behind his comically tiny cubicle. His shoulders beshawled in a beige cardigan his (now deceased) mother crocheted. If Fred Rogers had been a methodically empirical atheist and five times as large, he would be Albert.

"I find that, yes."

"Hmm. You're sure?"

Sylvia scoffed. "He's literally the gentlest and most supportive human I've ever met." Sylvia's Bloated Catering Boss floated by with his hands behind his back. He sliced her throat with his gaze. "Albert works harder than anyone to keep that library the way it is."

"And what if I and the board don't like the way the library is?"

"That was not meant to be an admission of status quo."

"And yet—"

"And yet you want to fire Albert for what reason?"

"Let me ask you: What do you think the purpose of a public library is?"

"To support the commonweal," Sylvia said.

"Too broad."

"Too bad."

Sylvia's tray drooped in her hand. There were only two prunebacon thingies left. She dumped the tray into a trash can behind her.

Ms. Gamelin smiled. "Oh, I see. You're one of *those* people. You don't like talking in the library. You think the library is a quiet sanctuary to education and study? You probably think we should keep all the books, right?"

"How is that bad?"

"Do you know how many homeless people nap in our reading room?"

In fact: Sylvia did.

"Here's my new charge to you. I don't want any of them sleeping in our chairs. Not even for a blink. Not even for a toothless tired sigh. I don't want them in the area, period." She paused. She touched the headscarf. Almost comforting it. "You think I'm heartless, don't you?"

"Maybe a tad."

"Well, running anything, even a library, isn't all handjobs and milkshakes. Do you think a mother of three visiting in the middle of the day wants to smell a drifter who stinks like shit and piss near the *New Yorker*?"

Ms. Gamelin didn't need to explain this to her. Sylvia had been waking up smelly—but kind and gentle—homeless people since she started. That was part of working in a library in the present era. Ms. Gamelin, on the other hand, wanted them moving like the flotsam she supposed they were. Something in that metaphor of fluids matched Sylvia's grand view of the public library as an Institution. The library was a pool filter, she felt. But not in a negative-Ms.-Gamelin-type of way. She loved the homeless people; those dogs tied with rope to the bike rack outside. On the contrary, Sylvia wanted to surround all the boring normies with farty, jacking-off homeless dudes. She wanted to keep the prim Tight-Assed Moms and Sockless Boatshoe Dads out of the stacks. Keep them on their well-manicured toes and uncorned heels.

Pool filters collected everything that drifted around the water and compacted it into one crowded weird space. Everything lost was found in the pool filter. Everything interesting got caught in the pool filter. Sylvia preferred that small, concentrated refuse area over the sanitized chlorine hole you were supposed to swim in.

So what in the hell did this woman want? What Ms. Gamelin wanted was a replacement. She wanted Sylvia to slide into Albert's cubicle and do *her* bidding and carry out *her* charges until Delores either died or retired. Or screwed up and got caught doing something wickedly dangerous.

Like ironing encyclopedias, Sylvia thought.

"Albert has a stalker," Sylvia said. "He endures a lot of crazy shit working for this library. He's started all of our most successful programs."

Ms. Gamelin adjusted an earring and wiped the edges of her mouth.

"Books represent everything gone wrong in the world," Ms. Gamelin said. A deliberately provocative statement, something Sylvia would've said. *Had* said.

"How can you say that? You read!"

The infuriated bride marched to the catering hall's doors. Her wine stain became a beacon. Her maids followed. Naked feet slapped the tile. The bride hoisted the guestbook above her head. No one took her seriously. She heaved it at the buffet table. Roasted red potatoes tumbled. Garlic butter sauce splattered. Propane blue Sterno cans spun on the floor like divine pucks.

Ms. Gamelin stared into Sylvia's brain through her eyeholes. "I don't mean literally, Sylvia. I mean in our sphere of business. Our work. Books instigate chaos in the budgets of smaller libraries like ours. Overspend? Overstock? Under deliver? It is hard to justify a dusty box of books to taxpayers. They want more bling for their buck."

Sylvia wanted to, but couldn't, respond with: *Yeah, well, people are stupid.*

"What you want is a conservative definition of a library. It's just not so anymore, dear. What people want is entertainment. They want computers. They want free, fast internet access. They want children's programs and adult education classes. They want farmer's markets in the parking lot and summer reading contests for kids. I used to think like you, Sylvia. I, too, wanted, needed, the ability to have all this knowledge around me in tall cathedral-like columns. We, though, are not a church. There's nothing holy about a book when there's Wikipedia. Digital books. Audio books. Instantaneous information. And from where I stand as the director of the board, we answer to the people. The public. Any other way is bad politics. It's bad civics. Your instincts are false. You're trying to send an email with a typewriter."

"And yet you'll replace Albert with me?" Sylvia said.

"You're as intransigent as you put on."

"Ah, grandmother, what big words you have."

"The better to eat you, my dear."

The catering manager reached max-irritation and stepped in to reprimand Sylvia for inattention to foodly duties. "I'm taking your tips," he said.

Ms. Gamelin turned and said, "Please buzz off. I'm having a discussion with my employee." Then she reached into her pocket and pulled out a hundred-dollar bill and handed it to Sylvia. Then she reconsidered and gave her two more. The manager's forehead beaded. Sweaty and stuffed, he scoffed and blushed like an angry anthropomorphic donut.

"Here's your tip, Sylvia," Ms. Gamelin said. "Take that uniform off and go home."

"If everything wrong with our local world is wrong with books—why bother saving them?"

"I'm a futurist, honey, not a savage."

"The future would terrify you. Anyway, you know I'll just buy piles of used books with this money."

"A cathedral of books, yes. I'm sure you will. It's your money now."

Sylvia narrowed her eyes. "*Blood* money."

Ms. Gamelin had stopped looking at her. She sipped wine. "Blood builds cathedrals, yes yes. Your threats hold no water. Now buzz off, dear, before I start to change my mind." Ms. Gamelin offered a meaningful smile.

Because Sylvia had no more appetizers, and no job really, she stood aloof from the reception. The bride raged on. The groom sulked behind a wall of fake ferns. The crowd enjoyed a free bar. Fried ravioli. Small bowls with olive tapenade and tiny garlic toasts. And Ms. Gamelin returned to a slim clique of golf-clubbing women in pricey but boring fashions.

Now Sylvia had a problem. She knew she didn't know how to sort out heroes and villains. She didn't even know if there *were* heroes and villains. She had lived in a pre-Oz world, filled with Kansan klarity. Monochromatic morality. She wanted to set herself against Ms. Gamelin like one holy warrior against another in the Crusades, but it wasn't as tidy as that.

The best thing about Ms. Gamelin was that she was a little bit like Darth Vader. Darth Vader was Sylvia's favorite character from any story, ever. Probably because what she couldn't shake about Vader was that he used to be a boy. The dramatic shift from light to dark and a sudden move back again. That kind of move warmed her un-microwaveable heart.

CHAPTER TWO

1.

NEXT MORNING. 6:30AM.

Sylvia sipped scalding black coffee. Ms. Gamelin's money flustered in her pocket, irritating her superego. The money burned at her thigh like a stolen jewel from a fairy tale.

Sylvia had checked on the boys and the scraping. They were heavy-lidded and mute. They slurped energy drinks and nodded with earbuds stuffed in their heads. They smelled. The moss had spread in the past few days. Parts of it hardened like stone. The work became more like chipping than scraping. Adolescent males had energy to spare. Sylvia wasn't worried. The books weren't melting. What was melting was Delores's mind. Whoaboy. She was a user. She dosed her meat circuits all day. She *looooved* her some fumes. She inhaled Elmer's rubber cement the way white trash trailer folk deface lottery scratch-offs. She'd brush on and dry the glue palm-side. Roll it into a ball. Then she'd chaw on it. A happy glue-chewing user. Breakfast, lunch, and dinner.

Sylvia knew she stashed cough syrup in her top right drawer. Albert had turned a glaucomic eye to this. Pints of booze were also laid up in the air vents. Cheap gin, cheaper whisky. Booze was emergency juice. But oboy—Delores *loooooved* glue.

Glue ruled. Glue ran the library.

Remember: what was wrong with the world was wrong with books. And glue held books together—a strong mucilage handshake down the spine.

Delores called the library her Bookstall, and she still ran it with some kind of order. That scared Sylvia. Scared Albert, too. Made one wonder how she did it. Made Sylvia wonder if Delores wasn't something other than human. Some alien that lived off glue fumes. A galumphing glue golem.

Maybe she'd arrive one day to work and find padlock and chains dangling from the library's doors like calumnious jewelry. Maybe Ms. Gamelin would reboot the library and hire all new staff. Maybe Ms. Gamelin really did want Sylvia to take Albert's place. But then what about Delores? Why not replace her, if anyone?

And then Delores's soapy face appeared from the doorway's edge. She asked to see Sylvia in her office. She wore her "Glumday" sweater. Her hair had wiggled into an efficient pastry shape on her head.

Dolores wanted an update on the moss. "Wow me," she said Today she drank a foul herbal tea with turmeric in it.

"It's coming along," she said to Delores.

"But what does that mean, dear?"

"It's moved from Jefferson to Adams. It's also moved from presidents to political science in general."

"It's colonizing. Would you say this change in the moss is the kind of thing we'd have to tell Ms. Gamelin about?"

"That seems like your call."

"Well, in the hierarchy of Dealing with Problems, what I'm asking is—is this the kind of problem you know you can deal with and not notify the higher-ups? The kind of problem you can kick under the carpet?"

"This is not a carpet-kicker."

"Shitsky."

The rear door squealed open and slammed. The sound of Albert launching his carrier bag at his desk. His massive steps would've given him away anyway.

"Do you want a diet soda?" Delores asked.

"I'm still in opposition to soda, generally."

"Noted. Do you have a timeline on the moss mold?—is it moss, mold?"

"Not sure."

"Find out. Collect some in a baggie. I'll send it to a friend whose husband is a biology teacher. Or to a lab. Where was I? Oh, timeline. Do you know when those boys'll finish up? They smell."

They sat silent for a moment. It began to rain outside. The turmeric tea smelled like a corpse farm.

"What'll it take for you to quit that catering job, money-wise?"

"Excuse me?"

"I've been instructed by Ms. Gamelin to raise your pay, so you don't have to have a side hustle as a catering girl. So how much?"

Sylvia said she wasn't sure a number existed right at that moment.

"Make one," Delores said. "Or I'll make one for you."

She must not have had her glue yet. She was so rational and businesslike.

"I'm behind on some student loan bills. So enough to pay those—not just the interest, but the principle—and maybe enough to put into savings every month?"

"An extra three hundred a month."

Sylvia mentally whistled.

"But you say *nothing* to *no one*," Delores said. "Not even Albert. Especially not Albert. Also: you can't quit for, like, five years now because of this." Delores wasn't finished. Something nagged at her. Sylvia shivered. The office—like Children's—kept cold.

"Moreover, I'd prefer you didn't talk to her, Ms. Gamelin, if you could help it."

"Oh, well, I mean, I'd prefer to not really have much of a choice but she's kinda my boss-boss."

"*I'd* prefer if you'd walk away."

"From the director of the board?"

Delores sipped corpse-tea. She nodded.

"This is a lot of preferring," Sylvia said.

"If you're to be bought, then maybe it would make sense."

Sylvia jumped at this. Delores shook her head.

"I didn't mean that to come out so bald. I just don't like answering to a woman who spends little time in the library and pretends like she actually runs it. It's maddening. I'm sorry. Forget what I said."

"Sure, but the money?"

Delores delivered an empty glare.

"Right, well I'll be off then," Sylvia said. "Gotta check on my oompa-loompas."

The boys were taking a morning break out back. Busting balls. Cursing. Talking nonsense. Vaping, dipping, picking their noses. The back door with the crash bar didn't close all the way. She saw, through the sliver of morning light, a boy dangling some moss over his mouth. The stunt was less for them as for him. It dropped into his mouth. He chewed as on a wad of bubble gum. He didn't belabor it but didn't relish it either. He did it with a rare sort of dignity. Of course, the others cheered, jeered, and retched. One passed a Mountain Dew to him, mentioning Moss Boy could keep it.

The speed with which the boys were over the novelty of the moss-eating scared her. If Moss Boy had social capital, he'd spent it before it was credited. Most teens, Sylvia thought, lived with social debt. Always climbing out of a personality hole dug for you by others.

The boys talked food. Sylvia waited for something salacious. It never arrived, so she went to the bathroom. Pissed, wiped, washed her hands.

The boys quit the break and headed back into the basement.

"Shut up, already," one of them said to Moss Boy.

"What?" he asked. "It's important in Fair Isle knitting to carry your main color in your right hand...and anyway, Fair Isle isn't actually as old as reported; it didn't originate on the Shetlands *or* Orkneys, and it may only go back as far as the mid-19th century, likely arriving from Latvia or other reaches of Eastern Europe." Moss Boy spoke with passion and earnestness. His friends put pure distance between him and them.

Sylvia snagged Moss Boy by the shoulder. She dragged him out of earshot.

"What are you talking about?"

"Fair Isle knitting."

"Why?"

"Why not?"

"Do you knit?"

Thinking. "No."

"Then how do you know all that? Is that stuff true?"

Unequivocally, he said, "Yes," and peeled off and walked away. But she jogged to him at the basement door and asked him where they were scraping before their break. How far had they come since they started that morning?

"I don't know. Art stuff."

"No, like a call number."

"TT...8...shit...TT819. Can I go now?"

She pushed him along. In the Library of Congress catalog TT819 was in "handicrafts." The kid was reading instead of working. She'd need to check on them after lunch and make sure they weren't jacking off in the stacks or sleeping.

2.

For ten minutes, Sylvia sorted materials going to outlying county branches and interlibrary loan orders that came in overnight. But she rarely paid attention to the details. When she was sorting materials, she transformed into a machine. There was a book on attracting Monarch butterflies. Three bestsellers. A book on the Cosa Nostra mafia. A book on how to get rich in 365 days. Sit com DVDs. Disney movies. Classical CDs.

Some of these materials may've had bits of moss on them. Hard to tell. She didn't touch or inspect them closely. She did this until lunch when a febrile patron began yelling, "Yeah, well *frick you*, pal! You think you run this place? This is weapons-grade bullshit. I pay my taxes. I pay your salary. I demand to speak to the head librarian. Where's your manager? My parakeet could run this stupid place. And he only has one eye!"

Albert manned the checkout counter.

A homeless patron applauded this tirade. The rest of the patrons paused, waited, and went back to browsing and reading. The security guard pointed to the door. The febrile man flipped off the guard and charged out. A second homeless person stomped their appreciation and wolf whistled.

Albert returned to his desk in back. His face calmed. "I never hate people so much as when they immediately need something from me without preparation."

Sylvia cocked her head. "You're too sweet, Albert."

"Yeah, sure."

Violence was a foreign language to him.

"How much did he owe?"

"Collections agency level numbers. $1000?"

Sylvia didn't think fines could swell like that, like a preposterous financial tumor. "What did you do?"

"Nothing. Fines are idiotic, anyway."

Albert squatted on a tiny shelving stool. It sang in pain. He was a misplaced rock troll from a Scandinavian folk tale.

It was only ten-fifteen in the morning.

"Do you think we'll be able to keep the library open?"

"What are you talking about?"

"I don't know. Seems like this place is always heading into a crisis. At least that's how it seems when I speak with Delores." She considered their last discussion. "Listen, can I tell you something, something totally dogdick bonkers?"

"Sure. But gossip is for the early lunch set. I'm not in a bonkers mood just now. Dogdick or otherwise."

They waited a quiet hour then walked to the nearby hell-pit, Cicero's. Everything was painted matte black and smelled of old onion rings. Every seat, handle, and spoon needed de-greaser. You could shave the walls.

Sylvia unfolded her napkin in which lay a dead fly. Albert didn't react. She wondered if he'd grown a little as they left the library and walked to Cicero's—wider shoulders, thicker neck, broader head—but that was impossible. All Albert could talk about was Deena's dark persistence. What made it worse, he said, was that Natalia, his wife, was pregnant. It was their first, after years of desperate trying. Doctors couldn't find any specific fertility issues in either Albert or Natalia. They had all their timing down. They ate well. Exercised. Got eight hours of sleep. Still: years of negative pregnancy tests. And now finally Natalia was pregnant. He wanted to enjoy it but Deena was dampening everything.

"Shit, man. This stalking is absurd," Sylvia said. "Can I call the police for you? You should be focusing on this great...*thing* that's happening for you guys." Sylvia turned dumb around kids. Even proto-kids. Even around kid-talk. She literally had no words.

Some ruction in his thoughts lifted. He touched her hand. His was oddly like a warm loaf of bread. "I'll call when I get back to work. Truly. I will. But thank you."

Sylvia imagined feeding Deena the baggie of moss she brought with her to lunch. Just stuffing this foul plant-fudge down her gullet. She didn't know why. The action sequence in her mind felt satisfying. Moss dangling out of Deena's nose attached to her lifeless body.

They ordered and ate their mediocre burgers in silence.

"What did you want to tell me anyway?" Albert asked.

She spun The Tale of the Basement Boys and their travails eating moss. Albert sniffed in disgust.

"It's hard for me to say I ever dared another boy to do anything. Maybe I gently urged a fellow student to read H.G. Wells's *The Time Machine* or maybe *Robinson Crusoe*, but I couldn't get another person to eat what's widely accepted as inedible."

"But why did he spout off on Fair Isle knitting afterward? That's pretty loopy."

Albert leveled his eyes. "You're saying you don't read the books as you shelve them?" He pursed his lips. "It's possible this kid is a reader and wants to learn more because he's curious, but because teenage boys tend to cast out whatever's different and seemingly non-masculine, this poor schmuck is forced to share his newfound treasure with whomever he encounters, no matter the consequences."

"I think there's more to it than that."

"Why is this stuff on our books at all? We've already got some consortium libraries refusing to ship us their items for borrowing and a few that don't want us to send them anything for fear of contamination. We're slowly being cut off."

Sylvia's stomach turned cold and hard. "Like a tourniquet. We're going to fall off like a dead limb, aren't we? I *told* you. Our jobs are potato chip thin."

Albert had eaten his burger in, like, two bites. The food on his plate was like miniature toy food. She imagined him chewing on the chairs and the table to satisfy his hunger.

"Let's stick to facts, Sylvia. Delores is going to test this stuff. I bet it's mold. Which means the whole library will be shut down and affected books liquidated. They'll tent the building and start abatement. Who knows what'll happen to the employees who've been exposed, like you, me. Those boys. I'm sure there'll be some lawsuits. Some settlements. If it goes that way, Delores will lose her job."

I have to actually send it off first, big guy, Sylvia thought. But so far, she had zero intention of doing that. So Delores still had a leg up on employment.

"Ms. Gamelin?" she asked.

"She'll step to the side and the tragedy will miss her by millimeters. Isn't that how it always works?"

"Maybe people are villains just because they know exactly where to stand when a tragedy strikes."

She pictured Darth Vader in the Death Star as Alderaan blew apart into a fine planetary mist.

Albert recounted the immense amount of labor and skill needed to remove all the books and all the taxpayer money and the loss of the community public library and how so many people relied on it for internet access and entertainment and a place to stay dry or cool or warm or—

Then in the middle of all this, Sylvia caught sight of Moss Boy roaming outside Cicero's. He walked away from the library. Head down. Intent. Talking to himself. She tried to focus on Albert's discussion because her livelihood probably was being explained in it. But she couldn't quit thinking about Moss Boy and what the hell he was doing. But then, a few minutes later, coming back the other way was Moss Boy with armfuls of yarn and needles.

"No flipping way," she said.

"I know!" Albert said. "That is an expensive way to reformat the catalogue system, but I think we could—Wait. What are *you* talking about?"

Sylvia pushed back her chair. She walked to the window. Moss Boy talked to his purchases and seriously ignored everything around him. He walked into traffic. A pickup truck skidded to avoid him. Sylvia fled Cicero's and also ran through traffic to catch up with Moss Boy.

"I guess I'll pay for this," Albert called after her. He ordered another burger. He wanted fifty. The pit of his stomach ached.

Sylvia caught Moss Boy about a block from the library. "What the hell are you doing?"

Yarn spilled out of his arms. Moss Boy's face was empty.

"What?" he asked. He fingered the yarn and rubbed it between his fingers.

"Why aren't you in the basement scraping with the others? Why are you out here?"

"I'm getting yarn."

"I know. I see that. You've got about a paycheck's worth of fabric there. Do you feel okay? Did something happen between you and the other guys?"

He dropped hard to his ass and sorted the soft yarn. He arranged the colors and chose three glinty needles and started knitting. Sylvia wondered if he was on meth or speed. He didn't look like an addict.

He didn't look like Delores, either. He knitted fast, he was so keyed up. As he started the pattern—had to be Fair Isle—she knelt down.

"What's your name?"

Diligent knitting.

"Trent."

"Hi, Trent. I'm Sylvia. Did you eat that book moss earlier?"

Trent nodded. He'd already finished a row and started another.

"I know you did. I saw you out back. Now what happened after you ate it?"

"Nothing. I ate a sandwich. Drank a coke."

"Were you reading the Fair Isle knitting books while you scraped?"

He scoffed. *There* was the teenager. "No. I wouldn't be caught dead reading something like that."

"But then how do you know how to knit?"

His face didn't give anything away. Cognitive dissonance had no meaning here. Trent's hands were on automatic. He didn't answer. And he wasn't going to answer. She stood him up best she could while he worked the yarn. His wet pants darkened with residual dew. Sylvia glided him along to the back of the library. He couldn't be bothered.

"Stay here," she said. He didn't acknowledge her. She pointed an instructive finger at him. "Good boy. St*aaay*. St*aaay*."

She ran back to Cicero's, picking up what yarn had fallen and found Albert on his third burger. He was gripping the table with anticipation as he ate.

"What the hell, man?"

"I'm ravenous," he said.

"Stress."

"Desire, more like."

"Eww. Maybe you have a tapeworm. Hey, this kid is nuts. I have to call his parents and have someone pick him up. He's gone off the deep end." Now Albert was lost in a burgerworld. Yarn, meat. What was next? "Hello? Are you listening, Albert?"

Through the burger, "Uh huh."

"Do you care if I stop by your house later to talk more about what the hell is going on?"

Albert set the burger down and turned to her. Suddenly he was back. "You're always welcome in my home, Sylvia. Please stop by." There was a sadness in his eyes. The sadness sat there and curled and spread. The sadness rooted inside him and pulled Albert's limbs like a Punch and Judy doll. She wanted to collapse into her friend and hug him to death. But instead she patted his shoulder like a reticent jerk. Albert hung his head and considered his uneaten burgers.

Sylvia turned to leave and dropped a loop of yarn. She knelt to pick it up. The air smelled metallic. Like a rusty swing set chain. The smell knocked her brain apart. She straightened and looked across the street into the opposite storefront. What used to be an ice cream parlor, but now abandoned. The signage had been pulled down and the shadow of a logo remained. A huge lock on the door pull. Typical business transition shit. She expected something like a monument. A tall, terrifying shape. Instead, inside the storefront a woman stared at her. Her eyes glowed like weak bulbs.

The metal smell strengthened. Almost incapacitated her. A smell had never done that to her before, that she remembered. Sylvia clutched the baggie of moss-stuff and ran outside. Albert called after her to slow down. She knew the woman staring at her. It was Deena. Sylvia didn't look away. Deena's head was cocked forward, and she faintly grinned as if her face was stuck in a videotape glitch. The smell swelled in her nose as she crossed the road, and when she touched the locked door, the smell changed to clay, deep earth, and wet leaves. Like an old house let to sit for years with vagrant animals pissing inside. The lock mechanism gave when she pulled on the door. Deena still had that dozy look on her face. But looking past Sylvia. She was ramrodding Albert with an otherworldly stare.

"Hey," Sylvia whispered. "What the are you doing here?"

Deena didn't move. She appeared to have been sitting there for millennia. Sylvia nudged the table with her thigh. Deena blinked slowly, staring away into the long distance. The smell of metal returned. Sylvia's jaw ached. She felt a phantom tapping on her hands, then her teeth.

Deena was dressed like she'd been a mannequin in a department store from 1964. As Sylvia stood there, all the street noise came to a stop. Cars glided by silently. Slowly, the sensual world retreated.

Sylvia's hands and feet felt heavy, as if she was holding them underwater. Then she started to get pins and needles in her toes and thumbs. Then everywhere else. This, Sylvia told herself, was an anxiety attack. You've had them before. *Breathe.* There's nothing wrong here. You're just—

Sylvia was instantly paralyzed. If this was anxiety, then it was total and complete.

All the flattened memories from her time in the wood behind her house were reanimated. Flush with blood. They flexed with muscle and bone. The wood, the waiting, the tickle spider, the spindles. The investigation, the interrogation, the weighing of something intangible in her.

Deena wasn't Deena. Sylvia knew that now. The clingy awkward woman from the library with a crush on Albert was no more. She wasn't inside the body that sat at the table and now stood up. Sylvia could see parts of Deena were patched in moss, vibrant and beautiful.

And a sound, like a trapped bird deep within a cage somewhere, maybe Deena's torso, sang out.

fa fa fa fa

Sylvia squeezed her eyes and her mouth shut the best she could.

fa fa fa fa

She opened her eyes and Deena had her mouth open. There were no teeth, no tongue. There was no throat. There was nothing. It was just a gaping black hole. Then a tumbling wad of moss rolled out and twisted around. It racked Deena's body and fought her. And Deena fought it. The mossy tendrils flicked and flopped their way to Sylvia. They seemed to sniff at her, to taste her. But they fell back, sensing danger or recognizing a certain unwelcome flavor. The moss tongue whipped back up into Deena's body and shuddered her backward. Unfazed, Deena rose and shuffled out the back of the building.

Within minutes, Sylvia's limbs were pins and needles, then tingling, then full of feeling. Still she dared not move. The old fear had her. She wept. She wept for her childhood, for forgetting what had happened in the wood, and she wept for the stupidity of pretending that her memories were cheap and fungible.

Behind her, she heard a crash. The door swung open.

"Sylvia?"

She couldn't turn to see. Correction: *didn't want to see.*

"Albert," she whispered.

He came alongside her and placed his hand on her shoulder. It almost crushed her. As soon as he touched her, she was able to spin around and grip him.

"What are you doing in here?" he asked.

"Can we please get out of here?"

"Sure."

He'd watched her run out and into this storefront. She stood there for ages, he said. Finally, after finishing his burgers, he came to see what the hell was going on.

"Looked like you were praying," he said.

"That is nowhere close to what I was doing."

Moss Boy was missing from where she'd left him. From his pocket, Albert brought out the yarn Sylvia dropped in Cicero's and placed it on the ground. It felt like putting flowers on a grave.

Before they returned to work, Sylvia sat down by the library's employees' entrance. There was no good place for Albert to sit, so he stood cheerfully.

"Can I tell you about something odd? Something that I've long carried with me but never told anyone?" She rubbed her wrists then her knees. Parts of her still buzzed with fear.

Albert smiled. "If you can't trust your local librarian, then who can you trust?"

"Have I ever mentioned the word *Grasshands* to you?"

He shook his head.

"How do I explain this without sounding insane...Grasshands is the way I used to think of how the world experienced life. Like, if we live in our daily lives, going along at a 'normal' city life pace, then the world, as an entity, goes along at a different one. Does that make sense?"

"Sure. Although, you have to think the world is an entity. Like Gaia."

"Eh, not really. But for the sake of the argument, yeah."

"This isn't crazy. But what does this have to do with you standing in an abandoned building looking terrified?"

"I used to think Grasshands was an adjective. But now I think it's a noun."

Albert thought about that. He pinched his lower lip. He tried to sit as best he could beside her. It didn't work.

"In what way is Grasshands a noun?"

"It's a thing. I saw a thing. I saw Grasshands when I was a little girl. I forgot about it, but it's, like, here. In the city."

"Hmm," Albert said.

"Crazy, right?"

"Yeah, a little. But some famous philosophers and thinkers have done much worse. This psychoanalyst, Wilhelm Reich, thought that there was a sexual energy that permeated the cosmos and could be captured and put into a box. He called it 'orgone.' People believed that. People built boxes that stored orgone and sat in them. Total idiocy. What did this look like, this Grasshands, when you saw it the first time?"

"Like a huge statue of moss."

Albert turned to her. He narrowed his eyes. He pointed toward the library, as if to say, *like the moss in there?*

Sylvia nodded. Then, remembering, she pulled the baggie from her pocket and held it out in front of them. It looked green, dumb, and harmless. It looked like a goddamn baggie of moss. She poked it. Flicked it.

Sylvia said: "And that's not even the whole story, man."

Tap tap

CHAPTER THREE

MOSS BOY'S MOTHER picked him up. One of the boys called her to say he was acting dumb. Sylvia sent the rest of the teenagers home and roped off the basement until she could figure out what was going on. Albert urged her to leave early with sick time, but to be honest, she needed the money.

Delores knocked on the top of the cubicle Sylvia sat in. Her turmeric tea's funk was merely mild today.

"You look the way my tea smells, Sylvia."

"Gee, thanks, boss."

"Did you send that sample off yet?" Delores looked around as if she was being spied on. "Time being a quality of essence and all that jazz."

"Yeah," Sylvia lied. "Taken care of."

"Good girl. Oh, Gamelin will be in tomorrow. She wants to see the progress in the basement. So I suggest you scrap the police tape you have up now."

"It'll be fine."

Delores patted the cubicle wall like an athlete's butt and drifted off.

The last of the returned materials breezed past Sylvia's eyes with little notice. Then it was end of work. Would Deena be outside in the parking lot? If so, what the hell would—*could*—Sylvia do? Bite? Claw? Not if Deena—it—paralyzed her again. Even as she sat, placid, in the cubicle, her feet tingled. But was it anxiety or Grasshands?

She breathed in slowly. The tingling stopped. Then her mind suddenly switched tracks. She was defragging her memory. Who else was a danger to her? Who else was tainted?

People bunched in the break room. Conversing by gunmetal grey army lockers. Retrieving purses and man bags. Talking beers, fussing zippers, goofing. Pete—a library veteran—used a mophandle as a long thin whanger. Some guy she didn't recognize pretended to jack it off. Teresa B. flicked it with her finger.

Everyone hated work. No one wanted to leave. The best of worst worlds.

Sylvia didn't know what to do. She never commiserated with colleagues. Still, she felt pulled inside the library. As if leaving meant death or danger. Full tilt animal alarms rang in her head.

"You coming with me?" Albert asked. "I'll drive you."

"Nah. I'm wiped out. I need to decompress. I need to walk."

"I'll buy you ice cream."

"Tempting, but no thanks."

He nodded slowly and squeezed her shoulder. He left.

Sylvia scoped out Teresa. She was switching from slave sandals to sneakers. She asked if Teresa wanted her sweater. Something about keeping the clothes that Deena/Grasshands had touched freaked Sylvia out. She lied and said it made her itchy. Teresa jumped up and down. "I've always loved your stuff," she said. "Here, do you want mine as a trade?" Sylvia took it. She wanted to burn her wardrobe. But she had a hunch. She balled her hair up in a way she never did. She looked different enough.

When Teresa pulled away into traffic, Sylvia watched a car across the street follow. They both turned at a stoplight in front of the library. Sylvia saw the driver's face. Some older guy.

She was equally relieved and disappointed. She wanted to take back everything she said about stalkers. All her goofy experiment proved was that she had one less sweater. And she edged closer to paranoia—a country possessing shifting topography; a country that didn't like emigrants.

Her walk home was uneventful and it felt good to walk. To feel her legs, feet, face. To allow the air to brace her brain. Her patience with herself was thinning. She aimed to go straight to her room. Maybe read. Maybe take a hot shower later when everyone went to sleep.

Two of Sylvia's roommates, Johanna and Leigh Ann, were watching a show about cyst removal. Johanna, a warm-hearted former goth, waved. "Your aquarium has been making noises for the past few hours," she said.

Without looking up, Leigh Ann said, "And I borrowed a bra."

"I don't have an aquarium," Sylvia said.

Johanna pursed her mouth. "Oh."

"You only had one bra," Leigh Ann added.

Water leaked from underneath Sylvia's bedroom door, which she always kept closed. She rushed in to find the ceiling collapsed on top of her bed. Apparently a thin pipe ran over her bedroom and was slowly leaking. Water made a weak pissing sound hitting her possessions. Her sheets were stained various shades of brown. Clothes left on the bed leaked dye. It looked like the mattress was bleeding or crying. The room smelled like old wet laundry left in the washer. Moldy. Damp. Her few favorite novels swelled with water-logged girth. Absolutely ruined. A few notebooks filled with random thoughts were also worthless.

A voice from across the apartment: "What-in-the-fuck-is-this?"

This was Merrill. Merrill owned the apartment. Everyone rented from her. No one liked it. Tough shit, Merrill would've said. She owned the apartment outright and funneled a lot of her income into her mother's addiction. The mother had had a tummy tuck that went bad, got sick, and then was quickly addicted to opioids. Nothing about Merrill was lovely. Much was fine, acceptable, or even okay—but never lovely.

"Why didn't you tell me about this leak, Sylvia?"

Sylvia was picking through her ruined items. "Merrill, I didn't know there was a leak. And if I did, Merrill, don't you think I would've told you before it destroyed my shit?"

This wasn't entirely true. Sylvia had been staring up at a bulge above her head for months now. She refused to see it as either ominous or frivolous. She saw the bulge above her as more of a wonderful sign. But with everything at the library—moss, Deena, Gamelin, Delores—and now Grasshands proliferating her memory— none of this was a wonderful sign.

"Whatever," Merrill said. "You're paying for this."

"*You're* the landlord. *You* need to pay for it."

"I don't know where it says that."

"Somewhere in some fucking renter's rights, I don't know. There's a fucking law somewhere, I know that." She reeled around and spread out her hands in desperation. "Johanna? Help?"

Johanna leaned into view from the couch. "I mean, I don't even know. But I think it would be nice if Merrill paid for it. Half?"

Merrill turned on Johanna.

"I don't think you understand how renting works, Merrill," Sylvia said.

"No, I don't think you do, Syl. As the landlord, I know that I can ask you to move out while I repair damages."

"You have to find a place for her," Leigh Ann said. "I think."

"I'll sleep on the couch," Sylvia said. "It's not a big deal."

She felt her energy to argue being drained away by Merrill's tenacity to win. She was a logic vampire, sucking the will to think straight. But, no, this was just pure exhaustion. Sylvia wanted to stand up for herself, say something definitive about her experience. She wanted to ask: *Have any of you women been paralyzed by a force of nature from your childhood in the form of a friend's stalker in an empty storefront?*

But, you know, questions like that always seem to fall flat.

Merrill shook her head. "No way. I'm not having you live in our shared spaces. This may take weeks to get done. You're going to have to find another place to stay until this gets fixed."

Sylvia leveled her gaze at Merrill. "This isn't getting fixed any time soon, is it?"

"That's not for me to say, Syl." The expression on her face said, *The hell if I get this fixed for you, bitch.*

Sylvia packed the one piece of luggage she had. It was a small magenta carry-on. Absolutely hideous. She had to be discriminatory about her choices. Johanna and Leigh Ann helped her sort what was dry. Leigh Ann gave her back her bra. "I'll come back and get the rest of my shit later," Sylvia said. Johanna said she'd salvage and dry and bag her paper materials and photos. She gave her a quick hug and pat on the back. When Sylvia's grandparents died, their home needed a few dumpsters worth of space to haul off their belongings. They'd been collecting worthless tat for three score. Sylvia had barely enough to fill a lunchbox.

Merrill demanded her share of the rent for the next month to help fix the leak and hole. Sylvia parted with the extra three hundred that

Ms. Gamelin had given her. It hurt to hand it over. Literally, she had pain in her wrists and forearms. That was most of her savings, pathetic as it was. Now she had one source of income, no home, and a whopping case of spiritual madness. What was left?

She called Albert. Shortly thereafter, he pulled up in a whiny import that looked designed and built *around* him rather than for anyone of normal size to get in and out of. When she shut the passenger door, Sylvia cried for ten minutes. Albert held her awkwardly. It was the safest Sylvia had felt in a long time. That fact made her even more anguished.

CHAPTER FOUR

"YOU SHOULD'VE COME here after work, anyway," Natalia said, hugging her. She was being hugged a lot. Could hugging tire one out? "Albert told me you ran into Deena earlier."

Albert made a motion behind his wife to Sylvia that said: *She knows nothing about the weird shit.* That is—Grasshands.

Natalia and Albert's house was quaint. There was no other way to describe it. Walls covered with family photos. One of Albert years ago (much smaller) outside the library planting a tree. One of Natalia in a police officer's uniform shaking someone's hand at a ceremony. Another was a newspaper clipping of Natalia and another woman standing behind police tape, talking. The caption said that the two were detectives working on an arson case.

This startled Sylvia.

"You were a detective?"

Natalia turned to Albert. "You never told her?"

He shrugged. "I guess it never came up."

Natalia swatted at him. It was a real hit. "Yes, I was a detective for about five years before I left. An officer years before that. Sort of a self-imposed retirement."

"Why for?"

Natalia inhaled dramatically and pointed to her stomach. She smiled warily. She explained she suffered from a light case of hyperemesis gravidarum.

"Understood," Sylvia said. "I know that it has been hard for both of you. *That* Albert has shared with me. Congratulations, by the way."

Natalia thanked Sylvia again in that wary way. Albert ducked through the doorway and slid sideways to move from room to room. Sylvia never really noticed this perspective since the library's passageways were large enough to accommodate two people and more. Albert excused himself to change. He took Sylvia's luggage and left it in the guest room.

As soon as Albert was gone, Sylvia breathed in to ask a question, but Natalia handed her a glass of wine and said, "No, he's not always been that big. When we first moved here, oh, fifteen years ago, he was twenty-five. He was done growing by then. And he had plenty of clearance. Now he's having to take baths in the guest tub. He can't shower downstairs anymore. I'm thinking he'll be better off in the basement stall. It's just a showerhead coming off a pipe in a coal room." She shivered to think of it.

"Umm. What's that about? Is he sick? Shouldn't he get tested?"

"*Dios mío. Me gustaría que lo hiciera.*" She laughed to herself. "No, he hasn't."

"He hasn't? What the shit?"

Natalia leaned against the counter. Sylvia decided she couldn't be more than two months pregnant, tops. But she had no idea. "He won't. He's embarrassed. Or scared. I can't tell. You don't know me all that well, I know, but I obsessively research everything down to the dryer sheets we use. And I've found only a couple things"—she stopped to listen for him—"only a few things it could be. The pituitary gland is a suspect."

Sylvia laughed up a bit of her wine through her nose.

"What? Oh—yeah. *Suspect*. Sorry. Detective pun."

"I suppose I just don't understand why he won't sit in a doctor's office for more than ten minutes."

Natalia was re-chewing all of this anger and resentment, Sylvia could see. Her presence was acting as a catalyst.

"He doesn't like being researched. Even if it means he'll be healthy. He likes doing the research. That's kind of why we get along."

Sylvia said she was starting to see how they worked.

"Still, I'm starting to get concerned. Even in the last week, it seems like he's gotten larger."

As if on cue, the floorboards squeaked from the other side of the house. Albert's bulk was on the move. Natalia topped off Sylvia's wine and put a finger to her mouth. She appeared genuinely nervous.

"I know I won't get anywhere by directly talking with him, so I pretend it's cute. But. I'm waiting for him to get frustrated. He's wearing clothes that I could drape over a small car. Anything you can do to drop a hint would be helpful."

"I don't want to get in the way of anything—" Sylvia muttered.

Albert surprised them, silently shifted sideways and ducked to enter the kitchen. He was wearing a large red knit sweater. Sylvia immediately knew it wasn't Fair Isle. Natalia handed Albert a glass of wine. The contrast in size between the glass and his paw was disorienting.

"Shall we sit?" Albert suggested. He motioned for the women to go ahead. When they did, Albert said, "We want to offer you a place to stay until your room is repaired." Natalia touched Albert's knee in agreement.

"I don't know if you understand Merrill. She has no intention of fixing it anytime soon. It's just as possible she'll block off the room and never enter it ever again."

Natalia said, "That's...disturbing."

"Well, yeah," Sylvia said. "But can we talk about something else other than me? I'm tired of thinking about my life. I sometimes feel I only exist to provoke."

"That must be tiring," Natalia said.

"No, it's okay. I make my own hours."

"What do you want to talk about?" Albert asked.

Sylvia pointed to Natalia's belly. Both Albert and Natalia smiled weakly but looked down somberly at her midsection. "Unless that's too sensitive?"

Albert nodded but Natalia said, "We've been patient a long time. So patient. Every doctor has told us outright or in some form to 'be patient.' 'Have patience.' I finally got so frustrated with this shit that I decided to find out what the origin of the word was, you know, especially as I was being seen 'as a patient' over and over. What the hell, you know? *I* am a patient and also need to *be* patient. What the hell does that mean? Do you know what it means?" Sylvia shook her head. "It comes from a Latin word that means *suffer*. Being patient means suffering."

Sylvia could only offer a dumbfounded stare. Some patrons at the library gave off this stare when you asked them pointed questions like, *Why are you dog-earing those pages so violently?*

"I think we should beg off this topic, sweetie," Albert said. He gulped his wine.

"No, I don't think we should, Beto. We have done nothing but wait patiently. We've done our suffering, for years."

"I know, Nat, but maybe not this, right now, in front of Syl."

"Sylvia doesn't care, do you?"

Sylvia threw her hands up. "Hey, guys, like I said, I'm not here to mess up anything." Natalia wiped at her eyes. Her hands trembled.

"You're not," Albert said.

"Shit's already messed up here, Sylvia. Don't worry about that." Natalia slumped down. She protected her belly with a hand. In uncharacteristic fashion, Albert took his glasses off and aggressively rubbed his face. "I'll glad you're here. Seriously. Finally a witness to how *brave* Albert is."

"Please stop, Natalia," he said.

Sylvia set her wine down. She couldn't remember where she'd left her shoes. She could come back in the morning for her luggage. But where to go in the meantime? As soon as she asked the question, she knew the answer, but refused to acknowledge it. She would've rather spent the night in the park or against the back door of the library. She had a rear entry key. *Where the eff were her keys?*

"You can't keep doing this!" Natalia said. "See a doctor already! A dentist, a veterinarian, an actor who plays a doctor. Go see a goddamn witch doctor if you have to."

Albert rose slowly. Not out of drama but because of his massive weight. He and gravity fought each other. A lot. He didn't seem comfortable standing from such a low position. Sylvia and Natalia began to rise and help him. Albert waved them off.

Finally, he was on his feet and touched his temples and swayed. He listed to one side but caught himself. In frustration, he stood on his tiptoes and slammed a fist through the ceiling. Drywall crumbled over his head as if from a shitty piñata.

Natalia dodged the debris and covered her waterglass. "What the fuck, man! *Chingado!* Come on, goddamn. Can you watch where you're going, please? That shit cost money to fix."

Albert, shamefaced, held his injured hand to his side. It was bleeding. He nodded slowly, picked up his wine glass, and shuffled into the kitchen. Before he did, he turned, and out of the side of his mouth said, "Plethora moon bench."

To Sylvia's surprise, Natalia smiled. In just the most intimate and private way. She repeated the phrase back quietly, embarrassed to be heard by Sylvia.

Plethora moon bench.

As Albert walked on, all the objects in the living room sitting on shelves jiggled.

Sylvia needed to leave. She rubbed the top of her thighs. "You know, I really appreciate your hospitality, but I think I need to get back to my apartment and see about—"

"Nonsense," Natalia said. "We may fight, but we love one another. Those people you live with sound like they hate you to see your face." Sylvia leaned back. "But if you think you have to go, okay. Although, I'd recommend you just stay at least one night. We promise that our beds aren't soaked in water."

Despite her total honesty, Natalia seemed to clearly need a third person in the mix to take the edge off.

A phone rang in the kitchen. Albert's cell. Natalia brushed drywall off the couch. Sylvia pulled her legs closer to her chest as she listened to a muffled conversation between Albert and Someone Unknown.

Albert returned holding the phone out in front of him like radioactive material. "That was Delores."

"She never calls you outside of work," Natalia said.

"The boy who ate moss isn't doing well. As in, he's doing poorly. The boy's mother called Delores. He knitted fifty sweaters tonight. His knuckles are swollen and bleeding. He's also unresponsive to speech and movement and light."

Sylvia felt Albert looking at her. She also felt his anxiety about her having some moss in a baggie in their house. But this wasn't a concern. She didn't know why. Eating it was the idiot move. Not holding it.

"So what does that mean?" Sylvia asked. "Unresponsive."

"Yeah, is he still knitting?" Natalia asked.

"Apparently, but he's slowing down. The mother doesn't know that her son ate the moss. So we'll need to be discrete for now. She was calling Delores to warn her, to warn other employees about this. She thinks it's a virus."

Natalia shrugged. "Maybe it is?"

Albert and Sylvia's glares converged onto her. At the same time, they said: "It's not."

"Okey doke," Natalia said, and threw her hands up. "I'll just sit here in my Midcentury Modern drywall dust and watch y'all drink boxed white wine." She stretched her legs across the couch. "Anyone interested in starting a show and then falling asleep halfway through?"

Sylvia turned to Albert, like, *What do we do?* He was thinking.

"Delores said she wants to speak with you first thing tomorrow," he said.

"Naturally."

Sylvia's guest room had a cozy bed, a tapestry billowing from the ceiling, and the air smelled like books. Small stacks of them were up against the wall.

"Living the cliché, I guess," Albert said, noticing this.

"I'd be mad if they weren't there," she said. She kneeled to inspect them. Many of them were children's books or young adult. New and used.

"I don't know when you wake up," he said, "but we're often eating and drinking coffee around seven. Let me know if you need anything."

She sat on the edge of the bed and told him she was sorry for interfering.

He shifted his shoulders, uncomfortable under the low ceiling. "You weren't interfering. We're just having a tough time right now. And I'm...well, I'm in a weird spot. Literally." Total understatement. He took a long moment, then said, "The problem is I think I'm understanding her but I'm just trying to attend to my own wounds." He sighed. "We often think we're loving someone when what we're really doing is making them into a mirror. That's when I get into trouble."

Sylvia agreed in her mind-heart and found this plausible. She felt this was what her and her mother were doing to one another for years until she died. Probably what her grandparents did to each other. It was what she did with any girlfriend or boyfriend she had. It was what she did with all the strangers she tried to extend flawed human care to. All of it withered because she was trying hard to mold people.

Albert rubbed a finger on his left hand.

"What's wrong?" she asked.

"My wedding ring."

His ring finger was swollen and empurpled. Sylvia hadn't even noticed. It looked bloated and infected. It looked like a mutated sausage.

"Jesus Christ."

He peered at her over those professorial glasses. "I need to have it cut off soon—the ring, I mean—it's slowly amputating my finger. That's what my medical professional claims." He tried to turn the ring, but it was stuck in place. His finger had grown too fast and he'd not thought to take it off.

"I thought you hadn't seen a doctor?"

He snorted. He never snorted. This was amusing for both of them.

"I'm not an idiot, Sylvia," he rattled with kindly thunder. His face dropped and his eyes watered on the edges. "I'm just as terrified as Nat is. I've gone multiple times. I just haven't told her everything because there's nothing to tell and because I don't want to disturb her. We have to think about the baby."

Sylvia stood up and took Albert's hand. It was heavy like a piece of marble statuary in her palm. "I think she's intelligent enough to handle you and the baby at the same time."

"You're right, of course. I'm overprotective."

"Many people would argue that that's not necessarily a negative, you know?"

Albert tried to smile but it came off as weary and painful. He side-hugged her, snuggled her head into his chest. She couldn't wrap her arms around him. He was a human garden shed.

The daybed was cramped against the wall. Sylvia hated this. As a child, her bed had been shoved against the wall. Her mother was worried Sylvia would fall out or off the bed. So she corralled her in. Her mother sometimes laid piles of blankets around Sylvia's bed just in case she rolled out. Ridiculous.

Sylvia pulled the daybed into the center of the room and gasped. There was a series of holes punched into the wall. They were the size of fists.

Suspicious, she stood on the bed and pushed back the tapestry. There, another series of dark holes dotted the ceiling. She could picture Albert letting loose after an argument just like he did earlier. She covered the ceiling again and stood for a long time.

Sylvia slipped under the covers. She sat with the lamp on.

Outside, rain pelted the earth. Cars streamed by. A slishing sound took over. It was almost meditative.

She walked through the plot of *The Wizard of Oz* two times in her mind to fall asleep. And she listened for Albert's giant steps in the hallway. She hated herself for that. Treating her friend and confidant as a fairy tale villain.

But she had to keep watch.

At some point early in the morning hours before sunrise, she woke to a sound. What she thought was morning traffic. More cars slishing through rain. But it was more of a delicate sound.

Tap tap

She first thought it was the heat coming on. The radiators clinking alive. No. Sylvia reached out and touched the radiator by the bed. It almost shocked her with its coldness.

Tap tap

Cool air from the holes in the wall buffeted the daybed. Despite her covers, Sylvia couldn't stay warm now. The sound was growing and an iceberg of a thought inside her split in half. She recognized it. The sound.

Tap tap

Her palms dampened. Her mouth tasted of batteries. She began to feel tingles in her toes. How did it find her here? She didn't see any moss anywhere. Was Deena outside? She was absolutely trapped in the room.

A rush of air flew out of the holes in the ceiling. The tapestry fluttered madly.

From the ceiling came: *fa fa fa fa*

Quickly, Sylvia's feet were numb. But she stood anyway, which wasn't what she thought she'd do. Factions of her mind battled each other. One side wanted to cry and hide. The other wanted to burn the fucking house down.

She blearily looked up into the tapestry and ceiling holes. She stood. And on what felt like numb stumps, she sang back.

"*Fa fa fa fa,*" she sang in a whisper. Unthinkingly, she also snapped her fingers softly. Just barely touching her middle finger and thumb together. She did this quickly and rhythmically. She was running on instinct here, like she was riffing with an instrument or a musician. Vamping. Maybe it wanted to know if another of its kind was out there, listening. Preparing to help or attack. And Sylvia's singing was meeting this unknown source at the same register; that is, giving back as good as it gave. Does it make sense? she wondered, standing on the bed. She guessed speaking back into the abyss could silence it.

The sound from the ceiling was responding to her. Not by changing pitch, tone, or words, but almost tying in with her singing. Then it was like a challenge. Sylvia's feet started to tingle again. And within a minute she had feeling in them. Her whole body anchored to the floor, really.

Fa fa fa fa, the ceiling sang.

"*Fa fa fa fa fa*," Sylvia sang back.

She finally noticed that the ceiling seemed to stretch down to meet her. It almost, she thought—although it was very dark—seemed that the ceiling was trying to kiss (or eat) her.

But as soon as she realized this, the ceiling stopped singing. The sound was gone. The cold air had stopped. And she was merely snapping and cooing into the blackness.

Tick tick clack.

That was the radiator. The heat hissed on through the pipes. With that sound, Sylvia felt at ease. Maybe she knew she'd told whatever was in the ceiling to keep away. Even though she had no idea what she was saying, singing. Maybe it was simply placated. Or scared. Or satisfied.

Whatever it was, she thought, it couldn't have been worse than what came out of the woods that day as a young girl. Grasshands had many forms, she figured, and that papery, spindly spiderthing was the worst. So far.

Those thoughts faded as she fell back asleep. She dreamed of Natalia holding a big fat wonderful baby with thick black hair. The dream baby was happy and laughed and laughed and laughed.

In the morning, Sylvia came down to the kitchen. Albert had demanded black carbonized toast. Natalia gave in.

"It's hard to watch him basically eat carbon bark," Natalia said behind his back. Sylvia shrugged. Although it made her gag to watch him choke it down.

Albert looked guilty while he ate it.

"Let me guess, he hasn't ever liked his toast black?" Sylvia asked.

Natalia shook her head. They sat down and began to eat.

"Since you're staying with us now," Natalia said to Sylvia, "why don't you get the rest of your stuff? Get settled in, you know?"

"I'll drive you," Albert suggested. Clumps of coalblack soot lined his mouth.

"No," Sylvia said abruptly.

Natalia and Albert looked at her, both in mid-bite.

"I mean—well, I'd already planned on getting a walk in and it's fine. I don't have much left. I'll get it, no worries."

She sipped some orange juice and stared down.

"Cool," Natalia said. "That'll be your room now."

"Then I'll tell Delores you may be late," Albert said. He didn't make eye contact with anyone. He wiped the carbon from his mouth. Then he spent an awkward minute trying to remove himself from the kitchen table. It almost tipped over. Albert didn't say goodbye or kiss his wife or even wipe his hands. He squeezed through the doorway and was gone.

Sylvia returned to the apartment to get her stuff, but it was gone. All of it. Her bedroom was unlocked, and the space was cleared. No one was around, either. Which was strange, considering the women had differing work schedules.

Sylvia knocked on their bedroom doors. Nothing. No one in the bathroom. She called out for someone. No one answered.

Her room had been a total clusterfuck. Now it was spotless. The ceiling was still broke open like a sore, but the leak stopped. The floor was dry. Her closet was empty. Every single item she'd left behind—pictures, clothing, books, letters—all of it disappeared. Not a goddamn scrap left.

Sylvia started to call Merrill when the front door lock shifted.

"Sylvia," Merrill said, as if she'd entered the apartment and discovered a walking tumor and not a human.

"Merrill, where's my stuff?" she asked, pointing.

She could tell Merrill was sincerely confused. Like, actually and honestly confused. In fact, Merrill looked unnerved.

"Talk to the other girls. I had nothing to do with this."

"Right." Sylvia stood facing the magically sterile bedroom. Merrill did, too.

What made Sylvia most upset, now that she thought about it, wasn't losing everything. It was really the loss of a few specific pictures. She'd had wonderful Polaroids of her mother. Those were gone now. Before heading to work, she quickly checked the Dumpster out back. Of course, there was nothing. Verdict: her possessions grew legs, stood up, and walked away.

CHAPTER FIVE

NOT MUCH ABOUT that morning could make the previous day feel any weirder. But when she walked into work and saw Delores, Ms. Gamelin, and the mayor, Eben Hardy, talking over a pile of moss on a desk, all bets were cancelled.

Hardy had a way of heaping his hands on top of one another as if they were about to fall off. Could've been from his days as a police officer.

"What we have is a litigation issue," Hardy said. "The mother wants to sue the city and the library for negligence."

"Negligence of what?" Ms. Gamelin said. "Her son ate moss."

"What we *think* is moss," Delores broke in. "Not sure yet."

"Whatever, Delores. Point is, Mayor, the boy could've just as easily eaten soap from the soap dispenser or chugged bleach from the mop room. Doesn't make us responsible." Ms. Gamelin was wearing a finely tailored hound's-tooth jacket and dark sailor pants. It was off-putting but fashionable. Only the head of a board of directors could do such a thing.

Mayor Hardy was overwhelmed. But he also appeared boyish, anxious to stir up manufactured trouble and then tackle it, Sylvia thought.

"Sylvia!" Ms. Gamelin said, spotting her. "Come."

Sylvia stood by her dark mother. Ms. Gamelin lovingly put an arm around Sylvia's shoulders and squeezed. Everyone beamed. Sylvia felt trapped. But it was a kind of trapped feeling that was remotely comforting.

Hardy shook Sylvia's hand. His skin felt like wet clay.

"Is Trent better?" she asked.

"Who's Trent?" the mayor asked.

Delores said it was the name of the boy who ate the moss.

The mayor beamed again. "Oh! Yes, he's just started eating liquids again. Doesn't remember his name, though."

Sylvia's chest tightened. *Hmm. That doesn't seem like he's better, does it?*

"Sylvia, dear," Delores said. "Could you please tell the mayor what happened."

"I was in charge of cleaning off the moss from the books downstairs and during their break I saw Trent eat some on a dare."

"Perfect," Ms. Gamelin said. "See? We had nothing to do with it."

"I don't know if that's the point," Sylvia said to her.

Ms. Gamelin glared at her, as if Sylvia was betraying a long-held secret.

"Did you have the moss tested?" Delores asked.

Here was a moment that Sylvia knew needed the "right" answer. Right as in, "what they wanted to hear." The untested baggie of moss was heavy in her pocket. She told them, "Yes, and it's just moss." She felt guilty. She *should've* sent it off. Instead she delayed and rationalized. She got scared allowing it out of her possession. She worried that if a scientist—while good-natured and well-meaning—perhaps got *too* curious, he'd send a smidge more off to another scientist, maybe in Atlanta at the CDC. Then the moss would be traveling over half the United States. Wasn't it better to keep it quarantined? She also had a strange attachment to it, like she knew it somehow.

Hardy nodded, obviously thinking about next steps. "Good. Please have the results sent to my office. I'd like to have them forwarded to the mother."

"Uhh, sure. How about I just send them directly to her?"

Ms. Gamelin squeezed Sylvia's shoulder again. "That's not how things get passed along in the adult world, dear," she said.

"I'm twenty-eight," Sylvia said plainly.

The boyish smile overtook the mayor's face. "Could I see this moss?"

Delores replied that it wouldn't be a bother at all. Her breath stank. Smelled like wood polish. Or linseed oil. Something not natural for a human's mouth to smell like.

They all began to head downstairs when a teenaged girl caught Delores by the sleeve. She was out of breath. Wide-eyed. Scared.

"Ms. Bardin wants you to come up to Children's," she said. "They found moss on the young adult stacks. And a few kids have already tried to eat it."

Before they were at the top of the stairs, Ms. Gamelin pulled in Sylvia. "I know you didn't test that moss, missy. Doesn't matter. After this, Delores is gone. You ready for that?"

Sylvia tugged away from her grip.

In front of them, Teresa Bardin, Children's librarian, stood like a defeated babysitter. She wore an avocado cardigan over her shoulders. She gestured downward.

Every other young adult novel was blanketed in bright Kelly green, damn-near sparkly moss. This stuff was radically different than what Trent ate or what Sylvia saw in the basement. If anything—*if anything*, this moss reminded her instantly of the broad soft blanket of green moss that she saw, stood on, and ran away from when she was a girl in the woods. The homebase of Grasshands.

The mayor knelt down in front of a shelf and peeled a sheaf of the fuzzy stuff off. He sniffed it. Then he brushed it on his cheek. He stuck his tongue to it. Shook his head, amazed.

"Kinda sweet," he reported. Sylvia looked over his shoulder and saw the moss had been attached to a middle volume of C.S. Lewis's *Narnia* books.

"I'd not do that, if I were you," she said. "Trent began acting strange and, as you said, he just eats soup now."

It was a strange way to persuade someone, Sylvia thought, bad-mouthing soup like that.

"I was an Eagle Scout, if you didn't know," he said without looking up.

"I didn't," she said. *How could I have?*

"Well, now you know. And I know that moss isn't poisonous. It's edible if prepared the correct way. Preferably boiled."

Hardy nibbled a small bit of the moss. She thought she heard him say *yum* quietly to himself.

This was madness, Sylvia thought. She reached down and yanked the moss from the mayor's hands. He stood and took it back. Looking at Sylvia, but speaking to Ms. Gamelin, he said, "Would you mind coming with me and discussing future moves?" They left.

Delores and Teresa Bardin were talking with a group of middle-schoolers. One of them said that two boys and a girl took the moss because they heard Trent got high and they went to eat some in the bathroom. No one knew where they were now. Sylvia, anxiety clenching her stomach, ran to the second-floor girls' bathroom and found an open stall. On the toilet seat were moss crumbs and fibers. Some vomit was in the toilet bowl.

Sylvia tried to work, checking in materials. But parents were in and out of Delores's office. They ranted, raved. Many of them blamed Delores herself for the moss, which was nuts.

"It's been tested," she heard Delores say over and over. "It's safe. It's fine. It's like eating lettuce."

"It's a fad, a dare," she heard.

"It'll pass," people said.

It would not pass, Sylvia thought. The basement was roped off and no one was allowed down there without Delores's permission.

She overheard Delores on the phone with someone who must've been Trent's mother. Trent was doing better. Maybe returned to normal? "Oh," she heard Delores say to the mother on the phone. "So you think this may've been a blessing in disguise? I see. Then I'll let Mayor Hardy and Ms. Gamelin know right away."

Delores shambled out of her office, worn from the visits all day. She came and leaned on Sylvia's area. She didn't smell like anything this time. Thank god.

"So Trent is fine now. No more soup. He knows his name. But he doesn't know anything about Fair Isle knitting. His mother showed him all the sweaters and he's utterly confused."

"As am I," Sylvia said.

"As are we all," Delores added. "Anyway, he'll probably be back tomorrow to keep scraping—"

"Wait, what? Scrape what? I thought we were keeping people away from this stuff. Those kids ate that moss in YA. What are we going to do about those parents?"

Delores looked confused, then sad. "Sylvia, it's moss. Not LSD. You had it tested, right? Send the results to Ms. Gamelin. Hell, let her test it again. It's going to come back regular moss. Hardy ate some!

He's fine. Stomachaches are what people will get with this." She sighed. Looked around.

"What I'm really worried about is Albert," she said. "He seems to be getting rather fat."

"It's not fat," Sylvia said. "He's growing. It's a pituitary thing, I think."

"Oh," she said, suddenly uninterested. "At least he has it figured out, then. I may go home early. Do you think you could keep track of stuff and close up?"

"Uhh," Sylvia said.

"Just kidding," Delores said. "I'll get Albert. Have a good evening, dear."

Sylvia wanted, more than anything, for Delores not to lose her job. Part of Delores reminded Sylvia of her grandmother. They both shared the same bad habits. What was worth talking about had little bearing on practical matters and they both lived for rumor. But the truth was: she was a horrible goddamn librarian.

Sylvia had an hour left before closing. Until then, she was locked in mortal combat with the curse of returned materials. She should've deplored the feces on the movie cases. Instead she fell into disavowal. People had no shame. Absolutely zero. They'd return anything to the library smeared in dried fluids. Blood, spit—even semen, probably. Where was the public storing their entertainment items? That was the real mystery. The first bit of advice she ever received from Albert was, "Keep your fucking hands out of your mouth."

She rarely heard him curse. It stopped her from chewing her nails.

The process of checking-in calmed her. She lost herself for a little while. She forgot about moss-eating politicians, Trent eating soup, her limbs tingling and going numb. Everything irrational in her slept. For a while.

Then a woman screamed. A patron. Out front. Sylvia nearly fell out of her seat.

A deep growl followed another scream. For a brief second, she imagined a wolf. Or a coyote. No, a pack of coyotes. Someone had brought a mutant pit bull? Or, no, a rabid German shepherd got loose?

Coming around the doorway, she saw Albert heaving in rage. Items on the check-out counter had spilled off. He must've leapt over.

The screams came from a long-haired woman. It was someone Sylvia recognized, but she didn't know their name. The woman wasn't afraid of Albert. Whatever Albert was facing and Sylvia couldn't see was scaring her. Sylvia moved behind the screaming woman. The woman held her child as it gripped her pants. The long-haired woman was shaking and tears were down her face. Ten feet in front of Albert was a man. This man held a gun at his side. There was an empty holster on his belt.

The man appeared normal except for the gun. Light down jacket, nice jeans, hiking shoes.

A visceral gurgling erupted from Albert. He looked rage-soaked. Unfettered and mad in eye and soul. Sylvia never thought he could hurt anything, but last night and right now were radically changing her mind.

"What the hell is going on here?" she said.

The man with the gun pointed up at Albert. "He wants to kick me out of the library and take my gun. He said he'd kill me."

"*No guns in the library,*" Albert growled.

This was true. No guns were allowed in the library. Sylvia never had to say that to anyone. Or worry about it. But there she was. Saying and worrying. She gently pushed the woman and her child behind her. "Go, now," she whispered. They skittered off. Sylvia took their place. They weren't this guy's target, anyway. The man with the gun was afraid of Albert. Who wouldn't be?

"Sir, my colleague, Albert, here, is correct. It's in violation of the library's rules. No guns are allowed."

The man was sweating. He didn't want to be here. She wanted to know what kept him from running.

"This asshole was going to attack me. I'm within my right to protect myself."

"Not if the gun isn't allowed in the first place," Sylvia corrected. "Why don't you just back away. Both of you," she said, pressing a hand on Albert. His skin stiffened like concrete at her touch. He seemed two feet taller than normal. His head almost skimmed the low ceiling above the check-out desk.

"How do I know he won't follow me?" the man asked.

"I'll keep him on a short leash."

In what she could only think of as *insurance*, the man raised his gun.

"This is unnecessary," Sylvia said.

Behind her, Albert swallowed more rage. She turned and saw that maybe insurance wasn't a bad idea.

"Hey," she said up to Albert. "Chill the eff out and back off, okay? Let this guy get out of here." She looked around. A few patrons on the second floor balcony were recording this on their phones. Some were surely already calling the cops. Uploading the video to the internet.

If she concentrated, she thought she could hear emergency sirens far away.

Knowing how way leads on to way, Albert would get shot. Not the asshole with the gun. Luck never broke that way. So she did something stupid. She walked toward the guy with the gun. He barely paid her any attention.

The gun was aimed at Albert. And she could sense her friend's eagerness to test the gunman's mettle.

"Can you please take your finger off the trigger? Or point it away from my friend, please."

The gunman's hand shook. Sylvia could feel Albert leaning toward them.

She asked his name. He whispered it. Jim, she said. No. He said it was Tim.

"Tim, hand me the gun."

Words she definitely never would've ever wanted to say prior to this incident.

Tim looked truly terrified. As if what he saw in Albert would eat him alive if no one was around. Sylvia believed it.

Sylvia stepped forward with her hands out, palms up. She had her hands on Tim's hands. She pushed up.

Albert blinked.

The gun went off in Sylvia and Tim's hands. A puff of fabric and blood popped off Albert's left shoulder. He didn't flinch.

Sylvia tore the gun away and Tim booked it toward the door. Albert roared (Sylvia couldn't dispute this later, but she always knew *roared* was the appropriate term.) He reached down and pulled the swinging door from the countertop off its hinges and launched it at Tim. It missed. But it shattered a window inside the foyer.

Patrons that were hiding and watching fled. Some cried. Some cheered. She told someone to call 911.

Meantime, Sylvia jumped onto the counter to look at his shoulder.

"It's fine," he said deeply. Her organs shook at the boom of his voice.

"Can I at least look?"

"So look."

She did. It was a small wound. Like a scratch. Nothing serious. She said so.

"I know. I said it was fine."

"Hmmph."

"Give me the gun," Albert said. His massive hand stuck out.

"What? No. Why? No."

"I want to take it apart."

"You don't know how."

"My father was a lieutenant in the Army. I know how to field strip a gun. It was a weekly chore. Clean dad's gun."

She made a face. "You're not exactly the most trustworthy fella right now, you know?"

He nodded. He was a battle giant, downshifting into kindly librarian. It was hard to go from Dr. Jekyll to Mr. Hyde and back again without a little awkwardness, a little seepage in personality. She handed him the gun, pinched on the top like a smelly diaper.

Albert faced away. He slid the top back and emptied the chamber. Then he removed the magazine. These went into his trouser pocket. The slide came off. A strange bunch of smaller parts fell into his hand. He'd crushed something on accident. The frame was next. Along with the barrel and trigger. When he finished, it was a heap of metal.

He dropped all of it into a gallon baggie Sylvia got from behind the counter. She shook them. They jingled.

"Christmas ornaments," he said.

Sylvia's armpits were drenched. Her neck was stiff with stress. Her body flooded with cortisol.

"I know you're my boss, but you're also my landlord, so I would kindly ask you to get the shit out of here before the cops show up."

Albert grumbled something about his wife knowing all the cops. But he awkwardly padded into the back and collected his stuff. She watched him barely squeeze out the back door.

By this point, the library was empty anyway. She called Ms. Gamelin and explained what happened. Ms. Gamelin would call Delores and all relevant parties. She ordered Sylvia to close the library with a note on the front door stating that the next day was closed for training. In a surprising moment, Ms. Gamelin asked, "Sylvia Hix, are you okay?"

Sylvia responded to her Dark Mother like this: "There is no okay."

And after a pause, Ms. Gamelin: "Accepted."

Sylvia debated on calling Natalia and did it anyway. Albert was a hero. Look for him coming home. It's just a small burn on the shoulder, etc. Natalia went into cop-mode. She was concerned for her husband but started asking a lot of questions about the shooter. Details. Descriptions. She'd give them to the cops. She was already calling them on another phone.

The cops arrived in a couple squad cars. No big. They took a statement and names to corroborate. Sylvia said she didn't know any names. Not the patrons'. Not the gunman's.

One cop said Sylvia was brave. Another said she was stupid. A third said it was the stupidest thing she'd do in her life. He said it with a grin.

Sylvia asked if they knew a former detective named Natalia. Two did. They said gold-tipped words about her. Wished her the best. Suggested names for the baby.

Conan, Hulk, Tony Stark.

They needed her to anchor down a few days. Might need to interview her. They taped off the scene and collected evidence.

As Sylvia left, a few cars showed up. Ms. Gamelin's. Delores's.

Sylvia hid in the parking lot hinterland. She gazed at the Throckmorton's sign. It now read *cock tons*. That was kinda funny. Ms. Gamelin and Delores shuffled into the library. Sylvia left. She was alone in an empty world. She walked toward Albert and Natalia's.

She had a twenty minute walk. She stepped on a folded picture halfway there. It stuck to her shoe. She plucked it off and opened it.

It was a picture of her mother. A picture from her bedroom. In fact, it was one of the only pictures she had of her mother. Sylvia looked around. Only the streetlamps were with her. What the *hell* was the picture doing here?

Loose paper cycloned around further up the sidewalk. She kept her distance. She walked. Then she ran. She caught some. She knew what it was before she flattened the paper out. Her diary from two years ago. The diary pages were like crumbs down the sidewalk.

As she tracked the breadcrumb trail, she finally realized where all of her possessions had gone. They *had* grown legs and walked away. But where they went, she'd have to follow.

CHAPTER SIX

SYLVIA WEAVED HER way through town. Down this alley, down that narrow street. She picked up more than she could carry. She started picking up more than she could have ever left behind.

None of the houses she passed had lights on. Houses with lights looked unwelcoming.

She walked for an hour. Her feet ached. Her hands were freezing. All of her possessions were folded and stuffed into coat pockets. She held a bulk of papers and pictures and an entire notebook that she thought she'd lost when twelve years old.

She was starting to find items that she didn't even remember owning. Figurines of cartoon characters with her name scrawled on the bottom. Old CDs. A VHS tape of a ballet recital.

She stole a rubber band off a newspaper on someone's porch to hold some of it together.

Then she snagged a plastic grocery bag that tumbled toward her. She felt homeless, and in a way, she was.

I was just involved in a shooting, she thought. *How odd is my life that that doesn't stay at the forefront of my mind right now?*

The moon was out. Full, bulbous. A fat illuminated onion, pitted with scars. Bright as a late-night diner off the highway. For a moment, she let herself look up at it. She allowed herself to realize it existed. That people—men—had been on the moon, walked around. That they had left shit behind.

She squinted to see the Sea of Tranquility. A bluish patch. So distinct. She had no idea how many times she'd looked up at the moon and stared at this area. And out of all those times—she had never seen a small black speck moving across it. Yes, there was something moving across the Sea of Tranquility on the moon. But she knew that if she could see it, then it had to be at least as big as the Empire State Building. She read that in a book about the moon while shelving months ago. She felt her insides pulled in all directions, as if driving swiftly over a rise in a country highway. That odd sexual tickle. She felt fast-forwarded in time looking at the speck, as if the far distant future had opened the door a crack and let her peek in.

Before she could synthesize this, something pushed into her thigh.

The road stopped. A wooded area met the road and ate it. Three red concrete parking pillars marked the boundary. She'd bumped against the middle one.

There were no houses for the last fifty yards or so. She wasn't paying attention to where she was. She didn't know which direction she was facing. Where was Albert's house from here? Where was the library?

She looked back up at the moon. The Giant Black Speck of the Future was gone.

Her heart raced. The cortisol from the shooting was still punishing her nervous system.

And there, about twenty feet into the woods, was another part of her childhood, impaled on a hawthorn tree. She debated on leaving her packet of possessions by the red pillar. She decided no one wanted her shit. She left it. But she took the picture of her mother.

The wood was cloaked in darkness. As soon as she stepped past the pillars, any light that made its way in vanished, as if a switch was thrown. She tried to avoid noises. Crunching leaves, snapping twigs. This was impossible.

The impaled papery thing was a drawing. She tore it off.

It was a likeness of the tickle spider from years ago. And the large moss creature. Done in crayon, she immediately remembered when she drew this. It was the night she ran home. She sat down, grabbed the closest writing instrument, and produced this.

She hadn't seen it in a decade and a half. She folded it and slid it into her hip pocket.

She checked the moon again. Still nothing. Although, its form was obscured by the wood.

GRASSHANDS

The slow crunching of plant material came from up ahead. It sounded like a drunk bulldozer grazing the forest. Something large was laying waste to saplings, small trees, dead oaks.

Further, much further in the distance, she saw a figure. Someone with long hair walking away from her.

Sylvia knew she should be afraid. And to be honest—she was. But not as much as she was *angry*. Fiercely upset, really. It was one thing to suffer under idiotic management at work. Another to almost get shot by a psycho with a gun. Then yet another to be attacked by a warped creature from the depths of the earth as a child.

But to have one's most private possessions strung across the town to be violated, soiled, and destroyed. All of one's memories annihilated. This was too much.

No sooner did this anger surface than a long string of objects lifted from the forest floor and into the air. She didn't even need to inspect it. All of it was hers. Underwear, bras, she saw a retainer, a few comic books, a bunch of saved receipts.

She tramped into the dark wood. The sound of the drunk bulldozer grew. A cacophonous storm ensued. The figure ahead never moved. Never shrank, never grew.

Sylvia knew it was Deena. Or, rather, it was whatever Grasshands wanted to be.

She began shoving her floating lifestuff into her shirt and coat pockets again. It was fruitless. The objects melted together like a child's modeling clay.

She'd smashed a swimming trophy into a high school history textbook. Hmm. Part of her wondered if she even needed any of it anyway. Maybe not even the picture of her mother.

The string of lifestuff kept glomming onto her original blob. She didn't want to leave it hanging. She didn't want to hold it. She smashed the stuff into the growing blob. She shaped the blob into a stick-shape as she moved deeper into the wood. Long, flat. Her rotating grip on it turned into a handle.

She felt like she was walking in the wood for hours. That made sense. Grasshands ruled here. The slow, galactic way of life. Creeping at an inhuman pace. She thought back to her naming of Grasshands. It was the clock that nature obeyed, slower than any clock ever made. She wondered which clock she'd been living by since those times in the wood behind her house.

Computerhands. Anxietyhands. Workhands.

In reality, she was seventy yards deep past the red pillars.

Again, there was the figure of Deena up ahead, never changing, like a demonic star Sylvia could guide her journey by. And luckily, no tingling or pins-and-needles. No numbess of limbs. She started to worry about the lack of numbness. What did that mean?

She heard a lilting through the chaos of the forest breaking apart. The same broken singing from her youth, from the hole in Albert's ceiling.

Fa fa fa fa

The singing burned her ears this time. It drowned out the mess of noise from the crushing of the forest around her. She still couldn't see what made the noise.

Fa fa fa fa

Sylvia sang back. It worked last time. It could work again. So the cure would be the poison, as it were. Her voice wouldn't carry, though. Nothing happened. Not far away, anyway. Instead, the stick-blob in her hands grew heavy and hard.

She swung it around and accidentally slammed it into a tree. A slice of the stick broke off. What remained of the end was a point. Sharp. Like a spear.

She held the pike out in front of her like a warrior. As she stalked deeper into the wood, the pike softened in her grip. So she sang. She had to keep singing to the pike.

The wood bristled with evergreens. A form of seaweed dripped and dropped from the branches. Like nothing Sylvia had ever seen. Long, loping strands of it. Glistening in the darklight.

Nothing obeyed the rules where she was. Past the red pillars, the rules grew moldy and rotten. She stopped. She pulled the baggie of moss from her pocket.

Curious, she opened the baggie and pulled some out. It looked normal enough. The sound of the drunk bulldozer faded. Then it died completely.

Deena wasn't straight ahead in the distance anymore.

Sylvia sang to the moss.

Fa fa fa fa

The moss sang back.

afa afa afa afa

Sylvia ate it. Chewed it. Swallowed it. Bits of it scattered over her face. The moss was gritty and mushy. It tasted of earth. It tasted the way the ground smells after a rain.

Renewed, she ventured on, now chanting her song to the pike. The only sound in the wood now was her voice. This bothered her. But she refused to stop.

Only, she had to. There was a clearing in the trees. A large circle had been mowed down. The forest floor was smashed into the ground, making everything muddy and sloppy. On the other side of the circle was a beautifully shocking sight. A sparkling vast blanket of green moss. And it spread back and back for what seemed like forever.

Sylvia was suddenly tired. Just exhausted. She wanted to lay in the moss and sleep.

Of course, that was exactly the same moment when a series of stiff arcing spindles appeared from behind a clump of trees to her left. There was no *tap tap* this time. It was a *thunk thunk*. Smash smash. This *thing* was the size of a tractor and it broke its way into the circle. It dripped with debris. Papers, chunks of moss, dirt, more of Sylvia's possessions. Sylvia was sure she could make out the door and rear window of a 1988 Honda Accord, her first car in high school. It was covered in band stickers. These shifted and morphed into the body of the thing. But even so, there was no distinct boundary to it. Like a fog or smoke, it purled and jabbed this way and that. All the same, Sylvia knew what it was. The thing slid along like a large black dissipating building.

Everything she ever owned, she thought, could be in that fucking creature. She realized she was still chanting softly to herself. The thing moved nervously within the circle. She could sense it wanted to pounce. It was that feeling that had haunted her since childhood. The feeling of knowing someone is going to call you right before they do.

Sylvia gripped the pike, leaned it forward, and stopped singing.

"Are you going to stand there all day or are we going to fucking do this?"

The borderless motherfog paused as if heaving for a breath. Which was stupid. It didn't breathe. What made it look like it respired was the constant shifting movement of the objects that comprised it. Everything writhed and folded over the surface of this creature. Her life scrambled in front of her. There. Right there. Her favorite paperback book, *Jude the Obscure*.

A small object dropped off the motherfog. As it scrabbled toward her through the leaves and needles, her body went slack and numb. This was the tickle spider. The *tappity* of it worked up the pike, her arm, and then her neck. With a fierce spindle, it snuck along her torso and began to tickle her until she couldn't help but laugh despite the utter unfunniness of the situation.

She struggled to keep her mouth closed. But a laugh escaped. The tickle spider jammed a leg in and pried her mouth up. It started to climb in, but either it slipped or Sylvia regained her jaw muscles.

She clamped tight on the spider's leg. It flopped in her mouth. The tickle spider fell, and, seemingly in shock, scooted away back toward the motherfog.

Sylvia wanted to spit the leg out, but it was dissolving into a foul-tasting gas in her mouth. She blew it out. A dark black steam emerged and hung there then seeped into the ground.

Her limbs tingled and regained movement. She re-gripped the pike.

"Hey!" she said to the motherfog.

Then it leapt toward her.

Terrified, she held the pike steady as it arc'd in the air and landed on top of her. She fell back into a squat and plunged the spike upward. The motherfog *tap tap'd* in some kind of painful glee.

It was two feet above her as she lay on the ground. Her hands were on fire. Her wrists felt hammered. She had no idea what she was doing. But she speared it again and again. Deep mud-colored blood-fluid cascaded out like old oil from a jalopy. She had no resentment about destroying her own life. It seemed that it was already up for grabs and disseminated into the aether without her permission.

The creature sank further on the pike until just touching her face. It was like being crushed by a parade float. It sank all the way onto the pike, then the motherfog rolled onto its back and Sylvia freaked and couldn't let go. She was carried up into the air with the pike. She dangled from the top. It started to push into her stomach. She could barely breathe.

Unable to stay there, and unable to jump away from the creature, she started to slide down the pike's shaft toward the rumpled belly of the thing. Down she slid into the increasingly torn wound that she'd ripped open with her pike's blade. As her feet started to touch the thing, the wound turned into a sphincter. It flexed open like a dark anus-mouth.

Sylvia screamed. It flexed and squeezed. And more ancient oily fluid leaked out. She thought she saw a report card in there. A Barbie doll. A Little Tikes Cozy Coupe, mangled beyond belief.

GRASSHANDS

She tried to hold on. She tried to climb the pike. Tried to push herself off and away. But nothing would work. The sphincter closed around her ankles, then her thighs. Her arms had lost all strength now, and she tried to scream. Her vocal cords didn't work.

The pins and needles had descended upon her all at once. She was absolutely numb.

The horrible mouth flexed and swallowed her into the body of the creature and she felt the moist cold pressure of the sphincter over her head. Then everything was black and floating. As if underwater in a pool at night. Hazy. Smelling of chemicals and night air. There was a frigid whooshing. Pressure at her back. The motherfog was spinning. Gravity reasserted itself and she felt like she was sitting in a seat. In a small room.

Lights flicked on. They were string Christmas lights. They were hers. She'd had them dangling around her closet door as a little girl. They twinkled weakly in pink, green, and yellow. Then it switched to red, blue, orange, and back again. There was also a lamp on the floor of the room/belly. The light was weak, as if traveling through brackish water. This, she figured, had something to do with the area she'd entered, inside whatever boundary the red pillars created.

As Sylvia gained her senses, she saw Deena sitting about five feet away from her. But this wasn't the Deena that harassed Albert. Nor was it even the Deena she encountered in the abandoned storefront. This Deena's eyes were made of moss now. All around her mouth, too, was a furry shambles of growth. She sat immobile, hands in her lap. Like waiting in a doctor's office. Deena was now a mummy.

Patches of hair had fallen out, revealing the skull underneath. Soil crumbled off her ears and sat in the divot of her clavicle. What remained of Deena's skin was paperwhite, nearly translucent.

The room shrank. Sylvia was unable to make out any distinct walls, but the lights and Deena's mummy pressed close together. Faced with the mummy's placid expression, Sylvia wept for the loss of the human Deena. Deena had been appropriated by Grasshands as its ambassador. *But for what?* Sylvia thought. Just staring into the dead face of Deena, Sylvia knew she was to understand that time is what nature deigns. Information belongs to it. Humans belong to it. Everything is it. But she couldn't tell if all of this was a reaching out to her, a way of communicating. Or a total act of evil.

"We're not the same anymore," Sylvia said to Grasshands. "At one time I needed, I wanted to know you. But there was no way

79

bridge that gap." She could feel an echo of the tickle spider wedging her mouth open as a girl. And then when it happened just now. She wiped her eyes.

It was cold inside the motherfog. She tucked her hands under her thighs to keep them warm. She felt the fur of moss underneath her. Instinctively, she pinched some between her fingers to keep.

The room shrank more. Deena's mummy was now a foot away from her face. Still. Pacified. Mouldering. The colored string lights dimmed down. The lamp went out. Sylvia felt tingling in her feet and hands.

This was the end.

"What do you want me to do?"

The motherfog shifted. The mummy's head tilted. The smell of decomposition filled the space. Sylvia was overwhelmed and gagged. "I can't—please—*stop*."

In a moment of what Sylvia would consider empathy, Grasshands rapidly decomposed Deena right in front of Sylvia's face. The body of Deena fell apart. It all caved in on itself and molded and crimped. The moss crept across her like a tide.

Before she lost all sensation for the final time, Sylvia shoved the moss into her mouth and swallowed without chewing. The lights inside the motherfog vanished. She felt as if she was floating in a sensory deprivation tank.

The veil around her dissipated and she saw the wood again. The odd moonlight trickling in through the barrier made by the red pillars. A hole had been cleared out of the sparkling mossblanket over the undergrowth. With great care, Sylvia slid into her mossgrave. Now she was completely numb and immobile. Even her thoughts felt sluggish and slow. Nothing moved at a human speed. The last thought was of Albert and Natalia. How they'd looked after her. She thought of the baby. Their baby. How good it would be to hold it. To watch them hold it.

At the bottom of the grave, looking up, she saw the moon. It was the last thing she saw. But, it wasn't really the moon anymore. How could it have been? It swarmed with a frenzy of black dots until the moon was blotted out. Everything empty. Everything dark. Like a curtain slowly descending over the stage of her mind.

BURIAL

THEY WERE IN a void, black and depthless. The entity known as Grasshands or the motherfog had all the time, ever, to play this fantasy out. And so did Sylvia, though she couldn't have known it. Time worked differently underground. Time was a desperate toy and not a master of anything—not a single damn thing—in this underground.

In this gravedream, Sylvia's mother was reconstructed through Grasshands on a dream-stage like a second-hand story told by a kindergartener, broken, filled with gaps. Her mother who, in reality, had been burned to ashes, spread into the wood behind her grandparents' place, some into a river in Italy, some into a lake in Canada. Some had been licked up by Mosby the dog on accident.
But Sylvia remembered quite a bit of her mother. And she could feel strong moments muscle their way into this fugue. Sylvia resisted the reconstructed mother but Grasshands persisted. Which is why Sylvia beheld, at first, different versions of her mother in this dreamstate. They were shown to her like slides on an old Kodak carousel.
One was young;
one was older than her mother ever was in real life;
one was embedded in a tree;
one was engulfed in flames on a bier;
one was trapped under a rock.
Sylvia pushed these images away; or, Grasshands took them away from her. She had no control here. So she tried to focus on one

aspect of her mother, one aspect that repeated over and over. She wanted to conjure her mother into view. To ransom her back from Grasshands. How could she do that? How to focus?

What did my mother do? Sylvia thought.

The dreamtime stretched out in front of her like a waking cat from a long slumber. Like this one black and white feral cat that used to hang around the house before her mother died. It slept near the back porch, caught and ate chipmunks, and licked the salt off pita chip fragments. When it would wake from napping, it would lengthen to an absurd span. Sylvia thought it would keep going in opposite directions forever. Now, here, time was just that, a thousand-year cat, stretching a thousand light years long. It was creepily comfortable and delicious to be inside of.

> (*The scene changes. The two of them were in a version of her childhood bedroom. The light from outside clocks into a different angle. Syl can tell it is late spring outside.*)

Her mother was always collecting and gathering her clothes and cleaning them. Sylvia spent so much time in the woods because her mother's need for cleanliness was overbearing. And she didn't want to burden her mother with more work. So she tramped along outside instead.

Nevertheless, there arrived then the feeling of her mother dumping hot laundry over her. Delicious hot terry cloth and cotton. Her mother often did this when it was still cold outside. Sylvia would be playing a video game or reading Lois Lowry or R.L. Stine and then *plowm!*—the towelfall. When the laundry load was large, she'd be completely covered under a weighty dome of clothes. Sylvia felt safe, hidden, slightly trapped, but in a strange way that didn't germinate fear in her. All that stored heat radiating out. Her mother then asked her to help fold towels. She'd taught her how to fold a towel in a specific way. There were four folds.

> (*Sylvia was both watching this from outside herself and simultaneously in the moment being herself as a young girl.*)

Sylvia: Mama, tell me how much you loved me.
(*It had been so long.*)
Mother (seemingly unhearing, folding towels): Sylvia, where should we go on vacation?
Sylvia (also folding): Hmm—Disney World!
Mother (frowning): In May? I don't know...could be bloated with tourists...
Sylvia: *Puh-leeze!*
Mother (breaks frown into a sly smile): Well, we can look into it, but no promises!
Sylvia (taken aback): Really? Do you think we could go? I thought you said we didn't have enough money?

> (*The mother's mouth is jerked back like a fishhook has snagged her where the lips meet in the corner. It's as if they are trying to meet the earlobe. It goes on for too long. It keeps going. Sylvia begins to reel back in fear, but the face snaps back and she eases and forgets. Sylvia had never heard a positive word about money in her house or from her mother's mouth. All vacations were bombed into purgatory from the first mention of them. She does not know what she's dealing with here.*)

Mother: Sure, we can make it work. You just gotta trust me, right, Syl?
Sylvia: Sure, Mama.
Of course, all of Sylvia's memories and understandings were corrupt and malformed.
Perhaps she knew nothing about her mother. Grasshands seemed to know more than she ever did. Or it wanted to convince her it did. Which wasn't hard when Sylvia was handing over all her data and

trust and keys to the Entity-in-Charge. Grasshands searched Sylvia, scanning her like a hard drive. Her mother continued folding towels, singing some hokey TV theme song they both despised. The bedroom door opened by itself, just a smidge. Sylvia could see into the hall, a seething vacuum. In the hall stretched the thousand-year cat, stretching further away than she could ever conceive. The hall was a refulgent black, a void of possibility. It took up the whole field of vision. Grasshands churned in there somewhere. Then: a tiny, nearly imperceptible eye twinkled in the darkness, like a distant quasar blinking and getting swallowed by the galaxy. Why was it looking at her? Why was it hiding?

She turned to ask her mother if she was serious about Disney World. But she was not there. The towel was still frozen in place, as if held by invisible hands on an invisible lap. Sylvia wanted her mother again. The mother who wanted to take her on vacation. The door to the hallway closed.

She understood every door could be entered from either side. Maybe this was why, as a girl, Grasshands's twig spider didn't get far with her—because in order to truly inspect her, it, too, had to be open for inspection.

There were no one-way doors, Sylvia knew. And Grasshands wasn't ready or prepared for any kind of poking around from a short-term creature like a human. But the more Sylvia let Grasshands indulge itself and search her memory banks, the more she could press forward into it. The more she could read the transcript of its intentions. In the aboveworld, she'd read on some hipster website a quote that reminded her of this situation. *When you look into the abyss, the abyss looks back into you.* Ah, Nietzsche.

What she gleaned from Grasshands was evergreen, yet no less horrific for that. Like anything else, it wanted to carpet the universe, particularly her planet, with its body, scent, taste, image. Life run amok, and all that. But it also wanted pure information. Her DNA, her brainwaves, her mitochondrial details. And it wanted more than that. It wanted to know the entire geologic record of Australia, the particular feeding habits of three separate cockroaches in Tirana, Albania, circa 1456, and much else besides. For what reason? she wondered. She pressed forward. All while still sitting on her old bed, with the frozen towel by her, she nudged the abyss. What bounced back was the horrifying part.

Just 'cause.

For the hell of it. Grasshands was nothing more than a galactic hoarder. It wasn't even going to use the information it took from people for a greater purpose! Each chunklet of info it absorbed from a book or a person—from anything—was simply stored away and mashed together with every other detail. Like Sylvia's possessions glommed together. That pissed her off more than anything. All the strife and pain and effort would be for nothing.

But then, there was another scene.

>(*Sylvia sits at the kitchen table. It's dusk. Autumn. Barely any lights are on in the house. Her mother is using a corded clamshell phone screwed into the wall.*)

Mother (distressed, wrapping/unwrapping phone cord around index finger): I didn't say that! Don't put words in my mouth, Mom. Don't put those thoughts into my mind! I've said over and over that you're the one who hated him. Just because he's dead doesn't mean you can tell me all about how you hated my goddamn husband.

(Covers the mouthpiece of the phone and turns to Sylvia.) Don't ever let me talk to you like this when I get older. Promise me. If I do, walk away. Just ignore my old dumb ass.

Sylvia nodded. Although she had little knowledge of why her mother said this. Here her mother looked much the way she did when she died: youngish, relatively healthy, serious. She had olive skin and black hair and many who saw her picture later in life would always ask, "Was your mother Mexican or Italian?" The answer was no, her grandmother came from Germany. Sylvia did not receive any of her mother's more genetically attractive traits.

Sylvia tried to ask her mother a question, but she put a silencing hand up. Trying to distract Sylvia from asking questions; from siphoning information about Grasshands.

Fed up, her mother let go of the phone, but it hung in the air. She walked to the sink and filled up a glass. What curdled out of the faucet was a fluid steam, the same kind that fell from the wound in the motherfog. It gelled in a glass tumbler. It was the same refulgent black of the thousand-year cat distilled into a beverage. Her mother downed it in one go. Something in her voice broke.

Mother (her body spills over the physical bounds, turns pixelated): You know you're all alone forever now. The earth is all nerve, not an altar made fat. There's nowhere to place grain, money, or blood.

Sylvia got up to stop her from speaking but the distance expanded exponentially.

Sylvia: Mom. Mama? Mama, can you hear me?

Mother (now sitting next to Sylvia at the table, tired-looking): I'm right here. You don't have to yell.

Sylvia: Are you my mother?

Mother (laughing): As much your mother as I can be, dearie.

> (*Begins to reach out and caress her daughter's face but notices the phone receiver is still hanging in the air.*)

Oops. We can't forget to hang these up when we're done.

Sylvia: Have we ever been to Disney World?

Mother (taken aback): Of course. Three times, silly. Are you messing with me?

Sylvia: Why can't I remember?

Mother (stern): Well, you've always had a bad memory.

Uh huh. *There* was her mother. The one who wasn't afraid to tell the truth, no matter who it hurt. Grasshands was trying to sell Sylvia what she wanted her mother to be, not what her mother actually was. *As much your mother as I can be.* Which is to say, not at all.

Mother (drinking from glass, ventriloquizing as she drinks, and the voice sounds drunk): A house is not a home. A house is not alone. A house is merely a construction. Humans build homes. A house is not a stone. A house is not a phone.

Maybe Grasshands didn't know what rhymes were. Or it was playing around. Sylvia pulled from Grasshands information that she hadn't known prior—that what this reconstructed version of her mother said was true. The house Sylvia spent most of her time in as a young girl was not built by construction workers. Her house was built by her mother because they dwelled in it. Her mother labored every day. Wiping, scrubbing, straightening. The placemats were aligned. The pill bottles on the counter were grouped. She was grateful.

Sylvia fought hard to remember that she was buried in the dirt by the motherfog. That she wasn't actually a young girl sitting in the kitchen with her mother. She clutched her head and squeezed—but was the squeeze real or was it all being fed through Grasshands in order to *seem* real?—and she felt the pressure.

Mother: Through work, I dwelled. By dwelling, the house was built, and to dwell is to be free, to spare something from danger, to let a thing be itself with no interference. I freed you. I will free you now.

Her mother's face was expressionless.

Sylvia: Mama. I just wanted something other than life.

Mother: I never interfered with you, Sylvia.

Sylvia (crying): I know, Mama. You took me to Disney World.

Mother: Well, then, you'll need to follow me. (*She blinked so slowly.*) You can have something more than life. You can join me.

Grasshands drew her mother's face into anger.

Sylvia didn't know who was really speaking now. The mother or Grasshands. She had no way to know. Sylvia kept losing herself inside of herself, in her *wanting* this to be reality, in her *wanting* to forget that her mother and father were dead. That she was alone.

Mother: All there *are* are things. The way we handle things says everything about us.

Sylvia: That's not true.

(What about all her stuff now? It was liquefied or clayey or disappeared. The way Sylvia handled her things was to make a weapon of it; or to not possess it at all.)

But the mother wasn't listening anymore. She was staring out the patio doors to the back yard which led onto nothing but more void.

Yet a new scene.

> (*Now both women are adults, almost close to the same age, which is impossible, and her mother and she are sitting at the kitchen table again—and she wished that her father could be alive in this scenario.*)

Her mother had been crying, and Sylvia understood that it was for her own dead, obliterated self, and for Sylvia's being alone. In some way, the reconstructed mother in front of Sylvia *knew* she was being controlled by an entity, although she was dead. (Sylvia didn't want to get into metaphysical questions about the soul at that point.)

Sylvia: Let me out.

Mother: Out of where? The kitchen? You're crazy. Get up and go.

Sylvia: You know what I mean.

Mother (squinting): Do I?

(*Mother produces a cigarette from thin air and lights it, smoking.*)

Sylvia knew her mother smoked in secret. She tried to reach out and touch the reconstructed mother. She felt certain that she could hold on to this knowledge now without forgetting. This was all bullshit and she was dreaming or dying or both. All the same. Here was something closely, almost exactly, looking like her mother. The small stature, curly hair, squinty eyes, short nose, sharp laugh. The mother turned away as Sylvia reached over.

Mother (flinching): No! Not unless you follow me. You're going to follow me, aren't you, Sylvia? Be a good girl and follow me down here. (stands up and gestures behind her) Just there, right around the corner.

(*There are no corners in the kitchen now. The light over the stove is being sucked away into the ragged void slowly gnawing at them. The mother points to some distance beyond her. Somewhere deep in the visible darkness.*)

Sylvia: What do you mean?

All she wanted was a touch, a hug, a face pressed against the cheek. Warmth. But where was the mother's cheek? Did she have one? Her mother inhaled the cigarette and the smoke curled out of the top of her head into beautiful fragments. The ventriloquizing voice spoke again. It groaned a red tone. The mother looked down at her lap. Sylvia followed and bent down to look under the table. On the underside, by her mother's knees, was a mouth, bearded with moss. It had her mother's teeth and tongue, which licked the mossy lips. The table-mouth coughed. Her mother offered the cigarette to the mouth. It inhaled. No smoke came out. Sylvia sat up. More smoke whirled out of her mother's scalp as if her hair were on fire.

The smell of smoke hooked her nostalgia. Sylvia caved. She wanted just one more fantasy. One more dreamscape. One more opportunity to believe that this was her mother. If she was going to die down here, in the moss, then she wanted to die in a sweet maternal oblivion.

(*Sylvia was five again. At night, before bedtime in their old house by the woods. She watched her mother floss. Very meticulous with the unwaxed thread, sawing between the teeth. She then followed her, learning the rituals within the home. The closing-up at night of the house. The woods pressed on the safety of the home. Her mother checked the locks on the doors. She checked the knobs on the stove. Sylvia padded behind and watched her mother apply lotion on her hands, knees, feet. Sylvia followed.)*

The mother said, looking down at her: What you think about a thing matters a whole lot less than how you deal with that thing. Don't forget that.

Again: was this Grasshands or her mother saying this?

Then they were in the borderless area again. Yet the smell of the lotion filled the space. It was like basking in a room full of hothouse orchids and wildflowers.

What are you building, Sylvia?

Mama?

What are you building?

Nothing, Mama. Why? What should I do?

Will you follow, Sylvia?

Mama, I will. Wherever. Just tell me.

You must give up, Sylvia. *Give up.*

Her face disappeared. Nothing was there.

Her mother stood and came to her. Now, more than ever, Sylvia was aware that this was Grasshands. It had no sense of physicality like humans do. Maybe this whole thing was a misunderstanding. Grasshands was aiming at something. Sylvia had to focus on that. What was its motivation?

It buried me in moss, she thought.

Its actions say BURY but its words say MOTHER.

What do I believe?

Mama, you're not my mother, Sylvia said.

The mother did not respond. Then, relieved, Grasshands finally said, No, I am not your mother. The smell of lotion decayed.

Sylvia struggled to think. It was hard to even keep her mind together. She felt that wherever she was, wherever it was would pull her apart across the universe.

So Sylvia thought: What you think about a thing matters a whole lot less than how you deal with that thing. How would she deal with Grasshands? Well, what the hell do creatures made of moss do or build? They don't. They cover, surround, and break it all down. They eat it. They digest it. They disarticulate the molecules of life and throw them into the solar wind. A profound sadness descended all around Sylvia like an old smoke-stained curtain. She wanted to embrace her mother, even if she was fake and she was only five. She didn't even know where she was.

But it didn't matter: there was no mother anymore. There was no *there* there anymore. Physical reality melted into voided blackness.

Mama, she said into it.

Yes, Sylvia? Grasshands responded, lying. It recreated the kitchen again. Then it made a fold-out bassinette by the table. Sylvia picked up something from it. She held a baby in her arms.

What will become of me, Mama? Sylvia said.

Sylvia didn't want the baby. The baby looked ill, like it needed immediate medical attention.

In a voice that wasn't human, in a voice that Sylvia knew was more electrons than flesh, more moss than electrons; a voice that was Grasshands as far as the known universe reached out.

You'll build soil, the voice said to the baby in Sylvia's arms. You'll become dirt, hun.

Then the baby looked into Sylvia's eyes. The eyes were distant stars. Winking quasars that felt nothing, had nothing, cared nothing.

Build soil, Sylvia. Dwell in the soil, honey.

Turn into dirt—

—and then the dream ended

CHAPTER SEVEN

1.

SYLVIA GASPED AT the cold air crushing her face.

Sound reverberated. A voice. She heard her name. The voice called to her. She heard crying mixed with laughing. She couldn't open her eyes. She couldn't feel anything except her face. She hyperventilated. She knew she was buried. Had been buried. Someone's hands brushed her face, pressed at the dirt and the mossblanket around her. Pin-pricks of ice hit her face.

Slowly, she could open her left eyelid. A blurry mess of faint color. Grey and white. Then the right eyelid. She couldn't speak. Her whole body was becoming uncovered. She was getting dug up.

She heard the fine *shinck* of a shovel blade entering the earth. Large chunks of moss flying up. She saw them as shadows across her frame of vision.

A warm hand touched her cheek. Then a face came into view. It whispered into her ear.

"You're alive, sweetie. Jesus. Keep breathing. I'm getting close."

Sylvia knew the voice—Ms. Gamelin. The voice was comforting. Not something she was used to—*comfort*. Though she recognized it. She welcomed it.

She heard rifle fire in the background. Ms. Gamelin dropped to the ground. "Quiet. *Shhh.*" Another rifle report. Silence. A male voice in the distance said something. Ms. Gamelin nodded and stood back up and immediately returned to digging.

It seemed like it was taking forever. How far down had she been buried? She was lucky that Ms. Gamelin followed her into the forest.

She could move her head now. Her vision was straight, clear, useful. Her arms were free and had feeling.

Slowly the rest of herself came to life again.

Ms. Gamelin pulled her out of a three-foot grave in a small hillock in the wood, covered in tough, thick moss—some of which she thought was trying to re-attach to her. "Here, dear, put this around you," another voice said. It was one of the homeless men from the library, Gerald. He was one of the people applauding the patron with exorbitant fines, the patron who'd shot Albert. Gerald smiled. He threw a ragged blanket around Sylvia. He said he'd been camping next to the red pillars since the library went nuts. Then he assisted Ms. Gamelin. Sylvia thanked him in a weak voice. He nodded and drifted off toward his campsite. She didn't see him again.

The women sat next to the gravehole. Ms. Gamelin handed Sylvia a thermos cup with something hot in it. Mint tea with honey.

Sylvia felt like her mouth hadn't worked in centuries. She felt like a puppet dug out of an ancient rubble-covered city.

Ms. Gamelin's hair was in a loose chignon. She wore a field jacket and a pair of dungarees. Work boots. Her small shovel was from an Army surplus store.

It was only then that Sylvia noticed all the snow. Inches of snow. Snow hanging off the limbs of trees and layering bushes. Snow drifting down around them. And then Sylvia noticed spread out in front of her all the different graveholes. The forest floor looked like a vast Swiss cheese. Some of the holes had been dug before the snowfall. They were just white dimples in the landscape. Somewhere in the center was a fire. The smell of camp smoke comforted Sylvia. She looked at Ms. Gamelin.

"Oh, all those?" Ms. Gamelin said. "Failed attempts at rescues. Guesses. Blind faith."

The mint tea warmed Sylvia and she sounded a few words.

"How long?"

Ms. Gamelin whistled. "How long were you out, you mean? Hmm. Well. Yeah. That's hard to say."

Sylvia turned to her. "One? Two?"

Ms. Gamelin shook her head. "Try four."

"Four days?" Sylvia said. She almost spilled the tea.

Ms. Gamelin blenched. She took one of Sylvia's hands between her own. "Oh no, no, sweetie. Four months. You've been buried there for four months. I don't know how. But you were. It's February now.

You disappeared in October. How you're alive is a supreme mystery. I expected to dig up a corpse." Ms. Gamelin couldn't stop staring at the dirty subterranean face of Sylvia Hix, alive, warm, drinking tea. She couldn't help herself and reached out, touching Sylvia's cheek.

Sylvia's first thought, foolishly, was that she missed Christmas. The whole season. It upset her for a microsecond. The sky above was overcast, leaden.

"Part of me isn't surprised by that," Sylvia said. She had bright static flashbacks of spearing the motherfog. The dripping of black blood. Getting sucked into the stomach. Deena's mummy. The long dialogue dream with Grasshands playacting her mother. "How did you find me?" she asked.

Ms. Gamelin reminded Sylvia that the night she went missing was the shooting at the library. Albert was grazed. When no one found Sylvia at her apartment, and after Albert said she was staying with him, but she never returned, everyone at the library started searching. Ms. Gamelin asked everyone who lived between the library and Albert's. She eventually knocked on the door of a house where someone saw Sylvia walking with a lot of stuff in her arms. Like she was trying to move houses without a van.

"I walked until I came to the edge of the forested area here. I saw your bag of stuff by the pillars. But when I tried to enter, I couldn't. It was like I was stopping myself. Or my mind would change as soon as I stepped toward the forest. Then I'd have no desire to. It wasn't until I tried to bring your stuff with me that I finally felt confident. It was a dull sense of optimism that I'd find your body, at least. *Very dull.*"

Surprising both herself *and* Ms. Gamelin, Sylvia leaned over into the older woman's chest. She wept. Ms. Gamelin held Sylvia tightly. When Sylvia stopped crying, she pushed her hair from her face. "Albert?"

Ms. Gamelin sat silently and didn't look at Sylvia, pretending not to hear.

"How is he?"

Ms. Gamelin sipped mint tea from the thermos. "He's missing," she said. "*Been* missing, I should say. Not that long after you."

Sylvia instinctively stood up. The blanket fell off her to the ground. The pit of her stomach ached. Both from anxiety and hunger. She wanted to puke, but there was nothing to bring up.

She clutched her stomach. "Oh god," she said. "Oh god." Before she could speak again, she retched something horrible. From her mouth a long dark nightmare blob of material appeared. It hung like a deformed tongue. She coughed and hacked. She gagged and tugged on it. It fell to the forest floor. Ms. Gamelin pulled her back from it. Then right behind that was a perfectly marble-sized smooth stone. She puked this into her hand. It was covered in saliva, shiny and black like a wolf's eye. She could see herself reflected in the stone. She dried it on her dirty pants. Ms. Gamelin tried to take it from her, but Sylvia clasped it and put it in her pocket.

Sylvia knew that clump of shit was the moss she ate from inside the motherfog. And she knew that it had kept her alive the whole time in the grave. The stone probably had something to do with it, too. An accidental traveler. Like that spider she ate all those years ago. The regurgitated moss wilted and reincorporated back into the forest floor. The stone stayed warmish in her pocket, though.

Undistracted, Ms. Gamelin said, "I'm taking you to my place. Come on. Before it gets dark."

"What about Natalia, Albert's wife? I should see her. We have to find Albert."

Another moment of pretending not to hear what Sylvia said. "What? What now?" she asked.

Ms. Gamelin gathered her things and started to head out of the wood. Over her shoulder she said, "You'll have to go visit her yourself. I'm sure she'll want to see you."

When they passed the red pillars, Sylvia felt relieved. As if she'd escaped some containment of atmospheric pressure.

The car ride to Ms. Gamelin's house was silent. And the house was a surprise. It was quaint, small. But cozy. Ms. Gamelin asked what she wanted and without thinking Sylvia said, "Breakfast." Sylvia ate voraciously. She ate fried eggs, buttered toast, nearly burnt bacon, a small tower of buttermilk pancakes, and a half pot of coffee. After all that, she still didn't feel fully human. Nor did a shower help. Nothing would make her feel the way she did before being buried for four months. The two women sat at the dining table for a long time.

Then Sylvia asked if she had to go back to work.

"*I* haven't been to work in two months, not since I started looking for you in earnest." Ms. Gamelin said this while looking out the window. "So I imagine you're absolved."

"If you don't want to go back to work, what do you want to do now?"

Ms. Gamelin wiped her hands on her jeans. Both were filthy. "I want to burn the library down."

2.

The day cranked.

The town hummed with moss. It folded delicately in bellies. It curled around water pipes. It slept in basements, beds, and bureaus. The library protected it as a mother its kin.

Sylvia had been in charge of scoring moss off bookspines and covers. Now the moss was treated with deep respect. Delores herself ate moss off books by Tony Robbins, Edgar Allan Poe, and a textbook on information science. It was a strange trip. That week she developed a maniacal system of book arrangement that ended up entombing the patrons in a sepulcher made of their own failures. She had no way to build it, though. Better was her eating of the moss on Dale Carnegie's *How to Win Friends and Influence People*. She gladhanded all week. She was in constant meetings with members of the Chamber of Commerce, the city council, Mayor Hardy, and public patrons stopping by for feedback.

She gave little to no thought of Ms. Gamelin or Sylvia. All her mind was taken up with whatever she'd eaten. Probably because she was already a serious drug addict, she was skirting the ultimate dangers of the moss. Other folks nibbled moss dripping from a book on origami. They turned into paper-folding autistics. These moss trips lasted for weeks, amping up or down, depending. Some compared it to doing Adderall or Ritalin. It was merely an attention booster, a focusing enhancer. But what always happened within a month was the slow powering down. Patrons were lost well-deep in their own skulls. Irretrievable. Buried in Information Overload. It was like sleeping with Wikipedia. But in this case, Wikipedia ate your soul at the end of the affair.

Delores sat in her office at the library. Piles of different colored mosses like different strains of marijuana heaped in front of her. Four months prior, she ordered Sylvia to destroy this stuff. Now she glanced at it like a connoisseur. One pile was *The Lord of the Rings*. One was *Helter Skelter*. And the last was *The Diary of Anne Frank*. She decided on one. The decision rocked her bones. She ate it before she could change her mind. The effects started immediately.

Others in town had hard choices to make.

Tina Blackford lived on Bridge St. near the river. The house was a tiny saltbox with a gravel driveway. The linoleum in the kitchen bubbled. The dishwasher was broke. The front door stuck. She had Christmas decorations in the yard year-round. She was the night manager of The Grey Cloak, the only "upscale" eatery in town. She had been going to the public library for decades. She was excited to start taking her three-year-old, Francis.

When the moss-stuff was talked up on social media, she didn't think much of it. It was like that year when everyone drank açai berry juice in everything. Or all her friends who dumped carbs, then pushed full bore into the paleo diet. Her aunt had sent an email to stay away from the moss. She had a neighbor whose son went into a coma. Then a girlfriend of Tina's from work, Alana, texted her the same day and said that her son accidentally swallowed some moss off an Eric Carle book. He began speaking full sentences. Crazy sophisticated rhyming vocabulary. He was one and a half. Tina watched a video of him. She thought it was faked. But it wasn't. Alana wasn't that smart.

Tina Blackford had been an alcoholic for years. But she had three years sober now. She dropped into AA meetings multiple times a week. The night manager gig was good for her. She'd have loved to do something else, something better. Go to college. Find a decent human who wouldn't skeeze on her. Something amazing. But she had Francis. And a little guy was tough. It was a serious thing, raising a kid. She'd be the best night manager she could be. But she didn't want Francis to do it. She wanted Francis to be more. To be a doctor or a lawyer. Maybe a teacher or own his own business. Better yet—a successful artist. Deep down, she wanted her son to land on Mars or some shit. Something grandiose.

She kept watching the video of her friend's kid. He said *vertiginous*. Tina had to google it. The kid had it right.

So Tina went to the library. She found some moss on a book about shapes and colors in the Children's department. Then she found a book on astronomy. Probably a high-school level book. She considered the college textbook but decided not to push it. Tina wanted to start small. Just see what all the fuss was about. She gave

Francis the starter moss. The easy stuff. Maybe he showed a smidge of improvement. He started to point out the difference between alizarin crimson and cadmium red while watching Bob Ross on PBS.

Tina couldn't wait any longer. Two weeks went by trying more and more basic moss. Finally, she pushed the astronomy moss into Frankie's mouth herself with a smile and a wink. Francis cried the whole time. "No, Mama! No yucky! Stop!" (She'd been previously feeding it to him in his applesauce.) But Mama promised him it would get better. Everything would be better. We'd all be better. She wiped his tears away with a thumb. She pushed back his curly hair. She kissed his forehead.

She said, "You'll go to Mars, baby."

The other side of town. Tall oaks, winding driveways, stately lampposts. 4605 Meadowlawn Drive. Gordon Ritterskamp retired five years ahead of schedule to care for his wife, Joanie. She had early onset Alzheimer's. She was a former kindergarten teacher for twenty-five years. Teacher of the Year Award, etc. Gordon only visited the public library to read the *New York Times* and the *Wall Street Journal*. Maybe check out an action movie on the weekends. At a winter chili cook-off, a friend mentioned the moss at the library. It was, some said, a wonder drug. Eat it, become a genius. Eat it, know god. Eat it, heal thyself. And so on.

Typical snakeoil salesman talk. Gordon paid it little mind.

But one Sunday after church, Gordon heard buzzing somewhere. It was in the kitchen. He called for Joanie. No answer. He came downstairs. Beautiful sharp winter light shot through the half-moon window above the front door. Something unknown set his teeth on edge.

The buzzing turned into a gritty burr. His wife stood in her housedress at the counter. Her back was to him. Jeanie turned with a smile.

She had cut off half her left pinkie finger with an electric carving knife.

On the way back from county ER, Gordon stopped at the public library. He checked out a book on early childhood education. Later, he put some library moss on their old photo albums and a stack of love letters he'd written to her in college.

He put her bandaged hand in his. He held it.

He waited.

3.

So, yeah, Sylvia found out from Ms. Gamelin that lots of folks were eating moss now. Delores was doing it regularly. The mayor, of course, had his share. And a growing faction of patrons demanded that moss be deliberately planted onto certain sections of the stacks. The most surprising supporter now was Moss Boy's mother. Ms. Gamelin had been at Applebee's and saw Trent's mother, the manager, chewing on some rank fuzz.

Much like Trent's experience with the Fair Isle knitting, the moss was allowing library patrons to grok the contents of books and films and records they checked out—or didn't check out. People were eating moss growing on spy mysteries, Greek drama, cookbooks, and poetry. High schoolers loved it. They were acing calculus tests and history exams. Teachers loved it because grades were high and state quotas were being fulfilled. That meant more money for them for passing more students. Everyone felt smart, content, and capable.

And the moss grew as fast as patrons could scrape it off and throw it down the gullet.

"But what's the harm of eating moss?" Ms. Gamelin said, mocking the Eaters. "You learn stuff, but you forget it immediately and then want to eat more moss." She pretended to be an Eater, shrugging. She stopped pretending. "You never have time or space for you own thoughts. That's the harm in it."

Of course, the moss affected everyone differently. Some gained a minor edge—remembering phone numbers from childhood, etc. Other, though, absorbed calculus textbooks with little effort and scrawled derivatives and limits on the walls of restaurants and the post office. After Sylvia was buried, and patrons both accidentally and purposely ingested the moss, everyone was thrilled. A Christmas miracle. The sudden rise in goodwill, knowledge, and wit. How could the moss be a bad thing? Many Caldecottians considered their town blessed because the moss was only found there. Some met in informal committees around town in living rooms to debate whether other cities should know about the moss. Or should they cultivate and harvest it in secret? Why share this with the world when they could be the sole purveyors and subscribers? No consensus was met because everyone was strung out one way or another on the stuff. And, slowly, over weeks and months, the most immediate effects drifted into distended discourses on whatever topic someone had eaten. Interest turned into idiosyncrasy into idiocy. The world would find out one way or another.

"No one spaces out the eatings," Sylvia said.

"Exactly. People are just jumping from one moss to another. Mayor Hardy was on about some massive glass atrium built on top of the library because he ate something on modern architecture. He was doing model constructs and wrote a report with the city engineers. He was on the verge of getting bids for contractors when the moss wore off. Then he ate something on citrus tree cultivation. You can imagine the confusion among everyone in the mayor's office."

Sylvia wondered if this was why Albert disappeared? Of course, it had to be a part of the reason. "Close the library, then," she said, as if it was like shutting a closet door.

"I tried," Ms. Gamelin whispered. "Delores went behind my back and whipped up the mayor and the library's board. They voted No Confidence in me. So I stepped aside."

"And you proceeded to dig for me."

Ms. Gamelin nodded. "I've never wanted the public to be more disinterested in the library than I do now."

"What do you want to do?"

"Destroy the library and start over. What do you want to do?"

"Two things. First, I want to tell you a story, then I want to see Natalia. I've got to find Albert. I need to know if he's alive."

"Why are you so intent on finding him? Does he know something we don't?"

"Because he was there for me when no one else was. And I think he basically saved my life that night in the library. I think he's got an in with the moss. Or it's got an in with him. There's got to be a connection between his crazy growth and that stuff. At least, I hope there is."

4.

Sylvia told Ms. Gamelin about Grasshands. She told her about Deena. About her battle in the woods with the motherfog and about what she remembered of her gravedream.

"'Build soil'?" Ms. Gamelin asked.

"Yeah, she said I should 'build soil.' What does that even mean? How does somebody build soil? You can't. It just happens over time."

Ms. Gamelin was staring at her new roommate like a moron. "Of course you can build soil. I thought you were building soil for the past four months." Sylvia wasn't following. "Being dead. Dead-o. Kaput. A dead thing. A corpse feeding the ground, making dirt. Building soil. Your mother wanted you to die."

"Grasshands did."

"Whatever."

"Fuck. That's dark."

"Indeed."

"But what's the point?" Sylvia asked. "Why chase me down and fill the library and various parts of town with moss. I'm missing something here."

They didn't speak for minutes, both thinking about alternatives.

Ms. Gamelin made a noise. "We've been focusing on one direction. When you eat some moss, you take in information. But we've not thought about what the moss takes in."

"Us. Our info."

"Yes. Let's assume that for now."

"I always felt like that first time in the woods was a test. Like Grasshands was checking on me for something. Almost like I'd have passed its test if I metabolized slowly like a Joshua tree or something, living a slower life. But how can a human live as slowly as nature does? It's impossible. I don't live in a fairy tale."

"You'll always fail the test, then."

"Exactly."

Ms. Gamelin dropped off Sylvia at Albert and Natalia's to retrieve her stuff. But she couldn't stay. She needed to speak with Delores.

Sylvia knocked on the door; no one answered. Natalia's car was in the driveway. She knocked again. Tried the door. Unlocked. The living room was a right mess. Take out boxes, crusted. Wine glasses, variously filled. There was a massive stain on the couch.

She called Natalia's name. She waited. Nothing. So she started searching. Natalia was in the spare room where Sylvia'd slept.

The bed was pulled from the wall with the holes exposed. The ceiling tapestry was torn down. For a moment, Sylvia viewed the holes in the room as stops on some kind of insane instrument that only someone 60 ft. tall could play. What sounds would it make?

Natalia was facing away from Sylvia. She didn't seem to move. Sylvia's heart raced. She didn't know what to do. She froze.

"Natalia."

She waited. Then she tried again. This time louder.

"Natalia?"

A last time.

"Natal—"

Natalia rolled toward her and said, "Please shut up. I can't hear what it's saying."

"Hear what who's saying?"

Sylvia tried to get closer to the punched-out holes. Faintly, ever so faintly, she heard the distinct syllable.

Fa, fa, fa, fa

Natalia began to cry quietly. "It likes you. I can tell. Stay here. Sit on the bed for a minute." She gripped Sylvia's wrist. The sound continued in a pleasant but forgettable way. "Albert's not here," Natalia added.

Understatement of the year, Sylvia thought.

"Where've you been anyway?"

Sylvia considered: tell the truth? Or change the subject?

"Sing back," she suggested. "Like this..."

afa afa afa afa

"Into the holes there," Sylvia added. "I'll do it in the ceiling."

They sang their assigned parts. It synced with the original syllable. It was oddly comforting. After about a minute of this, Natalia sat up on the bed.

Sylvia expected to see, was excited to see, Natalia's baby bump. Instead, her belly was flat. And that was all she needed to know about Ms. Gamelin's reaction in the woods when she mentioned Natalia.

She sat next to Natalia and took her hand. She kissed it. Natalia wept and placed her head in Sylvia's lap. Natalia flattened her belly as if willing her body to grow, or triple-checking that it was truly gone. Sylvia couldn't catch her breath while she cried.

"I'm so sorry," Sylvia said. "I'm so, so sorry."

The sight and sense of holding that unknown dark-haired baby in her gravedream weighed her down. Literally, it pulled her to the floor of the earth.

"I'm sorry I couldn't be here for you, Natalia."

"It's not your fault. I thought you'd been shot somehow. When Albert came home that night, I couldn't believe he left you behind. He terrified me."

"He didn't leave me. I sent him away."

"Either way, I had him go to the emergency room to have the wound looked at. He never came back. The ER said he never arrived. Said they would've noticed a kindly massive hulk of a man in their hospital." Natalia laid her head back down. The crying started again. Then abruptly stopped. "I talk to the holes in the wall because I think they can both hear me. Albert and the baby. Is that insane?"

"Not lately, no. Not insane at all. I think that's a totally plausible suggestion nowadays," Sylvia said.

"I talk to the baby. I talk to Albert about the baby."

"He wasn't here. He doesn't know?"

"I've told him through the holes in the wall. I think he knows. Wherever he is."

"Police?"

Natalia shrugged. "I have my people. They have their ears to the ground. Nothing yet."

"Have you been able to get out much?" Sylvia asked.

"What does it look like? I can't stand to face people. I haven't told anyone yet."

"Why?"

"I'm—I'm embarrassed, Sylvia. I feel stupid. I feel like I'm a massive fucking failure. I can't stand to bring myself to say it out loud. That it happened. And even though Albert doesn't know this, as soon as I found out I was pregnant, I told all my friends and family. Even though everyone said not to." She waited. "I'm the youngest of seven kids, okay? Which means everyone is committed to this being true still. If I lose the baby, I'm an idiot. I lost my husband. Where the fuck is he?" She beat the bed and pillows. "Where the fuck was he when I had my miscarriage! That pituitary asshole!"

Natalia leaned over to a hole in the wall. "Do you hear me, you prick, do you hear me talking to you, you swollen piece of shit? Come home! I hate you and you have to come home." She hit the wall over and over. The *fa fa* had died out before then.

Sylvia's eye caught on something by her foot. It was a baggie of moss. Natalia noticed her checking it out.

"Oh, that's some late-night reading material. I've become a regular library patron now."

As if it couldn't get worse. Sylvia's chest tightened with the thought of her as an Eater. "You've not—?"

"Of course not! I can't stand to think of what it tastes like or feels like. Just there as a reminder. And I wanted to visit the library to soak up whatever is left of Albert, I guess." Natalia worked a small piece of gold between her fingers. It was split, like an earring. Albert's wedding ring. He did cut it off then, Sylvia thought. Or he'd grown so much that it broke apart.

Sylvia hefted the baggie. The moss was variously colored. Specks of orange here and there. Sparkly stripes of blue and purple. It looked slightly liquefied.

"And what were they growing on?"

"You don't want to know."

"Yes I do."

"Then *I* don't want you to know."

Sylvia returned a withering look. Natalia could've handled it in any other situation. But here, she was broken. Sylvia was one of the few direct human interactions she'd had. Natalia told Sylvia that they were from books about suicide, embryology, bad mothering; everything designed to push her over the edge.

"I'll throw this away, that way you won't feel obligated to eat it," Sylvia said.

"I don't feel obligated to do anything. I *want* to eat it."

"But you don't have to suffer for what happened."

As soon as she finished this statement, Sylvia heard a devilish *tap tap* coming from the ceiling holes. She took a step back from them.

"What happened to suffering, then? I'm supposed to move on, I guess. To where? There's nowhere to move on to. I don't want to move on."

"Okay. Fine," Sylvia said. "But know this: the first boy who ate the moss went nearly catatonic. And I'm not sure he'll be the same again. So if you think that ruining your life is the only solution to this scenario then yeah, eat it. If not, and I suspect you agree with me, then let me take it away."

"You know what I heard from people at the library? I heard that when you eat the moss—no matter what the subject—it's like you've never had a selfish thought in your life. Every anxiety is replaced with a fact or a story or a string of someone else's words. How is that not perfect?" Sylvia didn't give in. She set her face. Natalia slumped forward. "Go ahead then. Take it. You know I have two other bags of that stuff elsewhere. You take that, I just eat the backup stuff if I need to."

Sylvia didn't feel like going on a hunt for these other two suspected bags. And it wouldn't have done Natalia much good, either. What needed to get done was finding Albert and bringing him back. *This*—more than anything—*bring Albert back home to be with his wife.*

"Did Albert ever talk about any place other than home?"

Natalia shook her head. "You're forgetting that I'm the detective. Not you, chickie-poo. I've already done all this. I have those thoughts going all the time."

Yeah, but you're too close to him. What was there that he never told you? Sylvia thought.

The *tap tap* had faded. But now the singing syllable returned in the wall.

Fa fa fa fa

Natalia, almost lifted up by this, pushed her hair out of her face and rolled back toward the wall. She started to pat the wall; to whisper to it.

Sylvia took the baggie of moss and slowly, quietly left the bedroom with her stuff and waited on the front porch for Ms. Gamelin. When she didn't arrive after a few minutes, Sylvia walked back to the Red Pillars. She scoured the area around her grave for the pike. And she found it. On the way back to Natalia's, looking like a medieval warrior, Ms. Gamelin pulled up beside her.

"Hey, Kerouac. Need a ride?"

Sylvia asked Ms. Gamelin if she was ready to venture out.

"For what?"

"Albert."

"I thought we'd head by the library so you can see what's what."

"I know what's what. Nothing's gonna change there. Not until we find Albert."

She wasn't ready to visit the library or Delores. Not yet.

"You're like a goddamn broken toy. *Albert. Albert. Albert.*"

Sylvia didn't respond. They drove on. Ms. Gamelin turned to Sylvia after a minute.

"Is this a bad time to ask about the spear you put in the back? Or should I put a pin in that?"

CHAPTER EIGHT

1.

ALBERT WAS LIKELY half the size of a light pole by now (or bigger). He wasn't going to bed down in town. So the women proceeded to try all the largest out-buildings in the 657 sq. miles of the county. Albert wouldn't have gone too far from his wife and unborn baby. What worked best was following the moss. It had spread so enthusiastically while Sylvia was buried. Driving through rural ramshackle villages and depopulated burghs, they witnessed old homes swallowed by the moss. Train tracks devoured by humps and waves of the green bristly stuff.

All Sylvia could imagine was that it desperately wanted to absorb information from objects. But then she didn't necessarily think it was sentient, either. This wasn't an alien invasion. Or Mother-Earth-as-Gaia come to take revenge on the human virus. It was neither good nor evil. It just *was*. And, in a way, that was more terrifying.

A few times they drove over mossy speed bumps in the road. Sylvia demanded they pull over into a gas station and spray down the tires. They'd want nothing sticking. Nothing that could latch on and spread.

"You're paranoid," Ms. Gamelin said. "I thought it wasn't evil?"

"It's not. But Moby Dick still took down Ahab in the end."

"I thought Ahab was the villain in that book."

Sylvia shrugged. "Yeah, well."

Every grain silo they passed was a potential hideaway. At first, they were comically quiet, tip-toeing up to it, not knowing what in the hell could be inside. After a few silo checks, it was obvious that people weren't around. Where they had gone, Sylvia and Ms. Gamelin couldn't guess. It was almost as if the furniture inside their houses soaked them up. Or the earth ate them.

The grain silos were giant, empty agricultural tombs. And once Sylvia declared this out loud, it was hard for both women not to see them that way. In the winter light, their dull rounded crowns sent shudders down their bones. So the drive turned into a game of tomb hunting. They also wielded flashlights into dilapidated barns and once-glorious farmhouses.

"What if he went underground?" Ms. Gamelin said.

There were plenty of coal mines in the area. Perhaps since the winter had settled in, Albert needed to keep warm and descended into a long vein burrowed out by machinery. Sylvia thought about it. She decided against it.

"He's going to keep growing. He's not stupid. He'll get stuck."

"How do you know that?"

"Because things get stuck when they expand in small spaces."

"No, no, I mean—how do you know he'll keep growing? I thought he had a pituitary issue?"

While buried, and with the motherfog moss in her belly, Sylvia came to understand a few things. One of which was this: Albert wasn't afflicted with a growth hormone problem. He was tied into Grasshands. She was willing to bet it was that gross moss under his nails all those months ago when he got Aristotle's *On the Soul* for Deena. This had nagged at her ever since Ms. Gamelin shoveled her up.

Ms. Gamelin's eyes widened as she took all this in. "Oh. Well, that's horrible. At some point he'll just..."

Float into space? Die from lack of oxygen? From collapsed veins? Lack of enough nutrition?

Yeah, maybe, sure. She didn't finish her thought.

2.

They drove past a massive farmhouse that looked abandoned. It was an absolute dinosaur. It could've housed Godzilla on Mothra's back. A barn twice as large was in back. The family's name was painted below the hay loft door. It was unreadable. Dormers slumped. Windows were cracked or newspapered over. It was dark. The afternoon carried a gloom in the air, as did the objects themselves. Like the weather was pissing off the disused tractors and propane tanks.

The house had a wrap-around porch. The exterior was once painted a stunning yellow. The barn, too. Paint flaked. Boards warped. The porch was sinking on one end. Nothing looked habitable about the place. But again this was another sign of potential shelter for a beast like Albert.

They didn't spot any moss from the outside. They'd begin in the house first. Then the barn. Further behind was a grain silo, but it seemed too cramped to fit Albert. As they walked the perimeter, Sylvia asked Ms. Gamelin about Delores again.

"Lunching on moss everyday." Sylvia didn't blink at this. "They've based after school programs around it already."

"What? How? I thought parents would flip their shit over this."

Ms. Gamelin shook her head. "It had too much immediate potential for the local school districts. And local employment has shot through the roof. I heard that the layoffs from the factories were able to skip the educational subsidies and get hired back on in more advanced positions."

"Because they ate moss on the books that had to do with...machines or whatever?" Sylvia said.

Ms. Gamelin shrugged. "Sure. Or they put the moss on *people* who knew it." She kicked a galvanized tin pail. Turtle doves flew out of a bush. They made a *wheedling* sound. "Then they ate the moss. It won't last. When the knowledge goes, it takes parts of the people with them."

Sylvia thought on this. She extrapolated.

"A city full of living bodies with nothing in them. But all around, the moss will have absorbed the knowledge. Grasshands will know us, but we'll be gone." She pictured the motherfog like a combine, sorting out informational wheat from chaff.

Sylvia turned and there was a dog. A mutt chained to a piece of rebar in the yard. Short-haired, white and brown. The dog's eyes swelled with an infection, but it was slow and full of grief. It must've been abandoned or forgotten about when the family fled. The farmhouse didn't look kept up. Ms. Gamelin's face fell and she moved to pet it. Sylvia stayed her hand. She pointed at the back of the dog's body. It had chewed through its hind leg down to the white bone. Yet the meat on either side—the paw below, the thigh above—were still intact. As if by magic, the center of its rear leg was missing. The dog's leg bone was the brightest object around. Likely it was infected with fleas and mites. Or it had horrific allergies. Sylvia said that the dog was sad, yes, but a mood about the mutt told her it wanted to gobble the first face it could snatch.

Ms. Gamelin wiped her hand on her pants, despite not touching the dog.

The screen door in the back hung open. The door behind it was cracked open an inch. Outdoor light takes on an obscuring quality in the winter afternoon. For a small moment, it's harder to see at dusk than in total dark. Sylvia hated this time of day. It held nothing good in it. Blindness. Frustration. Transition.

She pushed into the house. A bag of concrete mix blocked the door. It was partially covered in moss. Sylvia stopped. She poked it with the blunt end of her pike. The kitchen looked used and abandoned, as if in the middle of something. Neither knew how long the house was empty. Sylvia could've guessed five years or five minutes. They stood by the table. The air smelled like food. It smelled like people. Like life. They stood still. Nothing made a sound except their breathing. It was totally dark outside. Ms. Gamelin clicked her flashlight. Sylvia motioned for her to shine it on the tall pantry door. Sylvia opened it. The pantry was stocked. She grabbed a box of saltines and tore open a sleeve. The crackers were crisp. They made for the doorway to the living room when Sylvia thought she saw an arm reaching out for her from the pantry. She cried out and swung her pike. Ms. Gamelin screamed, too. The pike nearly took her head off. Turned out it was just a shadow.

"Jesus Christ, Sylvia! Watch that fucking thing."

Sylvia prodded the pantry's contents and pushed foodstuffs around from four feet away. There was no room for anyone to hide in the pantry. It was dark. She was anxious. She made it up.

"Sorry," she said.

"Don't forget I have a machete. Sharp end here. When scared, owner will swing around. You are not excepted from that." The machete was also an Army Surplus purchase.

"Yeah, yeah. I said I'm sorry."

The dining room opened into a parlor. Nothing was dusty. Not even the plate rail and the tacky parade of porcelain plates painted with quaint rustic scenes. Sylvia hated people who owned and cherished this kind of shit, but no one deserved to die for it.

Ms. Gamelin saw a person from the corner of her eye. They moved into the parlor.

"Sylvia," she whispered. "There."

"Hell*ooo*?" Sylvia called. "Anybody home?"

Dough for biscuits hardened on a cutting board. Flour dust whiffed under their boots.

Ms. Gamelin kept her sight on the parlor corner. Sylvia walked toward the main entrance and staircase. There was a family portrait, naturally. It hung above a side table in the hallway. They must've had money because the painter was good. Everyone was lifelike. The family was a good-looking, cliché Midwestern group of faces. The parents wore white dress shirts. The kids—three girls, one boy—wore different sweaters. Sylvia leaned in closer. *Not Fair Isle*, she thought. She was sort of disappointed in that. Two of the girls wore their hair in a large braid. The boy was expressionless but handsome, like his father. The mother made up for all of them with her unfettered glee at having a family portrait.

One thing was missing, though. Their limbs were cut out of the canvas like someone strolled up with an x-acto knife and *swish swish*. Ms. Gamelin was rifling through papers on a desk in the parlor. Sylvia tried to stop staring at the portrait. It was difficult. The only thing she could imagine was an angry spouse, drunk on vodka, or a vagrant drifting in and having fun. But nothing like that was likely. On second thought, it looked like their parts had been popped out from behind like they were perforated, like they were in a sheet in the back of a kindergartener's activity booklet.

Behind the portrait was a hole in the wall with a breeze coming out. Not unlike Natalia and Albert's house. She instinctively leaned her face into it. It sang to her. She sang back. Maybe it was Natalia. Maybe it was Albert. Maybe it was just wind whipping through the lathe and plaster. But as she sang, she started to see a vision in her mind. An outline of a shape. She tasted salt in her mouth. The same taste she remembered as a girl in the woods. After her first encounter with Grasshands. The taste got stronger, and a shape solidified. It was a small salt cellar, like from a restaurant. Automatically, Sylvia returned to the kitchen and grabbed a salt cellar on the table to the back yard. The chained-up mutt grunted at her. It shifted a bit. The bright bone white like a piston in this demonic machinedog. Sylvia kneeled. She reached into her jean pocket and pulled out the still warm, smooth black stone that she coughed up. It now had a perfectly yellow dot in the middle. Ms. Gamelin stood in the door, watching her. The mutt was a few feet away. It licked its maw. Anticipating food. Or touch. Or a lady's hand for dinner. For some reason, Sylvia extended the stone in her palm to the dog. "Hey," Ms. Gamelin said. The mutt licked the pebble, ever so delicately, with a saint's passion. Sylvia then pressed the pebble into the unscrewed salt cellar top. Deep into the salt. Shook it a bit. Then she screwed the top back on.

Instantly, it glowed green and shined like a flashlight. She threw the salt cellar's greenish light over the mutt. Nothing happened. She scanned the kitchen. Great creeping patches of moss were behind the walls and under the floor.

Sylvia said, "Salt's a preservative. A trick I learned from my mother."

"Quite a mother," Ms. Gamelin said.

Back in the parlor, Sylvia asked, "Do you think that evil is a part of nature?"

"Depends if you believe in evil," Ms. Gamelin said. She was rather in awe of the salt cellar.

Sylvia thought she saw movement from the corner of her right eye. A shadow down the hall by the staircase. She couldn't tear her eyes away from the portrait. Whatever she saw stopped moving.

"I looked it up once," Sylvia said. "I was bored."

"The word, you mean?"

"Yeah." Sylvia noticed the mother's eyebrow and eyelids had also been clipped out of the painting. As had the son's teeth and the daughters' ears.

"And?" Ms. Gamelin asked.

"Comes from some proto word that can mean overstepping your boundaries. Seems to make sense to me."

The shadow to her right began to move again. She turned and broke her attention from the painting. No one was there. She swung the pike toward the shadowed hallway. Then she held up the salt cellar. A brackish light phasered out and filled the hallway like ethereal foam. Nothing to be scared of. Except what they couldn't yet see.

"Check this out," Ms. Gamelin said. Sylvia walked backward until Ms. Gamelin could be seen in her peripheral vision to the left. Ms. Gamelin held a stack of books. "Recently checked out from the library." Suddenly she threw them down. "Can we be done here?" She was sweating in places she'd never thought could sweat. The tone of her voice downshifted into a nagging adolescent. Grand powers had switched between them. Sylvia owed little to Ms. Gamelin. Other than her life, really. But what was her life, that small trinket, valued at now that she knew how little it was worth? "I know I've seen a lot of oddness in the past half year, but this is a bit much, even for me."

"I'm not sure we've even seen the surface of the abyss." Sylvia waved her on. She motioned upstairs. "I wanna do one more thing. Then we can go. I need to satisfy my curiosity." Such a statement was never in her repertoire prior to being buried by Grasshands.

"Fucking research librarians," Ms. Gamelin said. She followed behind.

"Technically, I'm not a librarian. Just an assistant. But if that counts as a promotion, I'll take it. Wait, do I even still have a job at the library?" Her shadow outlined on the bottom step while holding the pike minimized any worry inside the last question. Warriors fastened with weapons rarely worried about work.

"That is a larger story we can talk about in the car."

Sylvia shook her head. "Okay, Grandma."

Ms. Gamelin flipped Sylvia the bird.

Petty distractions are the bread and butter of frightened folks. As it was here. As it should be.

But distractions also dampen the mind's tingly bits, those most useful bits, those old, reptilian, sparked-up meat junctions that root deep and exist solely to seek out the nasties in the dark.

When they reached the top of the stairs, a large mass of darkness lifted itself from a wingback chair in the unchecked family room. It was easy to miss. The dark masked it as a large duvet does a small child. The mass did not rise like a person. It almost seemed lifted up from above by fine-spun thread. Do not imagine humanity. Do not imagine a person. A head didn't tilt forward. Hips didn't flex. Knees didn't bend and push up. It had no head, no hips, no knees. Still, it followed behind the women at a slow but sure shuffle. An agonizingly aching pace. Besides its loping gate, the shape of it was hulking; its topmost point couldn't avoid the threshold from family room to foyer. The tip of the mass then lapped at the wood trim and made a sizzling sound. Like scraping a hand across a newly shaved face.

Sylvia and Ms. Gamelin found the family. They were dead. And if not dead, then doing a wonderful job pretending not to breathe or move or have a heartbeat.

The husband and wife lay in their bed. The turned poles of the four-poster shot up in the air like the legs of a dead beetle. The children hunched up together in the oldest girl's room. Of course, neither Sylvia nor Ms. Gamelin could see them. All the bodies lay smothered under an interminable blanket of moss. Sylvia immediately peeled some from the floor in the hallway. Thick forest green crawled over everything. It was simultaneously smooth and rough to the touch. The moss struggled to come up. As if tiny teeth sank into the pine planking. She yanked on a lobe of it. She expected it to cry or bleed when it tore. The sound of it ripping reminded her of tearing old blue jeans for shorts in high school. She handed the moss back to Ms. Gamelin.

Ms. Gamelin batted Sylvia's hand away with the machete blade. "Excuse me? Carry your own moss, miss."

Sylvia sighed. She plunged it into her hip pocket. She worried for a hot moment about it crawling out or attaching itself to her. What if it prodded its way up her asshole and chewed its way out her belly button? Where was her plastic baggie when she needed it?

Sylvia wanted to uncover the family. But her desire to break open the moss over the faces terrified her. She was aware of her breath. How shattered it was. How jagged. The plumbing in her chest squeezed and went cold.

Just see their decrepitated faces and rib cages and move on, she thought. *Acknowledge their death, then leave.*

But it couldn't happen. She'd have to act as a surgeon to confirm her suspicions.

Sylvia approached the head of the parents' bed when the shushing sound happened.

SSSSsssssssshhhhhhhhhhhh.

Ms. Gamelin swung her flashlight behind her into the hallway. Nothing.

"You heard that, right?" Sylvia said.

"Yeah."

"Did we leave the back door open?"

"I don't remember," Ms. Gamelin said. Sylvia paused to think. "Later! Later! Cut this open. Let's get this over with. We're supposed to be looking for Albert, not missing families."

Sylvia had changed underground. Ms. Gamelin knew it. Sylvia herself knew it. And she knew Ms. Gamelin knew it. This made it hard. But it was true. Her aims were clearer. Her directions were steeled.

Sylvia looked down her nose at her boss. "You're not at all concerned for these people?"

"*Of course I am, Wonder Woman,*" Ms. Gamelin whispered. "But to be blunt: they're dead, aren't they? Or sort of dead. Point is: we have a goal. This is now a diversion."

Sylvia seemed to understand. A flash of Albert in the memory. He was standing like a mastodon in front of that gunman the night she went past the Red Pillars. Immediately she set to slicing the moss.

Sylvia moved slowly with her blade. The moss quietly hissed open like young skin under an operating light. The pike was an unwieldy tool for this, but she managed a steady line to reach in and pull.

SSSSSsssssssshhhhhhhhhh

Only Ms. Gamelin heard the shushing this time. Though she couldn't swing the light back to look because Sylvia was cutting. She turned her head to see. Too dark. She did, unfortunately, keep thinking she was going to see the children lined up in the doorway, their necks bent in a horrific fashion to the side. Or they'd be bent and folded around like crabs and walking on the floor. She kept anticipating the heavy feel of a hand on her shoulder. Though she knew that was just total animal fear.

Sylvia delicately reached her hand into the incision and noticed that it was warm. She clutched what she could of the moss and pulled back to reveal two tawny, sunken faces. "Oh god," she said. For a moment she waited to see their eyes open like hers. Maybe they, too, had been buried and would wake. "Hello," she said. "Can you hear me? My name is Sylvia."

Ms. Gamelin couldn't see well from the foot of the bed. Sylvia's expression was all she needed. The roiling shadows flickered near her feet and around the windows. Her stomach suddenly dropped. She had to shit. Or vomit. Something in her body needed to evacuate.

The parents' faces looked scrunched and jaundiced. Whatever had happened to them wasn't what happened to Sylvia. She felt both relieved at her luck and immense grief for this entire family. All of them gone in a night.

The father's mouth fell open.

It said in a high pitch: *turn on the light turn on the light turn on the light*

Sylvia screamed. She tumbled back. The voice was harsh but quiet. It rattled in her head. It started to sound playful.

turn on the light turn on the light turn on the light

Ms. Gamelin's lightbeam followed Sylvia, not the faces.

"The bed! The bed!" Sylvia yelled.

When the light flew back onto the parents, the moss was slowly healing itself over their faces and, just as it sealed, a sallow female hand reached up, grasping for help and motioning for someone. But the moss enveloped the fingers like frosting over a cake and trapped them again.

Ms. Gamelin opened her mouth to ask Sylvia how they were alive when they heard—

SSSSsssssshhhhhhhhh

Always bring two flashlights, Sylvia thought. *Goddamn it. Bring a flamethrower while we're at it. Have we learned nothing from decades of horror films?* Ms. Gamelin swung her light back to the door to check down the hallway. But there was no hallway.

Instead, a green void filled the threshold.

The question that Sylvia wanted to ask someone with more info than her was: *Is every instance of this crap Grasshands?* The answer arrived betimes. *Yes, it was.*

Thick greenness heaved in the doorway like the decapitated undulating hair of a surly goddess. Sylvia grabbed the back of Ms. Gamelin's jacket and yanked her back. There seemed very little reason to chat with Grasshands. It had a desire to absorb, to learn, to spread. One could've said the same thing about cancer, though. Or a virus.

Part of her wondered if it was Albert. If this was where he was, trying to communicate. But no. Albert would've already been much bigger than this if he was still growing.

Sylvia wondered if she would grow numb. Only the tickle spiders induce immobilization. She lowered her pike and walked forward. Ms. Gamelin didn't move out of the way. Sylvia placed a hand on her shoulder. Ms. Gamelin didn't turn to her. The look in her eye was like the Tin Man in the Enchanted Forest.

"Help," Ms. Gamelin whispered, as if suffering a stroke. Her mouth was lopsided and cramped.

The ambassador of Grasshands come to welcome them flowed and rumbled into the room. Its shape was hard to define. Sylvia also realized how nonsensical it was to call this *stuff* moss. But what other word was there? It moved toward them at an excruciatingly slow pace.

Ms. Gamelin shined her light on the doorway. She saw the massive boiling green sheet of moss. Instantly she couldn't feel her legs, couldn't move. Her toes felt welded to the floor. Her knees compounded with cement. And ever so gradually her waist and torso and head lost sensation. She worked hard to say something as fast as it happened but could only squawk from the side of her mouth. Panic overran her limbic system and her chest tightened in what felt like a heart attack. The smell of decrepitude and copper decay thickened the air. Old milk and putrid, unwashed bodies. The smell of damp basements and moist paper. She couldn't look away.

When Sylvia passed on her left, she tried desperately to speak. To ask for help. She wasn't sure if Sylvia heard it.

Ms. Gamelin wondered what it would feel like to be buried alive.

A form emerged from the center of the moss's body. It pushed through the moss like giving birth. A rounded shape ruptured the surface and forced its way out. The shape was a dirty white color, pitted here and there. Calcium-faded. It writhed in the green and pulled itself up.

Deena's deteriorated head pulled itself up. One eyeball was partially enucleated, half-way out of the skull. A trickle of gelatinous spunk dripped from the center where it looked as if it had popped. The mouth moved in a wooden puppet kind of way.

Sylvia squeezed the pike so tightly it hurt her hands.

"I thought you were gone," Sylvia said to it.

The sound that leaked from the rotting head was deranged yet sad. Tortured. Part of Sylvia believed that Deena was ultimately still alive in there somehow. A figment of Deena's consciousness running on some arcane plant-based neural network. It spoke. The voice was sluggish like a slowly frozen runnel of water.

"I am not allowed to die. Nor will you."

"S*uurrre*. But, like, what's the point?"

Deena's mouth worked up and down, chewing invisible meat. It was as if she was gnawing on all the sound in the house. *Fuck waiting*—Sylvia lunged forward and drove her pike through the head.

Everything in the room rattled and reverberated. The bodies on the bed boiled under the mossblanket and their feet and hands shot through the thicket of plantlife. Their tawny hands flailed as if submerged under scalding water.

Deena's head caterwauled in a guttural and mucosal yawp. Ms. Gamelin moved her limbs and turned her head. Sylvia pulled the pike from the head. It quit moaning. The room went silent. She was having trouble breathing. A floorboard ached under her boot. She spotted someone in the corner of her eye—a flickering shadow. Applauding or weeping, it was hard to tell.

Grasshand's pseudobody unzipped itself. Sylvia recognized the sound as when a whole roast chicken is pulled apart. Deena's skeleton tumbled out. It caught itself and stood. The rotting head on top lolled and began chewing again. Remnants of hair stuck to the skull with swampy sludge. It stumbled toward them, unafraid of the pike or the machete. Deena had her hands together, the bones rasping in a supplication. A voice filled the room, begging, urging.

turn on the light turn on the light turn on the light

Sylvia yelled for Ms. Gamelin to move back, and she did so, but slowly. She was still numb. Deena shakily walked into the pike, which did nothing to stop her. The pike's blade and pole slid easily through her open rib cage. There was no meat to stab. Sylvia shook the pike. She wanted to toss her through the window or break her upon the wall. Left, right. Left, right.

The skeleton was fast. Shaken to the right, it snagged Ms. Gamelin's left wrist. The machete dropped from her hand. A short burst of worry came from Ms. Gamelin. She couldn't muster much more. Deena's skeleton grasped Ms. Gamelin's hand and pierced her wrist with the tips of her metatarsals.

Now Ms. Gamelin screamed in pain. Fat drops of blood smacked the floor.

Sylvia expected to hear the horrible *tap tap* of the tickle spiders by now. The anticipation was worse than the actual sound anymore. *We're being delayed*, Sylvia thought. *Kept behind for some reason.* The physical pain brought Ms. Gamelin fully mobile now. With her right hand, she gasped and swung the machete over Deena's forearm bones.

They broke at the articulation point. The finger bones tore more of Ms. Gamelin's flesh. She pulled her limb to her body like a wounded dog. The skeleton fell back off the pike and then redoubled its efforts on Sylvia. It charged forward again. But this time Sylvia two-handed the pike staff and brought it down, cracking Deena's jaw and skull. Deena's skeleton and rotten head fell into a pile of bones. The broken jaw still chewing the air.

turn on the light turn on the light turn on the light

Sylvia remembered the salt cellar. The mutt-blessed stone. The brackish light. She pulled it from her pocket. Nothing. She dashed some salt onto the floor for protection. Just 'cause. She unscrewed the top off the cellar and radiant and galactic light burst out. The father's hand was raised. She turned the light on him. The hand evaporated into sludge. As did the bodies underneath.

Then she turned the light onto Deena.

Grasshand's pseudobody pulled away from the doorframe and fitfully shuffled somewhere out of sight. The bones rearranged themselves into a familiar shape. The skull as the body. The remaining bones as some spindly legs. The bone spider *tap tap'd* away behind the psuedobody into nothingness.

Sylvia trailed behind with care. She uncapped the salt cellar on the children's room, as well. The same results applied. Bodies into sludge. The smell of decrepitude.

"No, no, no," Ms. Gamelin said angrily. She stepped into the children's room. She was crying. It was the first she'd spoken in minutes. She felt like she'd just come out of a long-distance telephone call with a demon wearing the skin of a child. Her voice sounded reheated—old leftovers in a crusty microwave.

"There's no one left here," Sylvia said.

"Not anymore," Ms. Gamelin said, crying.

3.

They fled the house. Or tried.

There wasn't much to go through. But the staircase, living room, and kitchen was a nightmare. Space-time distended and warped like a god crumpling tinfoil. These spaces possessed nightmare logic. Navigating the way *in* was easy, but the way *out* was shifting and obtuse. As they ran, their limbs slowed; their joints slogged. They turned and looked at each other but couldn't speak, as they moved at half speed, listening to the sounds of the family's bodies upstairs deliquescing into non-existence.

Despite this, Ms. Gamelin pushed against the warping as hard as she could and grabbed two books off the side table in the living room, though they seemed yards away. As they cleared the threshold of the back door, it was like an airplane landing with the flaps up. They were struck by a renewed mobility. Ms. Gamelin threw the books into the back with her machete and Sylvia's pike.

The mutt was parked on its haunches as it had been. The same sad and defeated look on its eyes. Ms. Gamelin noticed Sylvia hesitating to get into the car and staring at the dog. So she took her machete and broke the rusty chain off the pole it was attached to. The mutt stood. It licked the bone of its leg. Then, slightly limping, it trotted off into the woods.

Ms. Gamelin took the wheel. The truck growled. Part of her soul (though she didn't believe she had one) lightened to feel her foot press down and sense the gas pedal's resistance. They broke the speed limit onto the driveway, rural route, and state highway. Often, safety is in inverse proportion to the distance between you and a threat. Ms. Gamelin knew this from a broken youth. When your stepfather comes home drunk and looking for a better reason to hate his own life than his own poor life choices, the bedroom window transforms into an escape hatch. The neighbor's doghouse into a far-flung bunker. She could now (still) hear her stepfather's high pitched, whiny voice. She imagined his body hanging out her bedroom window, shaking his fists. Foam and spittle on his lips. Nose hairs rattling. *Clara, you'll reap what you sow!* She was in her fifties now. Her stepfather had been dead for over half that time. But his voice wasn't. It lived on in her meat circuits. That's what came back to her as she stood frozen in that farmhouse bedroom.

She drove along the pitch-black back roads. Sixty, seventy miles per hour. The headlights gave her a small swathe of visibility. It seemed as if the universe fell off into oblivion on either side of the road. She knew on either side were fields. Some empty, some full. *Clara Gamelin, you'll reap what you sow.* She believed it. But it wasn't terrifying to her because of who said it. Her drunk stepfather crashed a school bus off an overpass with four kids on it. All of them died. He was shithoused. No one who knew him had to even ask.

Nothing about the shrinking farmhouse in the rearview made the women feel remotely secure.

She checked on Sylvia. "Hey, you alright, girly?"

Sylvia leaned her head against the passenger window, breathing heavily. She was hyperventilating. She just kept whispering, *Where's Albert? Where's Albert? Where's Albert?*

Sylvia thought back to when she left her apartment after her room flooded. Albert had wrapped his arms around her and let her cry. He didn't know why she was upset. And neither did she really. If this was to end, they had to find him, and soonish.

Ms. Gamelin made random turns and exits. "We'll find him, hun." She drove an hour in the opposite direction until they found a diner, some greazy spoon called Aunt Helen's.

They wanted distance; they needed a change of space. They needed fluorescent lighting and linoleum and sassy big-haired waitresses who didn't take shit from anyone. But most of all, they needed endless cups of cheap coffee.

CHAPTER NINE

MS. GAMELIN PULLED the truck into the parking lot where a smattering of other brokedown vehicles waited for their owners. Witching-hour sadness emanated from the huge lit windows of the restaurant. It was like a neon tombstone. Ms. Gamelin wrapped her machete in a large cloth from the back of the truck. She hid it in her coat. Sylvia and Ms. Gamelin's breath hung like icy garlands in the air as they entered the building. A relief from the hellscape of the farmhouse. The sound of the highway in the distance—air brakes, backfirings, the odd, lonely motorcycle.

Inside smelled of a dinner rush—chicken fried steak, bargain ranch dressing, some vaguely tomatoey sauce. Over all of it: the pungent smell of french fry grease. The industrial berber carpet had large dark stains that looked like a poorly cleaned murder scene. It had probably never been shampooed since 1983. Same as the library's carpet, Sylvia thought. Berber carpet was, yes, the devil.

They sat in a sticky corner booth and ordered a carafe of black coffee. The waitress was polite but taciturn. Probably on her shift's last hour. Her nametag said JACKIE.

Neither Sylvia nor Ms. Gamelin spoke to each other for fifteen minutes. They were too traumatized. They sat separated by fat-handled diner mugs and two feet of Formica table. Ms. Gamelin stared at a piece of kitsch art on the wall. A little girl led a sheep through a fence gate with a stick. Ms. Gamelin switched to idly rearranging the sugar packets. Sylvia stared into her coffee when she wasn't drinking it. All she could see was the dog chained in the yard with the clean bone exposed.

One of two men sitting at the counter stools turned over his shoulder. He smiled. Whether at them or to himself was hard to say. He wore a baseball cap with a cursive "W" on it. And on the bill was a large silver fishing hook affixed at the side. He wore a cheap windbreaker with a screen-printed advertisement of a towing company on the back. Ms. Gamelin did not return his smile.

Sylvia looked up when they finished the coffee. Her face was drawn and worn out. She was crying and not aware of it. Her eyes ringed with darkness and distress. A trickle of blood beaded down from her left temple. But she wasn't cut. She had no idea whose blood it was.

"Are you hungry?" Ms. Gamelin asked.

"Not really."

"You should eat."

"Why? So you can watch me?"

"Maybe."

"Fine. Get whatever you want. I'll eat some of it."

"I hope so. I'm paying for it."

Sylvia ran a finger around the empty mug's lip. She thought about the three hundred bucks Ms. Gamelin had given her months back; how she wanted Sylvia to do something with it. *That money you gave me went straight to my lying landlord*, Sylvia wanted to admit. But then, most money was flushed down human-shaped toilets.

"Why is this chasing me down? What did I do or not do?"

Ms. Gamelin looked around to see if anyone could hear them. Jackie was at the waitress station scrolling through her phone. The two men at the counter laughed quietly and drank coffee. "Grasshands? I don't know. Why does a lion chase down an antelope?"

"Because it's evolved to eat antelope. And it's hungry."

"Okay, smart ass. What about Persephone?" (This was a move Ms. Gamelin pulled often with young people, especially young women, when they countered with complaints about the unfairness of life.)

Sylvia shrugged with disinterest. She didn't want the oncoming lecture. Jackie appeared out of nowhere and replaced the carafe of black coffee. She wiped the table where it stood before replacing it.

This touched Sylvia for some reason. She wanted to weep at the gesture.

Ms. Gamelin spread her hands out. "Okay. Forget for a second that this myth goes back way further than the Greeks. This whole thing is very old. Persephone is a young goddess. She's a subterranean goddess. She rules vegetation, crops. She's connected with fertility, right? Her mother, like any smart woman, keeps her away from the male gods who're interested in her. But Hades, the god of the underworld, wants her. So he kidnaps her. Abducts her in broad daylight. The earth splits open. He rides out in his chariot, snatches her, and they're off."

"I don't want to psychoanalyze this thing."

"We're not. We're just asking questions. Thinking it through. You've got me on this now, and I can't give it up. Why did Hades do that? Why did he abduct Persephone? What's the point of the story other than to explain a natural phenomenon? The cycle of seasons and death and rebirth."

Sylvia gave in. "All meaning in writing is overdetermined. Especially myths. If you have a character who likes, say, tea, then everything about tea becomes symbolic. The brewing of tea is like the brewing of life or something. Or how tea leaves are picked and stored in the dry and cool places of the kitchen is a metaphor for how our tortured souls are kept away from—" She stopped.

"Rotting?"

"Ugh, no."

"What?"

"Don't you just want to read a story that doesn't make plain how it's trying to make you feel?"

Ms. Gamelin was exasperated. "*That is the point of stories.* But you're not answering me. Why did Hades abduct her?"

"I don't know. He was lonely and wanted a girlfriend."

Ms. Gamelin nodded. "Probably. I'd say that. Shows that we're all in need of companionship. Even the most desolate and terrifying of us. Or that he desired something and wanted it but didn't know how to get it. He was hungry for a missing part of his life. The idiot."

"But hungry for what? Flesh? Blood? Grasshands clearly wants info. Why was it taking over the library? You even said so yourself. People are feasting on the easy intake of knowledge and having their minds carved out because of it."

"Info," Ms. Gamelin corrected. "Information is just stranded facts. *Knowledge* is a way to travel from island to island in an efficient and productive manner."

Sylvia scoffed. "How poetic."

Ms. Gamelin kicked her under the table.

"Ow!"

"Well, quit being rude."

Jackie returned for their order. She could sense their need for food. Ms. Gamelin got both of them a short stack, bacon, and two eggs.

"Maybe," Ms. Gamelin said, "it was at the library because you were at the library."

"But why?"

"I don't know. Did it ask you on a date? Did you turn it down?"

Jackie came with the food mere minutes after ordering.

They ate quietly.

The trucker guys at the counter left. They eyed the women. They strolled out into the parking lot and loitered by a large pickup truck. Stretching, scratching. The one in the windbreaker laughed a lot and chewed a toothpick. The other dug around in the truck for something. They both climbed in. Truck started. It flicked the lights on and backed up and drove off.

"Did you know Albert studied Aristotle?"

"I did."

"You did. How?"

"I hired him."

"You did?"

Ms. Gamelin nodded and chewed.

Sylvia said, "The director of the board hires?"

"No, I was the head librarian then."

"Whoa, whoa. Slow down, priestess. You had Delores's job? Why did you leave?"

"Bored, I guess. Tired of watching hard work go to naught."

Sylvia couldn't argue this. She didn't know what *hard work* meant for Ms. Gamelin. But she could guess. "Did Albert ever share Aristotle stuff with you? Like facts or theories and whatnot?"

"Not really, no."

"I begged for it. Some people I love to hear talk. And a few people I beg to talk because what they have to say is interesting. Albert was one. Aristotle was apparently real big on moderation. Had this idea about 'the Golden Mean.' All things would move toward this."

"Seems like a sound piece of advice."

"I think so, too. I can't help but think how un-Aristotelian all of this business with the moss in the library is. How outrageously pissed off Albert has to be where he's hunkered down."

"Go on."

"Well, the moss is all the reward without the effort, yeah. Eat this. Know this. Move on. Rinse, repeat."

"Everyone knows the answer but doesn't have to show their work?"

"In a way, yeah, that's it."

A really old pair of ladies waddled in. Arm in arm. Peach slacks. Blue hair. Canes. Jackie sat them across the aisle in another booth. Between the two of them there were enough years to reach back and touch Shakespeare's teeth. Which one of them probably was wearing in her mouth right then. They were up late. Or up early.

"And you mentioned that after a while, their brains go kerplunk. Fall out their ass or whatever."

"Something like that, I suppose."

"But it could be anything, couldn't it? Always the same model. Something in moderation is good. Get a taste for it. Want more than you should have. Glut yourself. Die or get ruined."

"Drugs. Work. Sex."

"Pity. Pride. Food."

Ms. Gamelin shoved a massive piece of pancake into her mouth. Syrup glazed her mouth. She swallowed after a minute. "And now, it's information."

"The *having* of info, yeah. Even if it's Fair Isle knitting for a teenage boy. He was compulsively knitting. Unable to stop. He had to express the info in his head, or he'd explode."

Ms. Gamelin picked her teeth. It didn't seem like a normal thing for her. But what about the past few hours had been normal? They sat quietly for a minute.

"I debated on telling you this," she said. "But now I think I should."

Sylvia tilted her head.

"The guy who pulled the gun on Albert?"

"Tim."

"Yes, Tim. He'd apparently checked out a book on paramilitary procedures and history. Whether he knew there was moss on there or not, I don't know, but let's say he did. He ate some of the moss on it. This was a few days before you disappeared, by the way. Well, we know he ended up shooting *at* Albert. Grazing him. And the weeks after you disappeared, the police were getting calls about traps set up around the city. In public places. Parks. Garages. Yards. Large holes dug with sharpened sticks inside, covered over with greenery. Bad shit."

"What happened?"

"Three people died."

"Why were you hesitating to tell me this?"

"Because two of the three people who died worked at the library. One of the pages, Denis, and…oh shit, what's her name. God, this is horrible. Uhh—the Children's librarian who's always cold."

Sylvia was talking to Ms. Gamelin but staring into space as she said it. "Teresa Bardin. She always wore that beige cardigan."

"Oh my god, yes. *Teresa.* Jesus. Why did I forget her name?"

Ms. Gamelin was honestly embarrassed. She folded her hands in her lap and stared at them.

"What happened to them?"

Ms. Gamelin didn't look up. She spoke to her breakfast. "A pit with poisoned stakes. The two of them were walking in the park at night. They fell in."

Sylvia couldn't un-see their deaths. They were impaled, writhing. The hot smell of each other's blood flooding their noses. The smell of burst intestines, shit. The shock of pain. The realization they were about to die. Had very little time left. The sudden coldness of their limbs. They had probably just been talking, walking. Maybe even kissing. Teresa was way older than Denis, but who cares. Love is a crooked path. Was Teresa Bardin wearing Sylvia's clothes when she died?

Sylvia's vision was gruesome to behold. She needed to picture brutality. It was the only way she could feel anything. Everything was far away now.

"What happened to Tim?"

"Caught and arrested. They charged him for the shooting at the library, too. But since he's been in jail, he's gone catatonic."

"No great loss there."

"No, but as long as Delores keeps the library open, people are sacrificing themselves. And psychos like Tim eat up moss and think they're Rambo. Or an architect or a pilot or a doctor."

"What do we do if in a week or a month, the whole city is a mindless glob of useless flesh? Do we move to South America and hope this moss dies out? Or what?"

"Finish your food. We need to get going."

Sylvia's appetite was dried up. She pushed the flapjacks around. Built a wall with them.

She couldn't quit the thought, though. In the woods, all that time ago. She waited on Grasshands to show itself. Or the even worse version of it—the motherfog. She wanted to see something other than what she was expected to see. Finally, it did. It sent the spindly thing, the tickle spider. It sized her up. Judged her. Now that Grasshands was finally here, she wanted to obliterate it. Something silly about that, no?

Well, no, she decided. That was then. This was now. She wasn't going to be abducted and taken underground (not again).

Whatever ancient power Grasshands meant to represent, it would have to stay lonely or find a better way to woo. She thought of the books in the Children's section. The sweet-tasting moss. She wondered which children she'd seen ambling around the library were now slavering husks of organic material. Which children were brainless, senseless, taken over by a mental ice-cream scoop that was Grasshands.

She wondered what had become of the library's homeless population. She asked Ms. Gamelin if she'd changed her tune on the homeless.

Ms. Gamelin bit her lip. "I have been known to be harsh on certain policies. But. And I think I speak for many people when I say this—the last four months have changed my expectations of reality. In such a way, mind you, that I have no problem with homeless folks in the library. Again, not my choice anymore. I have zero power."

"I hope they got the fuck out before shit got bad."

"If it means anything, I've seen a few tents by the woods where I found you. I mean, Gerald was a big help in finding you. But it's hard to say where the homeless are going now that it's winter."

The library had been a sanctuary. Now it was Mount Doom.

Lightbeams swung into the diner lot. Glare flashed over their faces. The two truckers returned. They loped in. They weren't laughing anymore. They didn't glance at the women. They took their seats. Jackie appeared like a magician's assistant. *Abracadabra.* She warmed up their coffees. She disappeared into the kitchen. *Shazam.* Both Sylvia and Ms. Gamelin monitored them from the corner of their eyes.

The guy in the windbreaker pulled a chewing tobacco pouch from his hip pocket. The crinkling was loud.

"How big is the library consortium? The whole county?"

Ms. Gamelin sighed. "Of course it is, Sylvia."

"Is there a branch near here?"

"An annex, yes. Did you never pay attention at work? And there's a bookmobile for the most rural northern area. Why?"

Mr. Windbreaker flung something wet to the floor. It caught Sylvia's eye. Old chewing tobacco and juice. A small fecal pile of it. He was scraping it with a pudgy finger from under the lip and throwing it onto the berber carpet. That explained the murder stains. She expected the old biddies to notice and tsk-tsk. But there was not a peep.

Then Mr. Windbreaker leaned his head back in a dramatic fashion. Sylvia now had that ole Telephone Feeling. The telephone was about to ring and she knew who would be on the other end.

Mr. Windbreaker pulled out a large chunk of moss from the tobacco pouch and dropped it into his gullet. The other guy did, too. Less dramatically, though, as if he was embarrassed. Sylvia's stomach dropped into her ass.

"Goddamn it," she whispered.

"What?"

"Get the blade. Set it next to you."

Ms. Gamelin didn't even ask why. She did so without looking. It lay next to her in the cloth remnant. She pulled back a piece of the cloth. It exposed the handle. She returned to her pancakes.

The trucker guys slid off their stools and sauntered over. The sound of their butts gliding off the seats' vinyl reminded Sylvia of the pseudobody hushing along the hallways of the farmhouse.

Jackie *alakazam*'d from the kitchen and Sylvia motioned for her and pointed at the table. Jackie nodded.

These guys, Sylvia mused, were what the library boys scraping moss grew up to be when no one was paying any attention.

Pay attention, she thought. *Pay close attention.*

The truckers walked up to their table. They made it hard to exit. "Do either of y'all wanta have a bite a moss?" Mr. Windbreaker held out the tobacco pouch and shook it. Like Sylvia and Ms. Gamelin were dogs eager for meat.

"No, thanks," Sylvia said. "I've got some pancakes here. Moss usually fills me up too fast."

"You sure you won't have a little bit?" the other asked. "It's been growin on some interesting stuffs."

"I bet," Ms. Gamelin said. "Lemme guess? Racine? Apollinaire? Or maybe Goethe?"

The other man didn't recognize the names. "Uh, a sex book."

"Oh, right. That sounds fun."

Sylvia tried to play it off.

"Now why would we want to eat some unknown moss given to us by a couple of strangers?"

"We don't have to be strangers. We could join you for breakfast."

"It's dinner time."

"It's 2AM. You're having pancakes. That's breakfast."

"You already ate."

"We'll eat again."

"Maybe we don't want company. Maybe we're about to leave. Maybe—maybe we're a couple of lesbians on a road trip and just stopped to eat pancakes."

Up to now, she thought the men were loutish and dumpy. A couple of gravy-lickers. Laborers or long-haul truckers who had little to no decorum and were taking a chance with a couple of unknown women before heading home and drinking the dark morning away. Mr. Windbreaker's hands were beat up and dry. Cuts and healed-over scars marked his skin. It was deeply cracked by the knuckles. Dried blood smeared near his thumb. Neither man had a wedding band.

Something about that fishhook at the end of Mr. Windbreaker's hat she couldn't figure. Was it a symbol? Or a practical thing?

The other guy was taller than she first reckoned. He was small-town handsome, actually. But he looked clueless, empty. He clearly just followed what Mr. Windbreaker dealt out. He wore glasses and a collared shirt. Maybe he wasn't a laborer. Sylvia decided right then that she'd miscalculated these two. Which meant they were more dangerous to her and Ms. Gamelin than previously thought, only because they were now unknown elements.

She could sense Ms. Gamelin edging her hand closer to the machete's handle.

"Nah," Mr. Windbreaker said. "You're not lesbians. You're too hot for that. And I think you're up for a bit of moss, but your mama here won't let you." He nodded his head at Ms. Gamelin.

"I'm not her mother. I'm her insurance agent."

The men looked at each other and laughed.

Ms. Gamelin continued, "And we were about to—"

"Invite us to join you, that's right," Mr. Windbreaker said. His eyes narrowed.

Both men scooted into the bench seats, effectively trapping them. The biddies across the way turned and smiled. Sylvia scowled. Mr. Windbreaker, who sat next to her, placed the tobacco pouch near her plate.

"Honestly, we're not interested in chatting right now. We'd like to pay and leave."

"Sure," he said. "But why rush, you know? We're being nice, aren't we?"

Jackie sidled up to the table out of nowhere and swapped the coffee carafe. Then she refilled the two mugs to the top with fresh coffee. She vanished as quickly.

"Well, we're tired," Ms. Gamelin said. "It's been a long night."

The other guy spoke up. "But we've been sitting over there and finally got enough courage to come over here and talk with you."

"Congratulations. But no one asked you to come over here."

"No need to be mean, now, lady."

Ms. Gamelin wanted to smack the flat side of the blade into this kid's face. Smash his glasses. Chip his teeth. Ruin his visage.

"Hey, Casanova," she said to Mr. Windbreaker. "Where's this moss from?"

"Library."

"Which one?"

"The main one. Downtown Caldecott."

"Oh yeah. Again, let me ask you the pertinent question. What book did you get that hilljack Viagra from? I don't take strange drugs unless I know their provenance."

Something in Mr. Windbreaker's face change. It smoothed. The muscles went slack. He gained posture. Maybe the moss was kicking in. Hard to tell what information was coursing through his skull now.

"*The Kama Sutra*," he said. "The most sophisticated sexual manual in existence." That sounded like it was directly lifted from the dustjacket.

Their eyes glowed dull orange, which wasn't possible. But she saw it all the same.

Sylvia clocked the physical size difference between the men and the women. Even with the machete as a threat, the men were twice as big as the women. She didn't think they'd do anything stupid in a restaurant, but then again, they had eaten moss. Overconfidence bred recklessness.

She didn't break eye contact with this guy because she didn't want to come off as weak or submissive. Orange eyes or no. She kept her exterior firm and cold. She'd just stabbed a reanimated skull of a former stalker with a magical pike not but two hours ago (four hours ago? who knew when? time had been melting all around them). She wanted all of that shit to come through her face and blast Mr. Windbreaker in the balls.

He scooted closer to Sylvia. He tipped his hat back. There was a sweaty indent where the hatband had pressed into his forehead.

Sylvia poured more fresh coffee, topping off the mug to the lip. "I'm sure some of that moss was on other, more interesting, books as well, huh?"

He nodded slowly. Now Mr. Windbreaker played the Calm Game. Not too eager. Patient, understanding. She admitted to herself that it may've worked on her under radically different circumstances.

"I could tell you—but then I'd have to kill you."

He didn't laugh. Sylvia froze. Then his face widened. There was an impossibly long grin with no teeth showing. The guy's friend was now just staring at Ms. Gamelin. His whole body turned toward her. He leered. He breathed heavily. His lips hung slightly open like a slavering wolf.

"Sorry, your mouth smells like a camel's rectal area," Ms. Gamelin said.

This guy didn't react. He was on moss-guided autopilot.

Sylvia heard Mr. Windbreaker fumbling under the table. There was a rustling of fabric. Metal grinded on metal. There was the telling sound of a zipper. Ms. Gamelin and Sylvia made eye contact. The exchange said: *We will kill them to get out of here.*

She turned back to Mr. Windbreaker.

He had his dick out. It was hard. He was leaning back in a proud display. As if merely exposing his cock to a young woman was ample seduction. Whip it out. Reap the reward. The dick wasn't small, but it wasn't big. It *was* ugly. The head was warped, dented like an old World War II helmet. The shaft was a sickish purple. A wild tuft of black pubic hair crawled around it. Whatever it was that made men think dicks had aesthetic appeal—it was dead wrong. Dicks needed lots of cosmetic attention.

Sylvia could see from the side of her eye that the friend had closed in on Ms. Gamelin. He snuffled at her ear. Maybe his tongue was out. Sylvia couldn't deny the fact that this man might eat her. They might eat both of them. Like something out of a George Romero film. *Sex Moss Zombies Devour: The Virgin Meat, Pt. 2.*

And then—

Sylvia poured hot coffee on the dick.

She first noticed that some of the scalding coffee got into his urethra. That pleased her. She also noticed the coffee flood around the pubes. It made the dick look like a dying sea anemone.

Mr. Windbreaker doubled over. He covered his cock with both hands. He cried out. It was a squeal crossed with a scream. Like when an eagle dives at prey. The whole crotch area steamed. Sylvia didn't move yet. The old biddies craned their heads back.

She could see the erection had melted. Faster than a candle in a microwave. The friend had reacted by grabbing Ms. Gamelin's shoulders. He'd have anything he could get at this point. Violently, sloppily trying to kiss her face and neck. Ms. Gamelin pushed him with her left hand. His weight forced her back. It was hard to grab the machete with her other hand. She needed it to prop herself up.

Despite the Hot Coffee Dick Trick, the women were still stuck in the goddamn booth. Sylvia grabbed her plate. She brought the plate down as hard as she could—harder than she thought she'd needed to over Mr. Windbreaker's head. The food exploded like a science experiment. It broke into five large pleasing pieces.

"You fucking—" he said.

"Cunt," she said, finishing for him. She pulled her legs into the booth and spun on her sit bone. She fixed her legs on his shoulder blade. She kicked. Mr. Windbreaker tumbled to the floor. He still cradled his boiled cock. His pants were at mid-thigh. This made it difficult to stand or walk.

The friend saw this but still persisted. He wanted his share. "*Sylvia...*" Ms. Gamelin said, begging.

Sylvia gripped her fork and crawled over the table. She stabbed it into the friend's shoulder. His face dropped. He tried to push her off the table. She slipped and fell onto Mr. Windbreaker.

Ms. Gamelin had enough space to grab the handle of the machete. The attacker yanked the fork out. Blood spurted on the table. A delicate jet of red. He chuckled at this.

Jackie had appeared from the waitress station and stared. She wiped her hands on the frilled apron around her waist. She had no intention of calling the cops. At this point, they may've been as dangerous as anyone else.

Mr. Windbreaker snagged Sylvia's throat like a doll. She immediately tried to find a broken piece of plate. Her hands scoured the berber. She knew she would slice his throat open. She'd tear it like wet paper. That was the only way she or Ms. Gamelin would leave the restaurant alive. She knew this. Her heart beat so fast she wondered how threatened animals weren't distracted by the sound of it. The *thunketta* of it. Panic rang in her ears. All movements were blurs. Everything seemed decided in the long moments before she executed them.

Mr. Windbreaker got another hand around her throat. He brought her close, squeezing her neck, closing off the air. He was propelled on moss, and whatever the hell it was had wallpapered his veins and brain canals like an adamantine barnacle. Her legs flailed. Her breath slowed. The fluorescent lights above winked and faded. The drop ceiling tiles had water stains and grease stains. The tiny black dots made faces. They were like the black dots she saw on the face of the moon. They started swarming. She could feel her panic subside. Then it slipped away entirely.

Blackness closed in around her like an unfeeling blanket.

And she didn't care.

She wondered how many times this was going to happen to her before she put a fucking stop to it.

Ms. Gamelin put everything into keeping the Nice Guy off her. She knew he wasn't giving it his all yet. When he did, she would be sauced. So she slid her left hand over to his shoulder wound. She jammed her fingers into it and pushed. He gasped. His grip eased a little. Ms. Gamelin had enough time—a second—to grip the machete and bring it up.

She slammed the blade into the table. The machete chopped her plate in half. Cutlery and glasses rattled. Food jiggled. Nice Guy took notice.

"Hey, listen," he said. "We're just funnin'."

She pointed the tip of the blade into his chest and nudged. He backed out of the booth. He stood a fair piece away. Hands up. Mr. Windbreaker was on the floor struggling with Sylvia, who was near passing out. Ms. Gamelin swung the dull side of the machete blade down into the top of Mr. Windbreaker's skull. She heard a thud and a bit of give. He instantly let go of Sylvia. It was like turning a button off. Sylvia rolled and coughed. She rasped for air.

Just then, Nice Guy bolted toward the kitchen, knocking down Jackie, clipping her shoulder. Ms. Gamelin looked down at Sylvia, who choked out, *Go*, and waved her on. Ms. Gamelin followed Nice Guy who'd burst through the galley kitchen's double doors and begun scouring the countertops for a weapon. As she came in behind, he reached out and grabbed the handle of a fryer basket. "You all are fucking crazy," he said. She crowed. "Excuse me?" He yanked the basket out and swung the residual burning grease at her. She stepped back, missing all of it. When it was clear the basket was worthless, he dipped a long serving spoon into the grease and flung it at her. Again, she stepped back, but this time got burned where the grease seeped through on her pant legs. The rest of the grease slicked the space between them. In an attempt to step forward, she slipped and dropped the machete. Nice Guy jumped for the blade and slid on his knees next to Ms. Gamelin. He clutched the handle at the same time that the line cook entered the kitchen from the other end, pinching an extinguished half-smoked cig between his fingers.

"The hell are you doing in my kitchen?" he said. But intuiting the danger of the scene he stumbled onto, the cook pulled a chef's knife from a block and walked toward them. He motioned for Nice Guy to back off. Instead, Nice Guy charged the cook and tackled him. Neither man cut the other. Their weapons clattered to the floor. Ms. Gamelin got up, steadying her steps by holding the counter. Nice Guy had the chef's knife and was maddeningly bringing it above his head when she dipped a ladle in the grease and poured it onto Nice Guy's neck. He yowled and fell over. The cook suffered a droplet of grease, too, but nothing critical. Sylvia opened the door on this scene, looking ragged.

"Help me drag him in there," Ms. Gamelin said. She did so.

Sylvia feared her companion's moves. It was like a jaguar dressed in all black had replaced Ms. Gamelin. She had no idea what would happen next. She had no idea what *should* happen next.

Out front, the old biddies took almost no notice of the scenario.

Ms. Gamelin knelt down by Mr. Windbreaker. He wasn't dead, just knocked unconscious. But Nice Guy didn't know that, who was screaming in pain. She told him Mr. Windbreaker might die.

"That moss you ate was from the *Kama Sutra*."

He swallowed. "Maybe—I don't know! I don't even know what that shit is, okay? He just handed me the stuff—the moss. Said he'd had always been wanting to try out a fantasy of his. It was from a fantasy trilogy or something." He was nearly yelling this. "It's called *The Dongslayer Trilogy* or something."

So they had no real idea where the moss was from. Nothing you'd gift your grandmother for Christmas, obviously. Ms. Gamelin placed her hands behind her back. Nice Guy tried to look away but was scared that if he did, she'd do something crazy. Sylvia approached and steadied the blade at his throat.

Ms. Gamelin pulled a small baggie of her own from an interior pocket.

"Where'd you get that? When you dug me up?" Sylvia asked.

Ms. Gamelin didn't acknowledge her partner. "There's been four months of this stuff growing on everything in the public library, and elsewhere. You don't think people haven't been harvesting this stuff for future use?"

Future use for what? Sylvia thought.

Sylvia asked what book it came off of. Then she realized it might not have come off a book at all. It very well could've been harvested off another person, a corpse, or something more sinister—like that pseudobody in the farmhouse. Then again, Sylvia wouldn't put it past Ms. Gamelin to have started a batch of anti-moss. Reverse the plague, as it were. She straight up asked her this.

"Wouldn't you like to know?" she said, smiling.

Ms. Gamelin touched Nice Guy's burned neck again. His face flared red with pain. Tears streamed down his eyes. Some blood appeared at the corner of his lips. She opened the baggie with her mouth and offered a plug of the moss to him like a priest with communion. Something about the whole act reminded Sylvia of the tickle spider. Forcing into the mouth. She tried to push the thought away. Afraid, he took it willingly. Sylvia had to be careful with the blade. She accidentally nicked a spot under Nice Guy's jaw. She put the machete down at her side. Then Ms. Gamelin released the guy. That's all. Crumbs fell from his mouth. Nice Guy slumped to the floor in a dazed manner.

Sylvia handed Ms. Gamelin the machete. She caught Jackie's eye. The waitress reacted as if she'd watched the whole thing impassively, as if this happened often enough.

"We're not paying for our meal. You know that, right?"

Jackie nodded. "I'm not gonna call the cops or anything," she said. "They wouldn't come anyway."

Ms. Gamelin shook her head. "No, no, no. You've looked after us." She searched Mr. Windbreaker's pockets and found his wallet. "Ah ha." She peeled a twenty out and slapped it on the table. Then Ms. Gamelin took all the cash—$214—and handed it straight to her.

"Have a lovely night, Jackie."

After they left, Jackie split the money with the cook.

They drove back to Ms. Gamelin's to sleep. Two topics floated around the border of whatever potential conversation they may have. They floated like globular ghouls.

Safety and Albert.

Forget the fact that the women couldn't even go to a waffle joint and eat in peace. Put that aside for a second. They drove in silence. Ms. Gamelin lay the machete across her lap. The end of it still dripped with blood.

Sylvia's neck and arms were bruised. Ms. Gamelin's shoulders had deep empurpled smudges where Nice Guy wrung her joints. Their hair was mussed. Pulled out and stringy. Ms. Gamelin had her own or someone else's blood on her. Sylvia's stomach was upset from stress. She checked herself emotionally. She found herself relatively stable. She was filled more with anger and burning revenge than anything.

They brought the machete and pike inside the house. They refused to let them go now. Ms. Gamelin poured red wine. They drank from juice glasses. Minutes crawled along. They camped on the living room floor in near darkness. It was 3AM.

"If we don't find Albert tomorrow," Sylvia finally said.

Ms. Gamelin waved her off. "Don't. Not right now. Give me a few hours."

"And if we don't have it?"

Ms. Gamelin drank all her wine. She poured more. Cheap cabernet didn't sit well on pancakes and eggs. She undid the black headwrap. Her hair fell down. Full black. Long disparate strands of gray here and there. An idea struck her, staring into the darkness. "What about that saltshaker?"

Sylvia rummaged through her winter coat. She hadn't thought of it in the diner. She'd left her coat in the truck. The salt was zipped into an interior pocket. She pulled it out and hefted it.

The salt cellar burned bright green. She scanned the walls of Ms. Gamelin's house. Not much moss hanging around. There were some itty-bitty spots in the walls.

"Use the salt to find Albert," Ms. Gamelin said.

"I don't know how to do that."

"Well, try. Figure it out. There's gotta be some kind of connection. You had the vision to make the thing."

Sylvia didn't say but thought—*My mother had the vision; not me.* She said she'd try, but that they'd still need to search tomorrow the old-fashioned way. Also, that she now wanted to drive by the library. At least look at it. Ms. Gamelin seemed resigned to this request.

Sylvia handled the salt. She rubbed a thumb over the cut bevels and the pointed sterling screw cap. Then her body stiffened with recognition.

"There's something we haven't considered."

Ms. Gamelin's face said, *Go on.*

Sylvia said, "Before I found out about this junk—how many materials were going out the door?"

"Oh Christ," Ms. Gamelin said. "Interlibrary loan."

CHAPTER TEN

DELORES KEPT TICKLE spiders in the library's basement. Perhaps it's better to say she *cultivated* them. The caretaking started two months after Sylvia's burial. Delores kept them because they came to her. They had pleaded with her, in their own way. That's what Delores thought, anyway. They had seemed insistent. Their spindles were persuasive.

She had been in her office, only a week after the shooting. Albert was long gone by then. Up and vanished. The library was closed. It was midnight. Delores had been sniffing industrial binder glue. She was drinking cheap vodka. Everything normal had been crumbling. Her staff had disappeared. Mayor Hardy had pushed for a rehauling of the moss from basement to main collection. Patrons had attended monthly board meetings. They wanted more moss. It soothed. It broadened. It was demanded.

She'd tried moss early that night, just as the library closed. She had chewed on spy novel moss. Who knows why. Delores had taken speed all day. It probably seemed like a clever thing to do. Espionage. Sneaking around. Dark corners.

But the spiders.

They came to her that night.

She had sat in her big swivel office chair, her head lolled backward in a drugged stupor. Mouth open. She had stared up into the one working canned light in the ceiling.

Tap tap

The pipes had been making noise. The heating was off.

Tap tap

A spindle appeared above her head, then, testing out her scalp. The tickle spider slid a spindle under the skin of her forehead. What felt like a smaller spindle off of the main one tapped her musculature. Then her skull.

It would be easy to think that sniffing glue or chewing speeds tablets all day made this a hallucination. But it was not.

The floor was smeared with vibrating and pulsing tickle spiders. The whole room swelled like a black wave. The spy novel kicked in. She was to secret this black wave away from the public. She was to bring it out at the right time.

The black wave parted when she stood up. This felt right. She directed them to the library basement. They heaved on down there. They covered the walls and floors and ceiling like a living wallpaper.

She locked the basement door and taped off the whole area as forbidden. Employees of a drug addict don't ask questions when shit like that happens. *Forbidden* was a totally normal word to see in everyday occurrence.

Many nights were filled with Delores opening the basement and riding the Black Wave. She let them crawl into her mouth. She let them feed her moss. Good moss, too. Not book moss. Pure moss. Not grown on anything. Just pure hunks of Grasshands.

Then there was the day Sylvia was dug up by Ms. Gamelin.

Delores had stepped once again into the Black Wave that night.

It was then and there that she had met Deena.

Natalia craved moss in desperation. She desired moss from fantasy books. She wanted to lose herself. And why couldn't she? What was to stop her from pushing herself deeper into a charnel house that had no ladder, no lift, no way out?

She had a plan. She collected fantasy novels from second-hand stores. She read boxes of them. She read them no matter how awful. She tore out pages of the most bugfuck crazy scenes. She wadded them up and shoved them into the holes in the upstairs bedroom walls. Then she waited.

She waited for the page that floated back up. When she had the page that floated back up, then she'd turn the lights back on.

Yet no one could turn the light on.

That's what she imagined a voice in the wall told her. The slow sludgy voice that sounded like it spoke syllables over eons. A voice made of hot stardust and sea mud.

She'd let that voice inside of her if it wanted.

People of the town ate Bible moss, of course. (There were two camps divided over this. The Indulgers and the Clamped. Indulgers gobbled moss. The Clamped kept their mouths shut. Many Clamped retreated to churches as the months went on, fortressing themselves in.) Over weeks, the Indulgers just ended up manic street preachers. They posted up on corners and tore their clothes and recited whole books of the Old Testament. Bible moss-eaters lived in ascetic fashion. They forgot their names, their family, everything about the modern world. Many of them proclaimed the world over or ended and the current world a crisp, fiery hell. Some slept in makeshift tents in blacktop lots or city parks.

Tina Blackford was overwhelmed. Right before Christmas break, Francis's teachers had phoned Tina warning her that he was too focused on the one subject and had no way of synthesizing the information. They asked if Tina had given Francis that moss to eat. Most teachers were against moss-eating. ("It's the journey, not the destination," etc.) To be fair, teachers could see the long-term, downward effects of eating the moss before many doctors did, but few listened to them. Still, Tina denied Francis's eating, though she sympathized with the teachers. All Francis talked about was the gravitational lensing of Jupiter. And about the solar mass. Tina felt lost in her own house. Her son was a foreigner. He had his information. She was now alone. And for how long, she didn't know.

A giant lived alone by the river in the old steel mill. He ate no moss, for no moss had crept near the mill. The giant ate whole deer when he could catch them. He entertained stray cats. He used large smelting crucibles as heating elements, starting great massive fires inside of them. He spent most of his time thinking. Planning. Trying to find a way to destroy the moss and everything behind it.

Grasshands, Deena.

The giant didn't question his size anymore. He didn't wonder or worry about how growing as large as a farm barn took him out of his original world and plonked him down into another, displaced one.

CHAPTER ELEVEN

1.

SYLVIA AND MS. Gamelin found Albert by accident.

It was early in the morning. It was the kind of early, the time of the day when you feel stupid for being out of bed, Sylvia thought.

They were tramping along the river north out of town. They both had flashlights, but Sylvia used the salt cellar light, checking for moss and nasties. Their beams were shaky and crossed often like a poorly produced, shittily acted horror movie. The old steel mill towered above on their right. Ms. Gamelin led the way. The ground on shore wasn't clear. Sticks, fallen logs, ferns. All of it was a marshy suck of gloopy foot holes filling with brown river water.

They chose to stay close to the river because moss didn't grow there. They were wary of anything and everything that even remotely looked like it.

Ms. Gamelin steadied herself in the muck with an old ski pole. The river to the left ran fast. Eddies swirled and disappeared, and a huge fallen tree lodged in the middle of the riverbank broke the stream against it two ways. The break created a churning and rushing sound. Foam frothed around it. The women tried to take some pleasure from the nature around them, but their mission deflated those thoughts often.

They were discussing when to make their way up to the top of the floodwall—maybe they'd search the steel mill—when it happened.

Albert appeared out of a stand of tall trees across the river.

How they'd missed him, they didn't know. They turned their lights off. He moved slowly. He was the size of a light pole. Thanks to Grasshands's moss, of course. *Life run amok*, Sylvia thought. That nagging phrase. She said it out loud, "Life run amok." Ms. Gamelin asked what she said. "Nothing." Albert broke through the treeline and stepped into the river. Sylvia saw his face tighten with the cold. But he forded the river ably. And fast. It came up to his neck and chin, so that he had to raise his head up a little to keep breathing. Sylvia gawped at how deep the river was. She never thought of it.

Ms. Gamelin and Sylvia didn't speak. Sylvia reached forward and grabbed Ms. Gamelin's wrist. She squeezed. Ms. Gamelin nodded.

Albert's giant hands splashed up and pulled himself out of the water. He stood massive and dripping like a mythic creature from a child's story. Three short steps and he was at the top of the floodwall, swinging a leg over. Water from his feet sprayed the women. They'd hunkered down as much as possible into the berm. Sylvia felt wet spongy earth touch her ass. The air was crisp but dank. Her nose filled with the steely aquatic smells of riverlife.

All this and then there was Albert. Sylvia wanted to call out to him. Run to him. Hug his huge ankle or calf. Let him know he wasn't alone.

But to be honest, Sylvia was the one who didn't feel totally alone anymore. Just seeing his hulking frame—even more fantastically huge than before—gave her hope that they'd be able to find a way to stop Grasshands.

She kept squeezing Ms. Gamelin's hand, the gesture saying, *We've done it, we've found him!*

"Yes, yes," she said over her shoulder. Which was lower than it should've been. "We have another issue, though."

"What?"

"I'm stuck. And I think I'm sinking."

2.

She was sinking quickly. "You goof," Sylvia said. "Why now?"

"Well, you know, I like to spoil everything by getting into situations that I have no control over, so..."

The part of the shore they'd paused on was gluey and clayey. Ms. Gamelin had stepped into a particularly soft area and sunk almost to her knees. When she tried to step up, she sank down further. What made it worse was the river water had found a way to runnel over and fill the holes. This made it doubly hard to pull her out. Sylvia pulled her legs from the muck. A boot almost came off. She got above Ms. Gamelin on the berm for better leverage. She slid her foot under an exposed humped-up tree root for anchorage.

Their blood was buzzing from the sighting of Albert. But here they were wrestling with nature. The pike and machete could do nothing for mud. The machete was strapped to Ms. Gamelin's thigh. The pike strapped against Sylvia's back.

They were so close and all they wanted was to be done with the hunt. Done with the worry.

Cold river water swirled in around Ms. Gamelin's knees, loosening the mud. It also brought in the swift current. The part of the shore they'd been trudging through began to break away. Sylvia realized that she was actually squatting on the *real* shore. What they'd been hiking on was only years of build-up—a kludge of logs, branches, sticks, twigs, mud, silt, leaves. Not to mention human debris. Litter, trash, all around worthless shit. Like an extended and sad beaver dam. Now it was crumbling. How appropriate.

Sylvia could've used the pike to drag Ms. Gamelin in, but if she released her hand, the older woman would fall backward into the rushing water.

"Can you swim?" Sylvia said.

Ms. Gamelin said, "In a pool, dear. Not a river."

It would be a shame to die in that dirty river, Sylvia thought. *After she saved my life twice and her job evaporated and—*

Ms. Gamelin lost what foundation she had and fell backward, feet first, into the river. Her face smooshed into the soupy mud of the kludge. The current swooped in and took her. Gone. She disappeared under the current. Sylvia fell back on her heels. When she stood, Ms. Gamelin was probably twenty feet downstream.

Instinctively, she yelled. But what came out of her mouth surprised her.

"*Albert,*" she said. Louder, again. "*Albert.*"

She turned and cupped her mouth. She screamed his name, turning to keep an eye on the floating and bobbing head of Ms. Gamelin. There was no way she could run back down the crumbing riverbank. She had no lifebuoy. No rope. She had nothing. Except her maniac voice, tearing her throat to confetti.

Five seconds ticked by, the longest seconds on record. Ms. Gamelin had bobbed above water, though her head dunked down occasionally. Sylvia was so flooded with adrenaline she was frozen. The flight or fight reflex pole-axed itself.

The metallic clattering of a huge door boomed behind her. The old steel mill access doors, tall as houses. They shifted open. Along the treeline of the floodwall, she saw Albert moving downriver. He turned and caught sight of her small face. She pointed the same direction and yelled, "Ms. Gamelin!"

It didn't take any time for Albert to suss what had happened. He broke through the trees and the sound winnowed the air. Trunks popped like lightning bolts. He moved swiftly for his size. Imagine an oak unrooting itself from the ground and sprinting. He leapt along the berm and in a few short strides caught up with Ms. Gamelin. When he gained some distance ahead of her, he jumped into the river and turned to face her. It was a terrifying and relieving sight. Ms. Gamelin darted right toward a massive head sticking out of the middle of a rushing river. Then his long dripping arms blasted up from the water and prepared themselves as a catcher's mitt, adjusting for the current's chaotic movements. Ms. Gamelin wasn't in the water more than a minute, at most. She was exhausted from trying to stay above the water.

Ms. Gamelin collided with Albert's open palms. He scooped her up. The giant held her about ten or fifteen feet above the water as he waded out onto shore. Sylvia was climbing up. She reached the top of the floodwall and sprinted to meet them.

Albert lay her down on the floodwall's concrete top. Ms. Gamelin coughed and choked. She looked shrunken. Her face was pale. Sylvia went to her and held her head up. Her lips were bluing. Her teeth danced across each other.

She looked up at Albert, who hadn't yet spoken. "She needs warmth. A fire. She's going into hypothermia."

Albert pointed toward the steel mill.

"Come," he said.

He once again gently picked Ms. Gamelin up and cradled her into the steel mill. Sylvia followed. Inside, Albert shut the access doors and threw a massive chain across the old lock mechanism. The weight alone held them shut. On the far side of the mill floor were huge crucibles that once held molten steel or slag. Inside one of them was a psychotic blaze. Medium-sized tree bowers stuck out the top. The flames licked up and nearly touched the girders. That fire alone warmed the entire structure. Sylvia wanted to remove her jacket. The mud on her boots was drying and crusting. Albert brought Ms. Gamelin down on a gantry that crossed behind the crucible, far enough away to warm her quickly without smothering her or setting her on fire. Sylvia ran up the gantry ladder to meet her. Ms. Gamelin was vaguely conscious. Albert leaned in as closely as he could. His every move was silent as a cat. It shocked Sylvia more than his size.

Ms. Gamelin was trying to speak. She wanted to sit up a bit. She coughed. It kept going. Dark, brutal hacking. She'd gotten water into her lungs or couldn't catch her breath. Then she puked. When she was able to speak, she waved Albert in. She gently touched the end of his nose.

"*Tag*. You're it."

Albert smiled. It was the first time Sylvia had seen that in a long time. Pleased with herself, Ms. Gamelin settled back onto the gantry. Sylvia wrapped her jacket and placed it under Ms. Gamelin's head as a pillow. She turned onto her side and fell asleep. She still had her machete strapped to her thigh. It caught the light and glinted.

Albert noticed this. And Sylvia's pike.

Sylvia stood.

"You've been hunting?" he said.

"For you."

He nodded. "I'm sorry."

"Don't be. Not now."

His face broke into a partial weep.

"I thought you were dead, Syl."

"To be fair, I did, too. If it hadn't been for her. Intrepid Explorer back here."

"Tell me about it. What happened?"

"Oh, we've got some shit to discuss."

3.

She told the whole story of leaving the shooting to finding the pictures and her possessions and fighting the motherfog to being buried, the fever dream with Grasshands-as-her-mom.

"Did you see Natalia?" he asked.

"I did." She tore at her hair a second. "Albert. She lost the baby."

Pause.

"I know."

"You do? How?"

"Since I've been here, which was a month after I left, I've been hearing her speaking to me somehow. Through the drains in the floor. I lay there and cry and listen to her. I listen to her curse me and tell me about what's happening. The one-way conversation with a lover is the worst kind of hell."

"She speaks into the holes in your guest room. They sing back to her."

Albert looked worried.

"Bad and good," Sylvia said. "It's complicated. Is there no way you could ever see her?"

"Maybe in the future. But not now. Not any time in the present."

"How suitably cryptic. Jesus Tap Dancing Christ, Albert." Even at this mammoth size, like his silent walking, his voice was quiet. Calm. The voice of a librarian. A protector of knowledge, a lifer. "Hey. I'm, uhh, I'm sorry about, you know, the baby. By the way."

Albert bowed his head in acknowledgment.

He was depressed. Although, his demeanor said he was trying to focus on the upside. So Sylvia lied about the state of their house, its cleanliness. She also didn't mention that Natalia had been eating moss. Albert seemed to restrain himself from probing further.

Sylvia had no idea what to say. She wanted to jump on his back like in a fantasy novel and ride him into town and slay dragons. But she knew it wasn't going to work that way. Albert needed a tad more prodding and confidence first. The steel mill had been closed for over a decade. Maybe longer. She didn't know, didn't remember. Shit, she hadn't much cared or ever paid attention to it out here. But now that she did, it was clear that this place employed a hundred people at one point. It had to explain why this part of town was so absolutely scant with humanity. Just desolate like a plague ship.

"How much more have you grown since I last saw you?"

She felt like a weird old aunt who forces their nephew to kiss them on the lips when they visit.

"I would assume, based on the average height of this access door, that I have gained an additional ten feet." He said it as if it was a death sentence.

"What have you been doing since I've been missing? How do you survive here?"

She glanced around in the faded glow of that crucible blaze. Light was peeking in from minor cracks in the corrugated steel roof. It broke in between the panels that made up the massive walls. The whole place was a glorified pole barn. He whispered to her. And every so often he looked to Ms. Gamelin to make sure he hadn't woken her.

"My clothes grew with me. Why? I don't know. That was a blessing, of sorts. I do occasionally clean in the river at night. But I have no access to soap. I can only imagine how I smell." Sylvia didn't smell anything except industrial oils and solvents and cold steel. The smell of large machinery sitting alone for a long time. "I defecate in the old quench well."

"You mean you shit in a hole in the ground."

"If we're being crude, then sure."

"We're being realistic, Albert. Vulgar has nothing to do with it."

"I've learned I don't need my glasses anymore. As you may've noticed. Those are long gone."

True enough. He also slept on a train flatcar padded with old mattresses, coats, large canvas tarps used to protect cargo. A pile of deer corpses lay under the crane driver's box. The concrete floor around it was slicked with blood. Albert explained that he ate the deer. They were surprisingly easy to catch.

"Whole deer? Alive?"

"Oh no. I hold them over the crucible for a while. Burn off the hair. Cook them a little."

Sylvia's stomach turned. As a friend, she tried not to show her distaste.

4.

Cats had somehow struggled their way into the steel mill. Hordes of stray cats marauded about. A tangle of black cats threaded around the gantries near them. A tortoiseshell kitty nuzzled Ms. Gamelin's sleeping body.

There were layers and ecosystems to Albert's new home. She was slowly unraveling them.

"Cats," she said.

"Yes, they're my one network to the outside world."

"You speak as if you've been alone for centuries."

"Time has slowed for me. Or sped up. It's hard to say. I do know that I'm not feeling like it's only been, how long did you say?"

"Four months, give or take."

Albert looked shocked. Three cats rubbed their faces on his toes. He leaned down, careful not to hurt them or knock any equipment over. They leapt onto his hand. Even before standing straight again, the cats had curled around each other and were asleep.

"It's like they know what's going on," Sylvia said.

He inspected them. He appreciated them.

"They do," he said. "They tell me what I need to know."

"They talk to you?"

"In a way."

"About?"

"Everything."

5.

"How do we destroy Grasshands?" Sylvia asked.

"I don't think you do."

"What?"

"This is more than a one-person job. Moreover, Grasshands does not seem to be the sort of thing one obliterates per se. It could, possibly, be detained. Delayed. Set into hibernation, even. But annihilated? Never."

"Thank you for the vocabulary lesson. Some things don't change, do they?" She smiled. "Well, this blows major ass," she said, kneeling down. "Normally, when there's a bad thing, the good people get together and take it down. They aren't supposed to compromise on destruction and tamely escort the evil out of town and hand it a citation."

"You've watched too many television shows."

"And you've not watched enough."

She looked around his new living space. She was in his home. Devoid of books, obviously. No cultural tools. No entertainment. Much roomier than the house he shared with Natalia. No pictures of her. No way to see her. Sylvia wanted to hug her friend. Again, it was simply impossible.

There wasn't even any noise. She couldn't get over this. Except, if she strained her concentration, a boombox radio left behind years ago spouted a tinny whine. It picked up the university radio station an hour away. The boombox was plugged into an outlet near a fold down table. Ted Nugent's "Stranglehold" ripped through the speakers. The song was disturbing in its lyrics and sounded like it was told from the point of view of a rapey bigfoot. There was a total disjunction in the atmosphere. That song was the opposite of Albert. Well, the Albert she had known. The Albert who used to sit at his desk over lunch and tighten the screws in his spectacles. And liked it. The Albert who made sure to re-part his hair every few hours. The Albert who took it upon himself to spot check the entire catalog both digitally and physically. The Albert who always bought lunch for the entire staff on a random day of the week. She tuned the radio to a public station an hour away. It reliably played classical music or jazz all day, with intermittent weather and news reports. The tune was a creaky and crackly ragtime piano, the lyrics sung by a high-toned voice in a weird mid-Atlantic accent.

Did you hear it? Were you near it?
If you weren't then you've yet to fear it;
Once you've met it you'll regret it,
Just because you never will forget it.

As each verse progressed, her muscles clenched, and she felt the sweats behind her knees. The music swung but the lyrics spelled doom. The announcer came on a couple minutes later and said it was the early 1911 hit by Irving Berlin called "That Mysterious Rag." For a split second—and not that she *really* believed it—but could Grasshands or the motherfog get inside a radio or a radio station and broadcast this kind of terrifying shit to her? Or was that, like, Peak Paranoia?

Maybe the current Albert, the steel mill giant, was some mutated version of a future-man. A new, evolved Albert. One who took "Stranglehold" seriously, or—even worse—took "That Mysterious Rag" seriously. *Jee-zus.* It could happen. Sylvia had read about people who were normal, hit their head, woke up and started talking with a Russian accent. Or went to work a loving partner, got into a horrible car accident, and then left their family when they recovered.

Everything was mutable.

"What's it like not being able to read?"

Without hesitation, he said, "Agonizing. The truest and worst curse of my situation. I have no Aristotle, no Dickens, no Baldwin, no poetry, no detective novels. Nothing. Only what my memory holds. And I don't retain much in the wake of Natalia's miscarriage and the utter monstrosity that I've become."

"I'm sorry."

"It's very unAristotelian."

Sylvia laughed. "What is?"

"Growing beyond your allotted amount. I'm violating the Golden Mean. Taking more than my share."

"Who dictates that?"

"Nature."

"Hah. Well, I think Grasshands is in violation of that rule, too. And maybe the people of Caldecott, while we're at it."

Albert pulled a face. "What do you mean?"

"The whole moss-eating thing. Why do people do it?"

"I don't think normal people would."

"*Exactly*. It's not a rational move. A normal person wouldn't want to eat moss. So it would have to offer something exceptional."

"Like?"

"Something whole and complete and intact without working for it. That kind of thing just short circuits the need for a library. Or for the internet, come to think of it."

"I hadn't exactly thought of it in that way," Albert said.

"That's why I'm here."

"And yet," Albert said, "someone has to produce the books for the moss to grow on."

Ms. Gamelin coughed. She rolled over and her eyes adjusted to the flickering light. The cats strolled past her. She saw Albert talking with Sylvia. She sat up.

"I'm sorry," Albert said. "Did my voice wake you?"

"No," Ms. Gamelin said. Her eyes wrinkled at the corners. He was a welcome sight. "Miss Big Shot over there is loud as hell, though. You could have a future career as a lifeguard at the ocean, Albert."

"I'll take it under advisement."

"Do you feel okay?" Sylvia asked her.

"I feel like I fell into a river and a giant hand squeezed me. But I'll live."

"Good. Bring your ass over here. We have a discussion to finish."

6.

Albert admitted he'd put moss on top of other moss and then eaten it.

"Why?" Sylvia said. She was shocked, disappointed. "That seems like the stupidest thing you could do."

"You just said that people did it because it was a shortcut. I wanted to know what it was that brought people to this. For me it was desperate hunger and curiosity. And I'm not a normal person anymore. Think of it as an empirical experiment."

"Nothing happened, I assume," Ms. Gamelin said. She took a step backward.

Albert shook his head. "Possibly my size has allowed me to withstand any effects. Or maybe placing moss on top of moss negates Grasshands's power? I highly doubt that. I believe that I've already been affected by Grasshands in another way."

The women were confused. He didn't respond. They looked at each other and then at him, nonplussed.

He pointed at himself, his height.

Sylvia said she wasn't ready to claim that an ancient natural power blighted him with a growth curse. Him, Albert, out of everyone in Caldecott, or everyone in town. Why not her? Why not Ms. Gamelin? Why not Delores?

"You sound disappointed that you're not a giant," Ms. Gamelin said.

"No, it's just that I don't understand it."

"Join the club, little sister."

Albert nudged the sleeping cats off his hand and onto the gantry where Sylvia and Ms. Gamelin stood. The cats stretched and yawned. They cleaned their paws and ears and tails. Albert enjoyed watching them.

"In the end, it doesn't matter why I'm this way. There could be more like me elsewhere. I can't change it. I bet no one could."

"No offense, Albert. This is lovely, but," Ms. Gamelin said, "did I miss the part where we talk about destroying this fucking moss so we can get back to our lives?"

"Moss doesn't live in one place," Albert said. "Assuming this is moss-like. They have no roots. They have rhizomes. Which means they are very adaptable. They've been on the earth millions of years.

If we're talking about seniority, the moss-stuff has a basement-load of it."

"Okay, so what do we have?" Sylvia said.

Albert held up a finger. He strode to the far end of the mill. He picked up two massive support beams, the kind used on the underside of bridges. They were polished and tapered at the ends. They glinted. He clanged them together. The sound was insane. The beams had to have been the largest blades in existence.

"Those are impressive, but are you going to eat a salad or fight an ancient evil?"

"Ancient *entity*," he said.

"Whatever."

"If anything, Deena's incarnation is the source of this, no? The thing that is housed in what you called the motherfog. She has threatened me, you, and Ms. Gamelin. It seems the most efficient route. Find motherfog. Kill Deena."

"I don't mean to be a bummer," Sylvia said, "but the only thing I know of that works against these things is my idiotic singing back to them. That *fa fa* nonsense."

Albert considered this. "The singing isn't nothing."

"Well, what do I have besides singing? And the pike?" She hefted it in her hand. She knew it was dangerous. It would work against the tickle spiders. Though something about it felt...unfulfilled.

Albert and Ms. Gamelin thought about it. "Make the pike sing," Albert said.

"A singing pike," Ms. Gamelin said, smiling.

"It's basically made of you and yours, right?"

Sylvia nodded. She gripped the pike again. Her hands twisted over it. The blade's curve, the ease of it on the end, pleased her. She imagined the pike belting out Sinatra or Michael Bublé. Maybe Madonna.

"You know what he means," Ms. Gamelin said. Part of her sensed Sylvia's misunderstanding. "You're not going to crank out pop hits." She turned to Albert. "She'll use it like an amplifier of her own self?"

"Possibly. Or we could try to have the pike do its own singing. I've found in the last few months that objects don't follow the regular rules of the universe. For example, that pike. My body. The walls of my house. And so on."

"How do I make a pike sing?"

"How does a child learn to sing?" Ms. Gamelin said.

"You threaten it with housework and visits to creepy aunts."

"No, you dingus. You teach it. Start talking to it."

Sylvia was embarrassed. "You're the expert in singing pikes now?"

"No, but I'm going with the flow of this batshit conversation. Speaking of batshit, I'm hungry. Can I mention now that we've gone almost 12 hours without a meal? And, again, lots of offense meant, Albert. I am *not* eating a whole fire-toasted deer with a side of toxic fumes."

"No offense taken."

"I'll go out later and get something," Sylvia said.

Albert's face got serious. He eyes closed. His lips pursed.

"I wanted to mention that. This 'going out' business. The reason I had left the steel mill, which I don't often do, was because I'd heard the cats. They were coming through the woods on the other side of the river. Falling into the water. I had tried to save as many as I could. They were coming in droves. Of course, I went to check it out. The moss had spread over there. There are a few housing developments. None of the lights were on. Not even streetlights. I heard no dogs barking. Nothing."

"What the hell does that mean?" Ms. Gamelin said.

"Bad stuff," Sylvia said. "It means that something's going on and it's going on right now."

Albert said, "At least wait until it's fully light out. It's cold comfort, but it's something. You need to rest more, Ms. Gamelin. And, Sylvia, you have a pike to teach."

"Homework," she said. "Barf."

7.

Sylvia carried herself off to a solitary area of the mill, the break room. There were drop-leg tables and a microwave and fold-out chairs. The fluorescent light blinkered on. She laid the pike on a table and sat.

Before she spoke a word, she felt stupid.

Ms. Gamelin laid down on the gantry again. Albert took himself to a flatcar for rest. The cats split themselves evenly between the two.

They got to sleep. And here Sylvia was, taking piano lessons all over again. A pervasive unease melted into her hands and torso. First her mother and then her grandmother made her take piano lessons. Those all added up to Sylvia knowing a rough version of "Autumn Leaves."

All she'd wanted to see in the woods was a talking wolf or a gnome's hut. Now she was trying to teach a pike to sing inside of a giant's steel mill.

She leaned forward so her lips almost touched the weapon.

"I'm your mother. I want to teach you a few songs. But first let's start with the basics."

Sylvia cleared her throat and sang *do re mi*. She did this for five minutes, what seemed like an eternity. Then she squeezed the pike. She smoothed it. She touched her lips to it as she sang the solfeggio all the way through. She let the harmonization buzz from her lips to the pike.

"Your turn."

Nothing. The pike lay on the table, black and matte and sharp. A weapon, not a musical instrument.

"*Fa fa fa fa*," she sang. "You try it."

Again, nothing. But not an inert nothing. It was as if the pike *knew* it could sing—*if it wanted to*—but it didn't, so it wouldn't. Like a child, it obstinately lay there, defying its mother's wishes. She'd shelved a book once by Annie Dillard titled *Teaching a Stone to Talk*. She imagined one of the chapters was called, "Singing Handheld Weapon Lessons 101."

She sat there for two hours. She sat so long she had memorized the topography of all the hardened gum stuck under the table. She sang until her ass fell asleep, prickly with a lack of blood. She sang until her calves and thigh muscles cramped. Until her spine burned. Until her eyes stung. And she sang until she hated the sound of her own voice.

When her patience crashed into a red wall, in a rage she stood. "If you do not sing," she said, "I will break you over my knee."

A moment of silence hung like a bird on a thermal. It was a threat to herself more than anything. Then, in a creaky voice that was her own:

Faa

Sylvia's eyes widened. She leaned closer. The noise was weak.

"Again," she said. Then, louder:

Faaa

A sob broke in her throat. The emotion surprised her. This was insane. But she'd come to accept it, the unreality. The pike felt strained to her. She knew it because she felt it as well. As if this was all it could muster in the moment. She kissed it. It tasted of alkaline.

She thanked it.

"I knew you knew how to do it," she said. "You little shit."

CHAPTER TWELVE

1.

TINA BLACKFORD RUSHED her son into the house but only made it as far as the laundry room. She thought he was spasming, but he vomited. Francis's small body rocked with evacuation. He gurgled up foam and saliva. Tina kneeled to hold her son's shoulders. She didn't want to call 911. If she got up and left, he'd die. Large ropes of moss hung out of his nostrils and mouth. It was as if it had crawled out of its own accord. She beat on his back like it was full of money. A slimed chunk of moss shot from Francis's face. It wiggled. Tina pulled Francis to her. He was breathing. That was all that mattered.

A woman screamed outside. Through the kitchen window, the neighbor ran around their house. A newly married couple lived there; they fought often. The woman ran, looking over her shoulder. She was yelling at something chasing her. Tina asked her son if he was okay.

"Yeah, Mommy." He fell into her arms glazed in sweat. She picked him up. In their house, there was a noise like a crack of plastic. It sounded like a large foot stepping on a piece of ice.

"You hear that, baby?"

Francis nodded with his head on her shoulder.

She stepped toward the hallway where the two bedrooms were. The sound swelled. Then fell silent.

"Hello?" Tina said. "I own a gun." She didn't. It didn't matter.

Tina held her breath. Francis did the same without even being asked. Something was in his room.

Tap tap

Tina's limbs tingled, pins and needles. She collapsed, protecting Francis's head. He cried out.

Tap tap

Her view was upside down.

Tap tap

A pair of thin spindly legs appeared around the hallway doorframe, tapping away. What followed was horrific. Countless legs chittering on the floor. The whole thing made of brightly colored Little Tikes plastic—red, yellow, blue. She noticed a few pieces of Francis's favorite figurines.

"Baby, can you get up? Go, honey. Go."

Francis couldn't move.

With the last of her strength, she wrenched her head back. The spindly thing was on top of her. By then, she couldn't speak or defend herself. The spider composed of her son's toys sank itself into her mouth. Part of it broke off and *tap tap'd* toward Francis. She couldn't see it but knew from the sound that the same was happening to him.

2.

Sylvia slept a short time but woke up hungry.

Ms. Gamelin was still out, recovering, breathing heavy, on the gantry. A growing curl of stray cats nestled around her. Not that she needed them. The crucible fire was making Sylvia's armpits, neck, and crotch sweat from fifty yards away. Her stomach squelched. She searched the break room for a single peanut, a candy bar, a lost donut, anything. Someone had to have left a bag of potato chips, a sugar packet, or even a straw to stuck on. But she found nothing. She heard her stomach moving violently from emptiness. It would leap out of her viscera and eat her if she didn't feed it soon.

Albert, to her surprise, also slept. Perhaps his sheer size required more rest. She wasn't even sure what level of physics she needed to describe him. It terrified her to think that the same kind of physics *did* describe both of them.

She resolved to go out for a quick bite. Grab a snack, return.

Mentally, she mapped the city from above. It was a bleak part of town. Far from the commercial strip. Far from downtown. Although, she remembered driving by a tiny place. Maybe a bar, maybe a small eatery. She forgot the name, but it was worth a jaunt. She could be back in fifteen if she left now.

Leaving in the daytime, even one or two of them, could be dangerous. Better to stay and rest. But she couldn't sleep or lay down if she was doubled over with hunger. For a moment, she considered if she had the ability to hold off anything that came at her. What if she suddenly felt her extremities tingle and fade away. What if she went numb. Couldn't breathe. Couldn't yell for help. What then?

Sylvia made a huge mistake: She was optimistic. She based her outlook on life by the current weather. This was the most ridiculous fallacy humans relied on.

How could anything go wrong? The sun is out!

Of course you're sick/rear-ended/getting a divorce/having trouble at work—it's pouring cats and dogs outside.

It was a bleary day with a masked sun blazing hazy in the sky. It also snowed lightly off and on. She snuck out a small window in the break room. She strapped the pike to her back. That was her only concession in the daytime. She'd have to order her burger with a pike on her back. She'd say she was spearfishing in the river. No one would believe her, but who gave a crap.

She prepped herself to answer questions. To wave at passersby. To put on her Okay Face.

She was north, on the edge of town where the old state highway used to go. Folks mostly used it as a shortcut from one end of the city to the other. But no one came or went. Something about that struck her as odd. She walked, checking behind her every half-minute. She got more nervous about no cars coming instead of one or maybe five.

She walked by rows and rows of homes where the working poor lived. Postage stamp yards had rusted barrels in back for burning sticks or trash. She turned up an alleyway—one in a grid of alleyways that had open garage doors and cinderblock trash pits overflowing with dried leaves. She was glad to be out, breathing the hard, cold air. Waiting in the steel mill convinced her that she was inhaling tiny steel filings. Her lungs would be lined with metal.

It was taking longer than she thought to find this place. Still no cars. She hadn't seen a single human.

One house (well, lots of houses) had a crumbling tarpaper roof. A massive hole punched right through the top. Drifting snow fell in. She wondered how anyone could live there. Then she scented food. Like a homing beacon, her stomach twitched. She was close. The place she'd been thinking of was up the road, to the right. She spotted the exhaust pipe from the kitchen sticking up. Smoke wisped from the top and perfumed the air with greasy burger.

Across the street was a two-for-one winner: the city dump and the Jeweltron Glass Factory. Cars dotted the small gravel parking apron. One car's engine idled while in park. Workers on lunch, she assumed. But she didn't hear the dump. And she didn't hear Jeweltron. The glass factory should be buzzing. The lack of industrial noises bothered her.

As she turned the corner, the restaurant's name returned to her.

The White Kitchen.

A long plastic tarp advertisement announced it was serving Lite, Michelob, and MGD. She'd get a couple lunch specials. A grilled cheese sounded perfect. The smell of garlic and onions in the air made her head swim. Her mouth watered.

Her boots crunched the gravel. But it sounded flat. There was little life in the click of rocks. She stopped. She wanted to turn and run. The ancient lizard part of her brain told her to beat it. Another ancient part in her gut told her to get food. Her ancient parts battled.

Hunger won.

3.

As soon as she touched the handle of the screen door, she chilled. There was no sound coming from inside. It was lunchtime on a workday. There should be bustling. It should be boisterous. There was just hot fry grease smell and scalding urn coffee. She opened the door and a horrid stench filled her nose. Burnt food, scorched hair. Something rank and acrid. The smell took the place of sound.

The tables were full. No one moved. Buddy Holly was on the jukebox singing "That'll Be the Day."

Everyone at a table sat straight with their heads slightly tilted up. Their mouths were pried open.

Sylvia tensed. Her palms sweated. She dried them on her pants. She knew why these people were sitting still, their necks craned. She pulled the pike off her back. "Get ready to sing, you bitch," she said to the pike.

She neared an older couple at a table. They had their red plastic food baskets in front of them, their food half-eaten. The thumping pulse in the man's neck was visible. She leaned over from behind. The man's eyes nervously followed her. She could tell it took all of his energy not to move.

A tickle spider was sunk into his mouth. This one had pushed its spindles out to make room. So the old man's mouth and head was distorted and bulging. He looked as if his skull would detonate at any second.

"G*oooo*ddammit," she moaned.

She quickly checked the old woman. Same thing. Less bulging. A cursory scan confirmed everyone in The White Kitchen had a tickle spider in their mouth. She knew it was the same everywhere. Those ramshackle houses. The dump. The Jeweltron factory. Probably the entire city.

A young guy in overalls had a spindle coming out of his nose. A middle-aged woman in front of a plate of eggs had two spindles arcing out her mouth. They tented her eyelids open so she couldn't blink. Sylvia figured all of these people were numb, as well. Totally unable to move and defend themselves. The creatures in their mouths were composed of their own possessions. Their magazines, dentures, tools, kids' art projects. They would have nothing at home. But they may be alive. That's something.

She edged over to the dining counter where a derelict sat. It was Gerald, the homeless man who gave her the rag blanket after she was dug up. He shook with fear. The tickle spider in his mouth pulsed. It was smaller than the others. He was crying. The tears cut a clean path over the grime on his face. His eyes moved back to the kitchen. She didn't know if he was warning her or helping her. The tickle spider in Gerald's mouth watched her. She knew it. They had no eyes. No features that resembled an arachnid.

Pots crashed behind the swing door to the kitchen. A glass shattered. Sylvia heard a struggling gurgle, a short yelp, then the sound of a body hitting the tile. She hugged the wall and peeked into the porthole. The short order cook was sprawled on the floor in stained whites. The head cook bucked and kicked like a psychopathic revival preacher.

He flipped over and Sylvia saw the cook had pursed his lips tightly. She pushed her way into the kitchen with the pike leveled down. It felt good in her hands. It felt as if it knew what was going on.

"Hey," she said. "Back off."

The tickle spider paused. Moved a little.

Tap tap

The sound made her legs brittle. It was taking Sylvia in. It was made of warped and bent cutlery. The body was comprised of curved blades from the kitchen. A boning knife, probably. There was a piece of a cheese grater in there, as well.

The cook wasn't relieved she'd showed up. If anything, he looked more terrified at the pike. And at Sylvia's anger and distress.

"Don't worry," she said to him.

She sang softly. "*Fa fa fa fa.*"

The tickle spider didn't budge.

Louder: *Fa fa fa fa*. She waited for the pike. She shook it.

"Jump in anytime, lady."

Finally, it sang.

Fa fa fa fa

The creature startled. A spindle popped off and unraveled into a butter knife.

Clang.

That optimism that Sylvia started out with returned. It was tempered but sitting in her gut like stone in a river. Optimism had replaced hunger.

She sang louder, hoping the pike would help. If not, this would be a long time.

The pike sputtered a weak and pathetic sound.

Fer fer fer fer

It clashed with her singing. But it seemed to assist in popping off another spindle. This one unfolded into a soup spoon. The soup spoon pelted the cook in the forehead. He winced. Sylvia had a glimpse of the Nice Guy Ms. Gamelin tortured in the diner some nights back.

"Sorry," she said.

The singing continued for thirty seconds, but the pike abruptly quit. The butter knife and soup spoon shot back toward the tickle spider and torqued back into the lost spindles. It wasted no time.

She watched as the tickle spider tried to prise the cook's mouth open. His mouth was locked in defiance. The creature did its trick. This time on the cook's neck. Tickling, lightly brushing. The cook's ancient nervous systems overcame his more modern ones. He laughed. Against his own will. The tickle spider caught the teeth and flung open the cook's mouth to an excruciating width and climbed in.

4.

But it didn't stop in his mouth. It tucked in the spindles and slid down his throat. The cook's neck bulged like an anaconda swallowing an air conditioner. It was like she'd strengthened it by not defeating it all the way. The tickle spider gained immunity. Like not taking all of your antibiotics during a sinus infection. Or it was just super-pissed at almost getting killed.

Sylvia stepped back. Her optimism fell out her ass. Her stomach shrank. This guy was gone. She didn't know how to help. A quick look out the swinging door porthole—everyone was still locked into position, heads up. The acrid smell hit her again. And she took notice of the sound of sizzling meat. She stepped around a tall rack of pans and trays and plastic condiment jars. A second cook was standing in front of a flattop grill, turned on high. All the food was shriveled and wasted. Burnt beyond eating.

But the horrible smell came from the second cook's hands. They were pressed onto the grill, stuck like a fried egg. Skin, blood, and an orangish liquid bubbled. His arms were red and blistered. The head was so far back there was no way his spine was intact.

The head cook's body crashed into the pan rack, which toppled onto the grill cook. The grill cook's body crashed onto the flattop. Sylvia backed toward the door. The head cook was on all fours, his neck still bulged. The tickle spider was rearranging his insides. His legs bent forward, breaking the knees. Now they were more appropriately spindle-like. Various spindles emerged from the rib cage. And now the cook stood on two inverted legs, its arms, and metal spindles. It tapped around, sensing the environment.

Sylvia knew he was dead now. But the head swung around, staring at her. The face was still in pursed horror and fear. Its uncanniness resembled an animatronic from a dark Disney exhibit. Her apologies to him meant nothing. She wondered if all the tickle spiders could or would take over bodies like this one. If so, she was hosed. She rationalized that *just this one* was a rebel and decided to make an example of her.

The pike was mum.

Sylvia retreated from the kitchen to behind the counter. The door swung shut. She backed up to the entrance of The White Kitchen. Her ass bumped a side table with ketchup and mustard bottles. They fell and crashed onto the linoleum. Red and yellow explosions.

The kitchen door creaked open. The upside-down cook's head peered through like a curious animal. Then it skittered out and crawled up the wall and onto the ceiling toward Sylvia. She panicked and dropped the pike. She tried to open the screen door behind her but slipped. She fell hard on her left hip. Something hard in her pocket jammed against her.

The salt cellar light.

Anything was worth a go at this point.

The cook was above her, uncannily clinging to the drop ceiling. Two metallic spindles swung down and tried to pinion her head.

Tap tap

She reached into her pocket as the cook dropped from the ceiling on top of her. His inverted legs and spindles clutched her lower half and squeezed. She immediately lost all sense below her waist. More spindles crawled out of the cook's nose. One darted at her head, but she ducked and it struck her shoulder.

The pain was worse than anything she'd ever felt. Worse than waking up half-way through her wisdom tooth surgery.

She unscrewed the salt cellar cap, and instead of green light, a solid black geometric shape emerged. A vast black rectangle as dark as the thousand-year cat she witnessed in her gravedream. The shape trampled the cook's head.

She aimed the salt cellar down the cook's body and the whole thing rippled, eased, then melted. The goo coated her pants and boots.

Diner napkins would be powerless against this slop.

She stood up and made her way around The White Kitchen waving the black geometric eminence over the patrons. Those who were alive fell forward when they puked up the goo of desiccated tickle spider.

Those folks who were dead already melted in their seats. She had no time to apologize to anyone. In ten seconds, her work was over. She capped the salt cellar.

She didn't hesitate.

"Go," she said. She caught her breath.

Everyone sat there, dazed.

Thin Lizzy's "Don't Believe a Word" clicked on in the jukebox.

"What are you, fucking deaf? Get the hell out of town, now! Move those retired asses!" She clapped her hands in people's faces. "Go, go, go."

Chairs scooted, rustled, fell over backward. People got up and fled, crying, shouting, gasping.

Gerald came up behind her with the pike. He handed it to her. "B*aaa*d news, sister. B*aaa*d news."

He stumbled out the screen door. It slammed shut. She watched him walk up the old highway that went out of town. She wanted to join him.

Instead, Sylvia grabbed a handful of cold fries from the nearest table. Next to the fries: a library book, covered in moss. And another across the table. One book on watersports, another on horseracing. Every table had a book on it. Some just had a small mound of moss.

She shoved the fries in her mouth and made her way back to the steel mill.

CHAPTER THIRTEEN

1.

SYLVIA SLIPPED INTO the mill without problem. Albert and Ms. Gamelin chatted in conspiratorial tones. Albert standing, Ms. Gamelin on the gantry with some affectionate cats. They spotted her dragging her tired, adrenaline-soaked bones across the floor, covered in ketchup, mustard, and tickle spider goo.

"You found food, then," Ms. Gamelin said.

"Of a sort."

"And you didn't bring me any?"

Albert knelt down. It was like watching a small building collapse next to Sylvia. "What's going on? You look...weird."

Ms. Gamelin added, "You look like two McDonald's restaurants had sweaty sex in a truck stop."

"I went to The White Kitchen for a bite to eat and instead found everyone rigid in their seats with those goddamn spindle things in their mouths. I almost fought one off with the pike and singing but this thing crapped out on me. I had to watch a cook get savaged." She looked up at Albert, who'd tensed as she spoke. "I've never seen them this violent. The one in my mouth as a kid was scary, but it never attacked me."

"How did you get out of there?" Ms. Gamelin asked.

She pulled out the salt cellar and slammed it on the stairs.

Albert said, "Salt. They're like slugs? I suppose you can explain how that works to me."

Sylvia laughed. It was drawn and manic. Real end-of-her-tether kind of stuff. "No, Hodor. Not really. But this crazy solid black shape shot out and ate these things."

"I see," he said, not seeing.

"It made more sense last week," Ms. Gamelin added.

Sylvia said, "The takeaway is this: the whole town has likely got their heads jacked up like satanic angels with spindles in them. *Ev-ry-one*. And that means Natalia. It means my roommates."

Albert stood up. The change in altitude disoriented Sylvia and Ms. Gamelin. "Fine, then we're getting out of here right now. I can only think of one place to go first."

"The library," Ms. Gamelin said.

"Yes, that is where I think Grasshands is storing Deena. We may never be able to stop Grasshands entirely, but we can stop the moss and Deena from destroying Caldecott."

"Can we, though?" Sylvia said. "Seems like the kind of thing that defies logic. Not that that's stopped us lately."

"You want this to be a good versus evil situation, don't you?"

"No, Albert, I don't. Because those words mean nothing to me as of this moment. Take this psycho, for instance." She thumbed over at Ms. Gamelin, who acted surprised. "She wanted to axe you and put me in your place. But leave Delores. Hmm. Seems risky, Ma'am Gam. But now, here we are side by side like a Disney movie slaying dragons and shit. Delores was wacky but innocent and now she's probably chewing moss like Skoal. And the tiny weirdo-lady who only used to pester you with questions is now *the* scariest farking thing on this round planet. Anymore, good and evil boils down to explanations. Explain yourself. If you can, I'll probably give you a pass. If you can't—you're evil. Grasshands has no explanation for why it wants my information, or me. All I did was ask to see something amazing and I got this."

She knew that what she'd conjured up all those years ago *was* amazing. But she was done with amazement now. To amaze was to stupefy, and she couldn't handle any more stupidity.

Albert had no way to respond to her. And, truly, he didn't want to. She had a point. Much like the miscarriage had no explanation. He could argue that that whole moment in his life was evil. Not the baby or Natalia or even the actual miscarriage or his not driving his wife to the OBGYN for what he imagined was a horrific DNC and his not being able to take her home in tears.

No. None of that was evil. What was evil was the inability for anyone to explain *why* such a thing happened. The best anyone would venture is, *shit happens*. And so far as Satisfactory Explanations go, that one earned a giant fucking zero.

Ms. Gamelin threw her leg up on the gantry's rail. She pulled the machete from the harness. She checked the sharpness with the edge of her thumb. It satisfied her. Sylvia's rant hit her square in the chestbox. She'd been a woman of repute and influence six months ago. Now she was ready to slaughter ancient creatures with a machete. Where was a woman like her supposed to go? Was local politicking all she was made for? The moment she decided to search for Sylvia past the red pillars, Clara Gamelin knew she was committing her life to a new goal. It was the same way some people committed their lives to Christ as their Lord and Savior. She had no belief. But she knew those commitments were real. Real as the teeth in her head.

Good and evil? Wrong dichotomy. She preferred thinking of Less Pain or More Pain. More Knowledge or Less Knowledge.

"I'd like to think I'm a delicate psycho, Sylvia. And may I say I never thought an abandoned steel mill would've made me feel safer than my own home."

"They'd make their way here, Ms. Gamelin," Albert said. "Count on it. They must know we have a method to forestall them."

"Barely."

"Barely is more than nothing."

"How optimistic."

Sylvia pulled a face.

"Lord, can we get this girl a granola bar or something?" Ms. Gamelin said.

Albert retrieved the two beams-now-made-blades. He walked over to the main access doors, the ones he laid a huge chain over. With a kick, he blasted the doors off the hinges. The sound throttled the air. The stray cats clawed and skittered around the mill floor. Albert slumped. He whispered to the kittens over his shoulder.

"Goodbye, my babies."

He walked into the daylight, dragging the blades behind him. He crossed them over his shoulders so they created an X. He smiled in the half-sun, half-snow.

Ms. Gamelin turned to Sylvia as they followed.

"Hear that?"

Sylvia tensed. She listened. It came from less than fifty yards away, pealing out of one of those unassuming houses.

"What is it?"
"Laughing."

2.

The laughing erupted in certain areas as they walked. But it eventually died out.

They walked another ten minutes into town and heard more laughing. Followed by more silence. They saw a house on fire. Total chaotic blaze. Albert recommended they not check on it. They passed an elderly man in a fat Buick with a tickle spider in his mouth. The man's eyes followed them as they walked on by. Sylvia stopped and considered. She could use the salt cellar and risk killing the man, or she'd save him. How did one weight that? She tried not to think and pulled the cap off to zap it, but for some reason the cellar sputtered and almost coughed. Nothing happened. That was not heartening.

For lack of anything else, Ms. Gamelin waved.

Albert declared that he wanted to make a detour. Sylvia protested.

"I want to see Natalia," he said.

At that, she shut up. There would be, she hoped, food.

And Natalia, of course.

3.

Sylvia couldn't shake the feeling that time was warping or slowing down. That, somehow, Caldecott was ensconced in a break from reality.

Sylvia fixated on a sense of delay. It was something she witnessed in the faces of the diners in The White Kitchen. It was a sense of time stretching out. It happened in the woods as a girl. Then again when she was buried. She would've sworn that she was only buried for the length of time it took to have that dream. For her, it seemed like twenty minutes. But it was four months.

Engaging with Grasshands slowed down time. Maybe that was how you had to deal with an entity as old as it. That's why it numbed you. So you couldn't hop away. Time was its weapon. And it used it like the fossil record. It moved slowly. Inconspicuously. Then it coiled around you and crushed you.

"Albert, would it be possible to slow down time?"

Albert was currently distracted by a distant oak tree aflame. He was appreciating the beauty in the burning.

"Hmm. Possibly. Why, do you have a need to slow down time?"

"No, but I can't stop thinking about how I got into this. Just constantly categorizing stuff by how it experiences time. I mean, wouldn't an animal that lives a long time like a tortoise experience reality different than us?"

"Can you imagine never being able to see your ass?" Ms. Gamelin said. "Jesus. On the other hand, maybe I'd be better off never seeing my ass again."

Sylvia looked at her.

"No, I'm serious. Grasshands can afford to take its sweet time. The earth, the universe, they're all on much longer clocks than we are."

"Okay," Albert said. "We have no way to test this even if we wanted to. And what difference would it make if we could?"

"I wonder if Grasshands moves more efficiently here with us or if it moves better wherever it came from."

"And that would be...where?" Ms. Gamelin said.

Except for the old man in the Buick, they hadn't encountered anyone yet. Sylvia noticed this again. She was flustered by the question. "I don't know. The red pillars? The library? I don't know."

They walked a minute. Albert and Natalia's house was close by.

"Maybe it's the Green Man."

"Excuse me?"

"A pagan deity. It's often in architectural designs. A man's face with a beard full of leaves and vines. Or often it vomits up vegetation that swarms around his face. There are many variations on it."

"Is it evil?"

"Not necessarily. On the contrary, many see it as a sign of renewal and rebirth."

They were on Albert's street. Picture perfect. If the picture was folded over and left in the sweaty back pocket of a maniac traveling cross country with just a knife and a bloody teddy bear.

A window broke somewhere. The glass crinkled and echoed. No one moved.

High-pitched laughter fell into crying.

A large black lab came charging at them over a lawn from across the street. They almost didn't notice until it was upon them. It was head down, dead-on sprinting for its life. A dark demon dog flurrying out of a suburban hell. Then they saw why.

A spindly tickle spider labored after it. It was smaller than any other they'd seen. It came hurtling close toward Ms. Gamelin. She pulled the machete. As it flew by, she swung at it like a gold ball and sliced it in half.

Sylvia knew what would happen. She'd seen it at The White Kitchen. The whole thing reverted back to the original components like in a dream. In this case, the spindles and body changed into squeaky dog toys and a water bowl. A leash. A collar.

The black lab could still be seen leaping over shrubs and hauling ass.

"Good work," Albert said.

He brought the blades off his shoulder and held them down in front. The tips touched the street. He looked angry and sad at the same time. The emotions fought in a small spot near his eye crease.

"I realized I cannot check on her myself."

"Well, sweetheart, we can do it for you," Ms. Gamelin said. She stepped up to him and touched his lower leg. "C'mon, Syl."

"Holler if anything with more than four legs shows up," Sylvia said.

Albert didn't respond. He stood in front of the house with the I-beam blades. A fairy tale sentinel.

He started scratching something into the asphalt.

4.

It wasn't hard to find Natalia. She was between the front room and the kitchen on the floor. On her back. It looked as if she'd willingly lain down and settled her hands on her chest. Like she was receiving First Communion or laid out in a casket.

Her mouth was pulled open, like everyone else's, in a grotesque shape. This particular tickle spider was a beast.

Natalia's chest rose and fell in even movements. She appeared calm. Her hair sprawled out behind onto the kitchen linoleum. Her right eye was closed and her left one was half-open.

The house was clean. Something about that killed Sylvia.

She knelt down beside Natalia.

"Hi, sweetie," she said. "I'm going to ask you some questions. If you can understand me and answer them, try to blink once for yes and twice for no. Okay?"

Natalia's half-open lid blinked slowly.

"You're totally numb, I bet."

One blink.

"Are you in pain?"

Blink, blink.

Relief. "Do you want me to try and remove that thing?"

No blink.

From behind, Ms. Gamelin: "Is that wise, Syl?"

"It may be. I don't know if I don't try. It started to work in The White Kitchen."

"Until it didn't."

Sylvia faced Natalia.

"What do you say? Can I try?"

One blink.

As Sylvia pulled the pike from her back, she wondered if Albert's wedding ring was a part of the tickle spider. *Till death do us part.* They never say anything in those fucking vows about *Till magical curses making one partner a giant do us part. In sickness and in health, in composite spider-creature in my mouth and in not that.*

Sylvia squeezed the pike, as if to warn it, to wake it up. She closed her eyes and started softly in a somber tenor.

Fa fa fa fa

She felt like an idiot for a few seconds, but then Ms. Gamelin joined in with a soprano harmony. It sounded good. It felt *right*, like they were hitting some mystical note. Or like when you finally get the lid off a resistant jar and it goes *throck!*

They kept a steady rhythm. After a minute, the pike warmed and added a deep undertone.

Fa fa fa fa

The spindle creature wriggled. It was uncomfortable. That was a good sign. Sylvia hoped they'd only need another minute of this and it would pop out of Natalia's mouth.

But just as they started to weaken it, the creature redoubled its efforts. First, it shrank, which means it sank down deeper into Natalia's throat. She gagged. Every creature Sylvia'd seen, they didn't cut off the airways of their prey/hosts. But here it wanted to punish either Natalia or Sylvia.

Or it was scared. But she couldn't find that believable.

It got comfortable; it nestled. Then it shot two of its spindles through Natalia's cheeks and jaw. Natalia gurgled in pain.

Sylvia stopped singing. Ms. Gamelin also stopped. The pike kept going for a few seconds. Finally, it followed suit.

"Natalia, can you breathe?"

One blink.

"Do you want us to keep trying?"

Blink, blink.

Sylvia's head fell forward. She sighed. She looked back at Ms. Gamelin.

Ms. Gamelin said, "Tell her at least."

"Nat, we wanted you to know that Albert is alive. He's outside in the street. He wanted to see you, but he's too big now."

No blink. Wetness dripped from the corner of her half-open eye.

"Do you want us to try and take you outside?"

Blink, blink.

Sylvia started to cry.

"Do you want us to have him tear the roof off?"

Blink, blink.

"Do you want us to tell him we found you?"

There was a moment where Sylvia didn't know if she needed to repeat the question. But more wetness from Natalia's eye.

Then: blink, blink.

"Should we lie and say you weren't here?"

One blink.

"We're going to leave her here?" Ms. Gamelin said. "That's crazy. We can't do that." She stepped past Sylvia. She knelt. "Natalia, dear, we can't leave you here."

One blink.

The rage in Ms. Gamelin gathered in her joints. Had she been alone, she'd have attempted to pull that spindly bastard out with her bare hand.

Again: one blink.

"I didn't ask a question."

"No, you didn't. She was ordering us to leave," Sylvia said.

Despite the risk, Sylvia leaned forward and kissed Natalia on the forehead. It was slicked with sweat. The salt tasted good. Ms. Gamelin took Natalia's hand and pressed it to her cheek.

"I don't know when, but we're coming back. And that thing in your mouth will turn back to knick-knacks and potpourri."

They stood. Sylvia wasn't hungry anymore. They left.

Outside, Albert turned to them.

Sylvia shook her head. "We searched all over. Found a note saying she went to her mother's."

He looked confused, then nodded. "Sure. Yeah. That makes sense." The giant had to turn away. He knew it wasn't true. They knew he knew it wasn't true. But he turned to walk up the street in the direction of the library. Just like that. No questions asked.

In the meantime, Albert had finished the message. He'd tattooed it onto the surface of the street with a beam blade.

Sylvia and Ms. Gamelin couldn't properly read it from where they were. It would've been perfectly legible looking down from Natalia and Albert's second floor window.

Sylvia had a good idea what it said.

plethora moon bench

Albert didn't offer an explanation. Ms. Gamelin didn't ask. Sylvia didn't pursue it.

All the same, the phrase rattled around Sylvia's head.

5.

The library horrified them.

It loomed. Although nothing outside of it was suspicious, it had a presence. A knowing. Albert acted differently as they approached it. He was more cautious. Ms. Gamelin went silent. Sylvia's hands began to tremor.

None of them looked directly at the library yet. They were hiding in a parking lot behind Cicero's. Five building stories hid Albert. The Caldecott Library was midcentury modern brick and mortar. The long panels of glass windows. The different rooflines. The landscaping undulated and wobbled with malicious vibrancy. Everything green, the moss, had turned maroon. Even the mailbox on the corner wanted to chew them up and spit them out.

They had no plan of attack. They just exchanged dopey, unformed expressions with each other. The neon sign outside Throckmorton's was layered with fibrous, hair-like tentacles of moss.

Everything wrong in the world was wrong with books, Sylvia thought. *Yes yes yes.* Their spines were broken and needed taped or glued or re-stitched or altogether rebound. Their pages crimped and curled. They were just plants repackaged into another form, so it made sense to say that what was wrong with the world was wrong with books.

She knew this still to be true. Sylvia confirmed in her gut that she felt Deena there. Her sixth sense could've just been an upset stomach. But she felt it anyway. And she'd have to go into the one place this whole shitshow started—the basement.

Then a voice broke into her stream of consciousness.

Everything wrong in the world is wrong with humans. Their spines are broken and need taped or glued or re-stitched or altogether rebound. Their skin crimped and curled. They are just plants repackaged into another form, bodies, and so it makes sense to say that what is wrong with the world was wrong with humans. Yes yes yes.

She didn't recognize the voice. But it wasn't hers. She was cold now. As if someone had displaced all of her blood with the vacuous pain of space.

"Grasshands knows we're here," Albert said, waking the others out of their reverie.

"Then let's get on with it," Ms. Gamelin said. "Syl?"

She stuttered something and nodded her assent. She could barely form words for some reason. They started to move. Then Sylvia realized why she leaked worry.

"Stop."

Albert reeled back.

Sylvia remembered Teresa Bardin. The pit and the sharpened stakes. The death traps set up around town. It was a miracle they'd not encountered one. But if there was one they'd have to deal with, it'd be at the library.

"How do we find them?" Ms. Gamelin said. "That's a literal needle in a haystack."

Albert said, "I'll just walk out first. It shouldn't affect me like it would you if I got hurt—"

"No, no. Stop. I think I know what will work."

I hope it works, anyway.

Sylvia pulled the salt cellar out. She'd gotten a lot of mileage from this in the past 24 hours. She hoped it worked one more time.

The sky grew gray and cloudy. Fat snow fell, dotting and whiting out Caldecott.

She unscrewed the cap but didn't take it off yet. Sylvia walked into the road and stopped. Albert and Ms. Gamelin came from behind Cicero's. She moved the cap from the mouth of the cellar. Nothing happened. Some salt spilled out. Hit the pavement with tiny tinkles.

"Why does everything you own now need constant encouragement to do any type of work?" Ms. Gamelin asked. Sylvia did not acknowledge the shade. She put the cap back on and walked away from the others. She knelt down and rolled the cellar between her hands.

"Do you want me to use the pike? Because I can. I *will*. If you're too lazy to do your goddamn job, then—" and Sylvia felt the pike on her back wiggle and heat up a bit in response to this talk. "I'm just saying, you aren't the only weapon here, you know? So, like, c'mon. Let's make a decision. You going to make a red choice or a green choice today?" She'd heard the children's librarians talk to the toddlers like this. As if life broke down into simple binaries. The salt cellar jumped in her hands. She clutched it and returned to the others. "We're good," she said.

"Did you promise it a cookie later?" Ms. Gamelin said.

As she leveled and uncapped it, the solid green geometric shape blasted out. Like a light beam. But it didn't illuminate. If anything, it ate light; a canned green hole, hungry for yielding, ignorant light. It was hard to look at for a sustained amount of time.

Sylvia swung the widening green geometry over everything she saw. The library. Shrubs. The lawn. The sidewalk.

What lay under the green geometry shimmered. As if tested and then approved.

The salt cellar made a green choice, then. Okie dokie.

As Sylvia moved further around the library, Albert and Ms. Gamelin followed in her path. She swung around the front of the library and started on the landscaping by the front entrance and there was a flash. A sparkle or a glimmer drifted out of the boxwoods.

The whole front library entrance exploded in a shower of glass and brick and steel. Sylvia dropped to a knee and blocked her face with her arm. The others did likewise. But the shooting debris was stopped by the black geometry. It hung in midair, a billion shards of an impossible puzzle with no corner pieces.

Sylvia stood. The explosion was frozen fire and pure propulsion. Probably from an IED that Tim or some other mossed-up survivalist manufactured. And in an instant, the debris and explosion dissipated, eaten by the salt cellar.

"I preferred the employee entrance, anyway," Ms. Gamelin said, breathing heavily.

The residual smoke wafted and lifted. They moved forward and stepped through the blast hole. Albert stopped short. "I'm going to crawl in. I can stand in the main room."

True enough. But in a quick escape, he was hosed. Or he would have to jump up through the glass atrium to get out of the main reading room.

There would be no arguing with Albert on this. He needed to get in.

Entering the library, the dark geometry switched to the algae-like green light. Sylvia scanned the vestibule and the checkout desk. She scanned the main room and the bathroom area. Nothing. She waved him in. As Albert got on his stomach and crawled in like a megaworm through a dank tunnel, the women made their way back past the checkout counter. The front of the library seemed normal enough, with the exception of the books nearly draped over with moss. It had also covered much of the windows. Their workspace, their home away from home, had mutated into a subterranean cathedral.

The whole building smelled murky, damp, musty.

They found Delores in her office. She was splayed back in her chair with her arms thrown out to the sides. Her eyes were closed.

Sylvia and Ms. Gamelin tiptoed in. The floor was covered in moist moss and hung with webby connective tissue. Their feet squelched into the floor. Their steps left deep indents that slowly filled with water. Same as outside in the reading area, it was dark here with the exception of a dim desk lamp.

The women pulled their weapons.

Errkk—ughhhhhhh

Delores's throat moved.

"She's got one in her," Ms. Gamelin said.

"Her mouth's not open."

Uuuwwwerrrlllluuggghhh

Delores's neck swelled and deflated. Her whole body reverberated with an inhuman intensity. Her eyes snapped open. She panicked. She gripped the desk and braced herself.

"Step back, step back," she said.

Sylvia and Ms. Gamelin went as far back to the wall as they could in the swampy surround.

Delores vomited. But what came out wasn't digested food, bile, stomach juices. It was an illuminated stream of small crystalline shapes jostling around and sparking off one another. This lightstream shuddered Delores's body. The coruscating contents spilled over the desk like electric milk and swirled in eddies onto the floor where it solidified. Sylvia worried for a moment that they'd drown in this hot bright vomit. Delores didn't seem to have an end to it.

Then, like an automated sprinkler, the lightstream shut off and Delores fell back into the position they found her in. She was drenched in sweat and her mouth had blood around it. Blood dripped from her eyes and nose. She'd both aged and reversed back to youth, it seemed. The paradox made it hard to discern what the hell was happening to Delores.

Ms. Gamelin stepped forward. Sylvia grabbed her arm to stop her. Ms. Gamelin shook her off.

"Delores, what the hell was that?"

Delores's face curdled into a slow smile.

"That, Clara, was pure knowledge. A bit disappointing, isn't it?"

And her body reverberated again.

6.

When Delores finished with two more violent lightstreams of databarf, she tried to stand but fell. Sylvia came around to the side of the desk to help her into the chair.

"Watch your long knife there," Delores said.

"Pike. It's a pike."

"How Anglo-Saxon of you."

"It's actually older than that."

"Not a pike. You're thinking of a polearm. *Hatchet glaive halberd sword pole-ax fauchard falx sickle scythe—*"

"Hold on there, Delores."

Delores put a hand over her mouth. "I can't help it. I don't even know what I know anymore. It's hard to concentrate. Just random streams of information roost in my brain and take over. Or I spit them out."

"Where's Grasshands?" Sylvia said.

"What?"

"Deena. Where's Deena? Or the small spider things."

Delores looked humbled and terrified in the same moment. "They were in the basement. But not anymore."

"Where are they now?" Sylvia said.

Delores grieved for the spiders. Sylvia could see it in her eyes. The way she fumbled with her hands. Even as exhausted as she was. She cared for them. "It wasn't safe at the library for the 'spindle creatures' as you call them. They know you can destroy them...They're not that bad."

"Well," Ms. Gamelin said.

"They're actually kind of wonderful, aren't they?"

"Tell that to Albert," Sylvia said. "His wife is lying on their kitchen floor with one in her mouth. Its spindles pierced her jaw and cheeks."

"They just want to know you. They want to learn from you, from us. Just give them that chance. Don't deny them. Why would we deny the opportunity for a new species to try and integrate into our world? Instead of cataloguing, we could be discovering."

"But it's not new, and it's not just them," Sylvia said. "There's something much bigger behind it."

"Deena," Delores said, with reverence.

Sylvia nodded.

"That's not here, whatever that is."

Sylvia didn't believe this. Delores's body jerked around. She clutched her stomach but kept the data gorge down. The liquid knowledge swirled around their ankles. Like bioluminescent plankton.

"Alexander Pope said a little knowledge was a dangerous thing." Delores laughed. "Totally wrong. Lots of fucking knowledge is a dangerous thing. Obesity of fact."

Sylvia was torn: she wanted to leave Delores there to die. There was no sure way to know that she would, but Sylvia would be willing to bet on it. "How did this start?" She pointed to the vomit.

"It fed it to me, day after day. A little moss here. A little moss there. I loved it. I wanted more. The only way to keep it up was to eat more. Then it was full-on consuming. I've not had food in weeks to substitute one area of knowledge with another before my brain withers." She paused.

"I'm sorry," Sylvia said instinctively. Then she wished she hadn't said it. Empathy got a first shot at everything sometimes.

"I'm not," Ms Gamelin said.

Delores gazed at her boss.

"You should go," Delores said. "Before that, could you do me a final favor?"

"Hell no," Ms. Gamelin said.

"Clara," Sylvia said. "*Please.*"

"In the overflow stacks below, there's a book of poetry by D. H. Lawrence. I know it's there. All of the fiction and poetry upstairs was destroyed by moss. That's the only copy left. I want to read the poem, 'The Ship of Death.'"

"Why can't you get it yourself?" Sylvia asked, heading off Ms. Gamelin's next question.

"I can barely move. Please. It's the last thing I ask of you."

7.

"Fucking D. H. Lawrence. Can you believe this?"

"Doesn't matter," Sylvia said. "I was going down here, anyway."

"Oh." Mrs. Gamelin gave her friend a salty look. "Uhh, why?"

She would've said *Deena* but didn't want to scare her. So she explained that the Aristotle book that Albert handled, *On the Soul*, was still down there, somewhere. Which was true. He had originally checked it out to Deena. Maybe, in some way, it could reverse his size or help somehow. Maybe something in *On the Soul* was making Albert grow? What if a different Aristotlemoss would stop it? Or shrink him back? Aristotle believed in weird-ass shit. Maybe his impossibility was made real through Albert's ingestion. Ms. Gamelin asked if she really believed that. Sylvia didn't know. It was a long shot. Everything was a long shot. And if Deena was down here, in whatever form or shape, then she'd blast that crap away, too.

"I'm prepared to believe the impossible."

Ms. Gamelin said: "Aristotle isn't going to help any damn person, any damn time soon, sweetie. Believe that."

Sylvia and Ms. Gamelin stood at the top of the stairs. The police tape that had shut out busybodies was torn down and wadded like sad birthday bunting. A full minute went by.

"Clara, is she the devil?"

"What? No. The devil doesn't exist."

"Then what are we afraid of?"

"Whatever is down there."

"Books and moss."

"You're an idiot, sweetie. Have Albert do this. He'd do it gladly."

"You know he can't fit down there."

"We don't have to do this. Screw her. She doesn't need a poem. She needs a goddamn head transplant. You don't need that Aristotle book."

Sylvia's body language pleaded with Ms. Gamelin for some kind of humane leeway.

"Look, the lights are already on."

"*La-di-da.* What? No one dies with the lights on?"

"Fine. I'll go by myself. I know that basement like the back of my hand."

Sylvia squeezed the handrail in her left hand, her pike in the right. She tread carefully over the wet, slippery moss and growth.

"People say shit like that, Syl. 'I know it like the back of my hand.' No one knows anything about their hands."

Sylvia ignored her. Ms. Gamelin's sarcasm was a distraction and delay. Part of her was correct. Delores didn't *need* anything. Sylvia didn't *need* to do anything for her. But Sylvia expected to live beyond the day. She didn't expect Delores to. Circumstances like that change how one makes immediate decisions. Especially when they have a heavy moral compass. If Sylvia didn't give two fucks about Delores, she sure wouldn't have stuck around Caldecott long enough to come back and blow the doors off the library. Sylvia knew that Ms. Gamelin knew that.

Although, Sylvia and Ms. Gamelin's whole relationship seemed predicated on ignoring the obvious and substituting it with the indirect. Many marriages were built on that premise. Albert and Natalia tried to avoid it. Sylvia's parents probably succeeded in skipping it. She didn't really know her grandparents well enough for a verdict on them.

She could guess which way Ms. Gamelin leaned in her two marriages.

Sylvia twisted the door handle to the overflow basement.

From behind her: "Fine, hey. Jesus. Make a big deal of everything."

Along came Ms. Gamelin squelching the moss, gripping her machete.

The double doors were steel and had a window with diamond-shaped wire mesh inside. Through them, Sylvia and Ms. Gamelin saw the state of the basement. True enough, the lights burned. Four fluorescent fixtures hanging by chains off the ceiling. Various cellar rooms branched off this way and that. Junk filled them up like administrative tumors. Unlike upstairs, the basement's floor didn't have much moss covering it. It was still dry, smooth cement. Which was odd. So for Sylvia, the biggest danger would be at the beginning. The basement was shaped like an upside-down U with the door at the bottom. On either side, the basement broke to the left and to the right. She'd have to check the right side before she went to the left for the poetry.

Sylvia wondered what Albert was doing with his time. Rearranging books? She let herself smile at that. Then she shut her eyes to listen better.

Nothing. No tapping. No breathing. No HVAC. All of that nothingness bothered her.

Ms. Gamelin opened the door and Sylvia went in first with her pike down. She immediately swung to the right. One light fixture hung near the end of the U and one hung right above her. The stacks were set parallel facing her. So she couldn't see between them, but through the space above and below the books she could see there was no one there. She knelt down and looked. Nothing.

Yards and yards of empty walkways between stacks.

Ms. Gamelin got the all-clear sign from Sylvia and shut the door behind her so it wouldn't click.

The door clicked. The noise was considerable and bright off the concrete floor and columns.

Ms. Gamelin's face scrunched in pain.

Sylvia stood and side-stepped over to the left so they could both enter together. This side had two light fixtures as well, but the far one in the back was out. That whole area was in darkness. Moss spilled from the blackness like hairy frozen-in-motion syrup.

Ms. Gamelin's shoulders slumped. She turned to Sylvia and mouthed, *Are you fucking kidding me?*

Sylvia set her teeth. She whispered, "We're going to go along the inside wall. I'll go first. Don't feel bad if you have to push a shelf over."

Sylvia re-gripped the pike and stepped forward. She moved toward the Library of Congress letters "PR" where some literature slept. It took forty-five steps to reach the end of the light. Beyond that there was another twenty or so steps into blackness where she'd be able to see just enough to pluck the Lawrence off the shelf. If it was shelved correctly. The book was on the topmost shelf. Green buckram-bound hardback. But Sylvia couldn't reach it. And there was no step stool. Ms. Gamelin checked on her and sussed what was wrong. "Use the pike," she said. Sylvia slid the edge of the pike's blade up underneath the spine of the book. She pulled it toward her and it fell into her free hand.

Then all the lights in the basement went out.

Ms. Gamelin gasped. Sylvia stepped back to the wall. She gently reached out and pushed Ms. Gamelin against the wall, too. She stuck the book in her waistband, hoping it would stay. If she had to run and it fell out—too bad.

"We just go back the way we came, Clara. No big."

"Uh huh. I guess finding the Aristotle is out?"

"Yes, I guess. Switch me spots."

"No way. I'm going first."

They felt along the wall. After ten steps, they heard a noise upstairs. It was hysterical laughing. Delores. She was laughing so hard she was ripping just these shredded coughs in between. A high-pitched squealing that turned into a wet haggard choking. Then it ramped up again.

Sylvia knew that the blackout was planned. How, she didn't know.

Further up ahead of them, it sounded like books were scooting on the shelf, moving. Or like the basement door clicking open and shut. Sylvia nudged Ms. Gamelin in her back. Ms. Gamelin didn't want to go first anymore. She didn't want to move. If she didn't move, she rationalized, then nothing could happen to her. She moved because Sylvia urged her along.

As they rounded the corner, a little light spilled through the two windows in the basement doors. It was like an island of safety in a video game. A place with an extra life or a bottled potion. Ms. Gamelin got excited by the weak shapes of light and flung open the door. Sylvia had crossed the pike over her chest to get through, but the door hit her.

Sylvia fell and the pike rolled behind into shadow. The Lawrence book slipped out of her waistband. Something else in her pocket cracked on the floor and spun around.

The salt cellar. Sylvia knew this because the cap popped off, casting a soft, reassuring Kelly-green light that shot onto a section of shelves. She crawled quickly to get it, cursing for not thinking to give it a now-requisite enthusiastic hype-speech. (Maybe it was proving it could do more than destroy—it could also illuminate. *Yeeah great*, Sylvia thought.) Sylvia heard more of the shuffling-books sound. It got busier and rushier. With nothing else, she grabbed the salt cellar and pointed it down the right side of the basement where she'd looked before. But there, the green light illuminated the biggest tickle spider she'd ever seen. It was made up of thousands of tiny tickle spiders. (Why did the salt cellar need so much emotional support?) What, in a brief flicker, Sylvia figured were the possessions of all the library patrons eating moss and then were themselves possibly consumed, drained, or dried by information. And the overflow books. The creature was absorbing everything. Her pike rolled slowly past her toward it. She stepped on it.

"Run," Sylvia said.

"What?" Ms. Gamelin said.

"Run!"

A spindle shot out at Sylvia, but it missed her as she ducked to snag the pike. She started to sing, hoping the pike would join. Ms. Gamelin obeyed Sylvia and ran up the stairs, two at a time. She slipped on moist moss halfway up.

Shoved into the small space, the spindle creature shook and heaved. It squeezed itself out past Sylvia, whose singing and salt cellar light did nothing, really. It trampled over her and flung her against the cinder block wall. One spindle pierced the Lawrence book and took it along with it up the stairs after Ms. Gamelin. Sylvia couldn't breathe. All the air was knocked out of her. She clutched her chest, trying to revive her breath. She was drowning with no way to inhale. She panicked. Then, all at once, her stomach and lungs inflated. She sucked in the cool, damp basement air. It was the only time she was grateful to smell it.

Sylvia stumbled behind the creature's path. The steel doors were blown outward, warped and bent. Already there was shouting upstairs in the main reading room. Albert was growling. Deep clunking of metal and the thundering sound of bookshelves tumbling.

In the distance, Delores still shrieked with fear and glee.

At the top of the basement stairs, Sylvia could see into the main reading room under the atrium. The tickle spider had wrestled Albert to the ground. It was trying to pin his arms and legs down with spindles. It was like watching old Ray Harryhausen monsters do battle. She couldn't believe it.

Albert still held the I-beam blades in his hands. He had little room to maneuver with them in the library. Resigned, he swung one around and took out a brick support column to the mezzanine. The Children's section collapsed behind Albert's head. He shoved the beam blade between himself and the spindle creature and wedged it off. There was no mouth or pincers on it. Only the massive spindles that could pierce him. Which they did.

The hulking tickle spider reared up so as to force its front spindles deep into Albert's flesh. Nine of them sunk like stakes into Albert's shoulder blades. Blood jetted out like a car-struck fire hydrant. The floor and computers and checkout desk slapped with hot giant's blood.

Sylvia watched this, deadlocked behind the counter. Maybe a glob of her friend's blood had landed on her lip. She wiped without looking, without *wanting* to look. She heard a chirrup behind her. Ms. Gamelin stood against the wall with a hand over her mouth. The machete was loose in the other hand, about to fall.

"Don't move," Sylvia said. "I'll be right back."

She ran into Delores's office. Her old boss choked on wet chuckles. Sylvia trudged over the sick growth around the desk and wrung Delores's mouldering shirt in her hand. "You're coming with me," she said. She pulled Delores toward her, out of the chair.

"*I don't think so,*" Delores said, her eyes relieved.

Sylvia tugged, then yanked at Delores's upper body. Tiny vine-like structures and the moist moss blanket had crept up the back of her chair. Interweaving into her hair, and maybe her skull. Sylvia didn't want to think too much about where it ended. She yanked one last time. Delores still gurgled a sad laugh. Delores then came unglued, her head and body falling forward. But not the spine or the spilled inner organs or the back of her head. Or her brain.

Delores's brain was perpendicular to the headrest of the chair. Clutching to the moss; being eaten by it, really. The brain was a gray bulbous wrinkled raisin. Slick, glittering. Sylvia dropped Delores's shell of a body. Her headcase knocked the desk hollowly, then fell to the floor.

Sylvia couldn't metabolize reality.

Fine. Better this way, she thought. *It will be a bitch to rehire all this staff in the future, though.*

Not in the mood for remembrances, Sylvia left and grabbed Ms. Gamelin by the hand and escaped out the ragged blast hole into the street. No matter how the titanic wrestling match between Albert and the creature went down, Those Who Are Small had no place in that arena. Besides, she already knew that the salt cellar was losing its effect. She guessed that the pebble inside the cellar was deteriorating or maybe losing its juice. The pike wouldn't do much either, she guessed. They crunched over the glass and brick. Ms. Gamelin slipped a bit on Albert's blood.

Albert broke one of the tickle spider's spindles off and tossed it. The spindle slid outside toward Sylvia and Ms. Gamelin. It melted and reverted back to its original state. The appendage was plastic children's toys, a stuffed dinosaur, math textbooks, a stack of crumpled family photos, a sweater, succulents in a terra cotta pot in a macramé net, an oxygen tank, towels.

What she couldn't know was that Francis Blackford, Gordon Ritterskamp, Tim the Shooter, Trent the Moss Boy, Deena the Stalker, and others were some of the owners of that stuff. That they may never see any of it again. That it was also possible to have a fulfilling life without it, despite the circumstances. But what she did know was that the sweater (actually, a cardigan) was Teresa Bardin's. She felt herself move toward it. She bent down to touch the sleeve. As she did, it changed again. Now into a gelatinous glop. Sylvia screamed. But it went unheard in the tumult. She wanted to freeze everything for one goddamn second. A panic roared inside of her. *What the hell am I supposed to do if my whole world melts around me?* She felt like she was drowning in a pool with rising sides and no visible ladders.

Behind her, Ms. Gamelin still stood dumbstruck.

The tickle spider still had Albert pinioned with the spindles. But Albert had pulled his knees up and his legs were under the creature. Albert kicked the tickle spider. It shattered through the atrium's glass ceiling.

Ms. Gamelin snapped to and followed the tickle spider's impact outside. It had flown up and crashed on top of the building across the street with Cicero's at the ground floor. Albert, with his blades, climbed out of the atrium and roared at the creature. The spider righted itself and leapt south onto the post office then into a parking lot behind it. The tickle spider fled, like a homing beacon had clicked on. Even at its size and speed like a semi-truck, there still was a *tap tap* to its spindly running. Sylvia's spine tingled.

"It's going away," Albert said to no one. His voice boomed in the deserted streets. Sylvia ran to where the giants had scrapped. "It's hurt and going home," he said, lightly amused. The holes in his shoulders dripped with bright blood. He looked like something ancient Celts would've sewn onto a tapestry. Or a futuristic Maasai warrior. He looked down on her. "Where do you think it went, Sylvia? Where do these things feel safe?"

A thought fired off inside her skull.

"It went home."

CHAPTER FOURTEEN

1.

IT TURNED OUT Sylvia's old home was now the Spurrier Christmas Tree Farm. Not long after her grandparents died, the land was sold off. An out of state tree farmer bought the land, tore down the house, and planted white pine, blue spruce, and Douglas fir. A small parcel was also sold for tract housing. McMansions. Those skeletons of pretension. The comfortable housing for the comfortably middle-class.

2.

Sylvia remembered cutting down a Christmas tree with her parents once when she was little, maybe six or seven. Surely one of the last family trips before her father died. Memory faltered, but images floated up. Images limned in static and the weak glow of string Christmas lights. Her father wore a lumberjack checked flannel and a deep blue down vest. Her mother wore Red Wings and a neon pink sock hat. Her father brought a trash bag with him so when he sawed down the Frasier fir or white pine he wouldn't get soaked by the water-logged soil or the snow on the ground. She remembered her father being a tad prim despite the lumberjack flannel. Her mother was a perfectionist. Especially about trees. They'd arrive around dusk, drinking hot cocoa. They'd leave in the dark, tree strapped to the roof with twine and bungee cords. Their hands covered in sticky lemony sap—Blood of the Coniferous Sacrifice. They hauled their reward away for another series of hours at home trimming and laughing and fighting. Every major holiday for her family was a psychological endurance test that no one would've ever agreed to otherwise. Sylvia wore, famously, her navy blue, fur-lined jacket with an old-world Santa imprint on it. Her prized possession. Worn from September to April at all occasions with no shame or second-guessing.

That jacket would be gone if she tried to find it. The jacket was absorbed. Eaten. It was obliterated into a tickle spider. Or the motherfog. Or maybe her pike. That thought lightly cheered her. But the chances were dim. All of her fond memories were likely annihilated to the detriment of her well-being. She knew this reality still hadn't sunk in and that it would be hard to grasp when the time came. *Nothing, or virtually nothing, she owned would exist anymore.* And what did that mean? What did it mean to tackle, battle, and wage against creatures made up of your own bedroom and childhood? It was a fluky nightmare. Maybe safety meant living like a druid. Someone who never resorted to material culture.

3.

Albert walked in his giant yet eerily silent strides to Sylvia's old home, dragging the sharpened I-beams behind him. Sylvia and Ms. Gamelin commandeered an abandoned truck to keep up. When they reached the old address, they proceeded on foot.

The shock of the missing house, the new stands of Christmas trees, the fast-growing shells of suburbia right next to it. Sylvia was ill with the speed of change. She didn't want to be buried again. But she also didn't want to hurtle through time so fast that all of her bearings broke off like disposable plastic tabs.

The sun was just burrowing into the horizon. Birds flitted silently from branch to branch. Robins lighted onto recently sawed off tree stumps. Old snow crusted on the ground. The women's breath hung in the air longer than normal. Clouds of exhaustion and nervousness. It was dark among the spruces. No one could see through the thick foliage. Boots cracked the old snow like glass.

The tree farm was young but looked well-aged. Specimens were tall. Healthy.

Sylvia carried the pike at her hip. Both hands in leather gloves she'd bogarted from the glovebox in the truck. Ms. Gamelin grasped the machete.

Albert listened intently. He scoped the farm. Then he knelt and stretched out in a long aisle between trees and set his basket-sized ear to the ground. He stood and shook his head. The blood on his shoulders had started to dry. The bloody dots like purposeful tattoos.

They walked deeper into a spruce grove. Then they stepped onto moss. Thick, lumpy waves of moss. Sylvia poked it with the pike. It was hard to tell in the morning half-light, but the moss seemed to flinch. She tore some off. Appeared normal with the exception that there was no dirt on the bottom. And it was much thicker. The section she tore was about as big as a Frisbee. The hole that remained was matte black. No ground, no dirt, no roots.

As an experiment, Sylvia found a pebble and tossed it in. She lost sight of it the second it passed the threshold.

"How far does that hole stretch?" Ms. Gamelin asked. She held the blade to her chest, as if the blade needed protecting from the gap in the earth.

"Underneath us? I'd say anywhere you see moss, there's this vast blackness."

Ms. Gamelin turned her head. The moss spread in every direction across the grove. She suddenly knew how worthless it was to hold the blade to her chest. It fell to her side, a mere accessory.

"What's holding us up, then?" she said.

"That's a good question," Albert said.

Deep from within the black hole spilled a trickling of noise.

Tap tap

Tap tap tap

The tapping grew into a vicious chittering. Like a nervous witch's steel teeth chewing on a robot's skull.

Ms. Gamelin knew what it was. She still held the machete in front of her. Sylvia also knew what it was. She didn't want to overreact. Knowing what was underneath them only eased her anxiety a small amount. She didn't have a tingling in her feet or hands, so she felt safe. For now.

"Do you feel numb anywhere?" she checked with Ms. Gamelin. She reported that she wasn't numb. Neither was Albert.

Far, far away up the hill of the tree farm, a line of Frasier firs swayed hard to the left. They swayed so hard they should've snapped in half. Then they swayed right. Sylvia recognized the sound of the drunk bulldozer. The snapping-sound of tree trunks shotgunned throughout the farm. What was left of the evening sun was buried behind a cloudfront. The sky faded into battleship gray. And the air stank with the lemony scent of pine sap and split wood.

The mossfloor underneath trembled then tremored. They ran back to the access road, tripping over limbs and clumps of dry pine needles. Sap and tree-shit stuck to their clothes and hair. They hiked up the road toward the new houses. Far along the ridgeline of the farm, Sylvia watching a row of Norway spruce quake. Then a pair of them dropped into the earth. Then another. And another.

Sylvia gasped.

Albert nodded. "Found it."

"What!" Ms. Gamelin demanded. "Gasping isn't allowed. Not now. Not ever. Shit—"

It wasn't the motherfog; two tickle-spiders big as minivans emerged from a sinkhole in the road ahead. One of them was Albert's former foe from the library.

Sylvia couldn't feel her thumbs or many of her toes. Part of her face. Her back. She was actually buoyed up by this change. When she clocked what was waiting for them twenty yards in front, Ms. Gamelin cursed. The creaturely things moved in jagged and blurry directions. Unpredictable. Their bodies heaved as if laboring with breath. But Sylvia knew they had no lungs. They needed no air. So what were they panting after? Sylvia steadied the pike.

Ms. Gamelin, unable to let Sylvia face these alone, stepped up reluctantly. She held the machete down. She tried to respect the weight of it, even though it was a cheap weapon. Starting to rust, probably not *that* sharp anymore, and oddly bent at the end. The sky was oddly still light with the cloudfront and nighttime and Ms. Gamelin could make out in detail the tickle-spiders. From this far away, she identified something on one of their bodies. It was a wall calendar from her kitchen.

"They've been in my home."

Sylvia shrugged. "Maybe, maybe not. Doesn't matter."

"I want my stuff," Ms. Gamelin said. She then saw a favorite book pasted to the body of the spider. Some of her family photos dripped off the underside where they had gone from solid to liquid and oozed into the ground.

Furious, violated, Ms. Gamelin brought back the machete to scream or attack—some show of violence. But the blade of the machete slipped out of the handle and fell backward into the ground with a *plonk*.

Tap tap

Tap tap

The two spiders in front didn't move. Sylvia could see where the others were coming from. Now they had only her pike. And Ms. Gamelin's bad attitude and sharp wit. And Albert.

Sylvia turned. Albert was gone.

"What—?" Ms. Gamelin said.

"Don't worry. He can take care of himself. He's around here somewhere. We have other shit to consider."

Sylvia charged the tickle-spiders that didn't seem much up for tickling. (She wondered how big their prey would have to be to comfortably fit in their mouths...) Sylvia's aim was to run them through or chase them off. No exceptions.

Ms. Gamelin held the hollow handle in her hand. She squeezed it and thought of all the luck in her life she'd already used up prior to this moment. Everything was absurd. It had to be. Or why would she be standing in the middle of a Christmas tree farm with one of her former employees facing down two large vile creatures made up of her own possessions while the floor of the earth chipped away into nothingness?

She howl-sang into the handle of the machete. *FAFAFAFA*. The handle sank in her hand. She struggled. She contained the singing. She popped a palm on it. The handle warmed, then burned her. She was surprised it worked.

The creature closest to Sylvia sped toward her. Its shape turned amorphous. The edges bled into dissipating smoke. She rammed the pike into the smoke's guts. Nothing happened. The dense cloud enveloped her. Then the spider's shape solidified. A return to body and legs. Sylvia was inside the tickle spider.

Tap

The machete handle now glowed orange and Ms. Gamelin cried in pain. She launched it at the tickle spider. Her shoulder blade clicked. The handle rolled under the flat, almost geometric belly of the creature. Tickle-Spider One crouched. Tickle-Spider Two lengthened.

Memories dripped off of them. Items. Possessions. Ms. Gamelin's First Communion dress peeled off T-S #1 and floated to the dirt. A sob bubbled up in her chest. She thought she'd lost it decades ago. She wailed in anger.

The machete handle exploded.

Singing pierced the sky. Ms. Gamelin's singing. Her own voice shaped as a weapon terrified her. It echoed off the trees. It pounded the moss blanket. It delved into the matte black gaps. It sliced up and through the tickle spiders.

4.

The spiders panicked. Ms. Gamelin couldn't see expressions on them. But they jolted.

They flailed. They chittered up and down the gravel road. They charged her. Nearly galloping. She couldn't move. Her body fell slack.

Tongue stoned. Eyes lacquered. Ears thronged.

The first spider leapt from a distance. It extended the spiny spindles at her neck but it fell apart into pathetic slender ribbons before reaching her. Papery ribbons of tickle-spider confetti'd down around her.

The second spider made to charge Ms. Gamelin. But it dissipated into a gaseous soup as it started to tap over. As the shell evaporated, Ms. Gamelin saw a large picture portrait of her parents as twenty-somethings. Her father sat on a large cardboard crescent moon. Her mother sat on his lap. The black and white of it shocked her. The picture disappeared—gone forever.

Sylvia floated in the space where the spider's body had been. She was unconscious. Ms. Gamelin softly made her way to her and reached up to pull her down. It took time to snag Sylvia down, and Ms. Gamelin used all her weight to tug Sylvia down toward the road. The pike was clenched in the younger woman's hand. Ms. Gamelin understood why these creatures, why Grasshands, was so powerful. She couldn't stand to have her past so perfunctorily destroyed in front of her. She also couldn't abide the source of destruction being *made* of her past and memories.

Sylvia looked pale. She didn't look worse than when dug up. Ms. Gamelin patted her face and stroked her hair. She wouldn't wake.

Caterwauling arose from far away.

Fa fa fa fa

Sylvia opened her eyes. She sat up.

"How long was I buried this time?" she asked.

"You weren't. It ate you, though. I sang into the machete handle, it got hot, so I threw it at them as they attacked me."

Sylvia waited. "And?"

"And it was like a bomb, sort of. They unraveled."

Sylvia loved this. She was nodding her head.

"Of course they did."

She pushed herself up with the pike. While in the beginning the weapon had started off as a bumpy amalgam of personal objects, now it had smoothed itself into a twisted ebony shaft with an obsidian-like blade on the end. Ridged and ragged. Flint-knapped like an arrowhead.

"Albert, what was this called again?" she said.

But he didn't respond. He wasn't anywhere to be found.

Nor was he anytime to be found.

5.

About where the original tree stump was Sylvia located the stalled bones of a four bedroom, three bath. The concrete slab for the garage was punched through. The hole lead downward.

Albert.

"I knew he'd try to go straight for Deena," Sylvia said.

"Grasshands," Ms. Gamelin added.

Silence.

"You alright?"

"I feel like my brain is downloading a huge update."

The hole in the slab was depthless and quiet. Ms. Gamelin kicked a chunk of rubble into it. The oblivion ate it right up. They had to go in. They knew it. Albert went in, which meant they must follow. No question about it. Sylvia took a moment. She pictured a scenario where they dropped in and instantly were evaporated. The crusading adventurers were utterly disposed of in a trice. It was not a thought she relished.

"I could sit deciding on the lip of this hole forever," Ms. Gamelin said.

Sylvia agreed. Then she screwed up her face. *That statement.*

"What day is it?" Sylvia said.
"I don't know. Maybe Feb. 27?"
"When does the sun go down? Six something?"
"No, probably quarter after six. Maybe later."
"What time is it?"
Ms. Gamelin checked her cheap Casio watch. "7:02 in the p.m."
"Exactly. It's too late for the sun to be up still."
They both looked at the pinkish and purpled sky to the west.
"Nothing surprises anymore," Ms. Gamelin said.
"Wait until you see the moon." Sylvia smiled. She eased herself into the hole.
"What's that supposed to mean?"
"I'll tell you when I get back."
"Whoa, whoa, Sister Christian. I'm coming with."
"You have no weapon."
Ms. Gamelin straightened herself. "I can still sing."
Sylvia considered this.
She waved Ms. Gamelin down into the hole with her.

6.

They scrabbled down into a crumbling tunnel. Dark, unwelcoming. Absolutely massive. Just the place Sylvia and Ms. Gamelin wanted to find themselves. The smell was different down here. Aboveground smelled of ozone, drying pine needles, clarity. In the hole, it smelled of spoiled meat. The iron and copper tang of blood and raw butchered flesh. Brilliantly colored moss covered every visible surface. Maroon, turquoise, umber. It was a hallucinogenic underground cathedral.

As they struck deeper into the tunnel—large enough to accommodate Albert easily—the smell turned sinister toward a charred stench.

Wailing sounds crawled from around a sharp turn in the tunnel. The sound of two gods disrobing each other of their sanctified powers.

Sylvia handed Ms. Gamelin the salt cellar.

"Just so you're not empty-handed."

Ms. Gamelin scoffed. She tapped her watch. "I can still tell you the time. I have uses." She peeked at her wrist. She squinted. Then tapped the watch. "It's frozen." She tapped it again.

"It's digital. How can it be stuck?"

"Stuck on 7:02. To the second."

Sylvia had an intuition of why it did that but couldn't say why. The pike lit up. Then it flashed. Phosphenes drifted in their vision. Sylvia felt the pike vibrating in her hand like a caged animal sensing an opportunity to flee. Or to strike.

7.

Albert was entangled in a colossal bear hug with the motherfog.

The motherfog had swollen since Sylvia last saw it. It'd grown to nearly Albert's height. And it extended further back than she could see. The tunnel turned sharply dark just beyond it.

The motherfog thrashed in Albert's grip. He'd somehow gotten both arms wrapped around it and refused to let go. Like a surly pig.

Albert saw them from the corner of his eye. He yelled out, "I had enough time to grasp it. Now I can't move. If I let go, I'm dead."

The massive blades were thrown askew against the far tunnel wall. Worthless. All that brute weaponry now idle scrap.

Ms. Gamelin unscrewed the cap of the salt cellar. A shattering bolt of green light burst from her hands. It struck Albert and drove right through him to the motherfog. Nothing happened. Like trying to control a wildfire hose in a cartoon, Ms. Gamelin stepped forward by degrees to get purchase over it.

Albert howled in pain. The motherfog feverishly crowed in nine different pitches. Small whips of foggy matter wriggled and wobbled against Albert's arms. When it struck him, the matter formed into points and thorns. Sylvia could see they were lacerating his skin and burning him. Now there was no way he could be mistaken for a portrait of a Duke of Habsburg. He looked far from professorial. He was simply a gargantuan barbarian in mortal combat with some unknown subterranean evil. Something many librarians claim to know about, but in a different way than this.

"Cut it," Sylvia said.

Ms. Gamelin shoved the cap back on the salt cellar.

"Singing," Ms. Gamelin said. "It's worth it. We have to try."

Sylvia started. This time she sang high and deep from the diaphragm.

FA FA FA FA

Ms. Gamelin met her at the same pitch. The pike jumped in with a steady, but lower, sound. Sylvia felt proud of the pike. She wondered if the pike could feel it.

But like the salt cellar, nothing budged.

"Keep going," Albert said. He groaned with effort. His face flooded red with exhaustion, fear, and playfulness. "Keep going."

The motherfog turned livid. Then it went nearly un-visible. As if Albert was holding pure, empty space. The vision was uncanny and disturbing. But the color returned, and the visibility. The women kept singing. The motherfog recovered anyway.

The motherfog shoved Albert into the tunnel wall. It bucked up and down. Squelching, squealing. A sound fell out of it like thousands of books on their spines, their pages flipping in the air. Furiously flittering.

The sound was a cathedral full of a million panicky birds.

"Albert, how long can you hold it?" Sylvia said.

"How long do you need?"

"Long enough to get inside."

"No!" Ms. Gamelin said. She grabbed Sylvia's arm. "I got you out of that thing once. I can't do it again."

Sylvia faced her friend. She threw her the pike. Ms. Gamelin caught it. "You won't have to," she said.

Sylvia put her hair up in a tidy bun. She kissed Ms. Gamelin on the cheek. Ms. Gamelin smelled faintly of Chanel No. 5, which was impressive considering she'd almost drowned in the river yesterday.

"You'll know when to use it," Sylvia said.

"Oh, so now I'm in charge of the psycho-stick?"

"Never too late to be a mother. It naps between 2 and 5. Toodles."

Sylvia pivoted on her heel and ran. She cut in right between Albert and the motherfog. She slid underneath the misty mass like a high school baseball all-star on amphetamines. Above her was the flexing anus-mouth. Little effort was needed to get in. She punched her fist into it. The motherfog sucked her up inside. It was the worst form of transportation available in the universe. Hands down.

That horrible feeling of the musculature or alien physiology it was made of, passing over her face. Her warm living flesh and the clammy dead flesh of the motherfog touching. Mingling. Exchanging smells.

Sylvia opened her eyes and cleared them of mucus. She found herself in the same cramped room. The same Christmas string lights twinkled. The same brackish lamplight from below. And, across from her, the same mummified Deena head. Still mouldering, still falling apart. Still psoriatic patches of hair clinging, drooping.

Instead of the room shrinking, she felt it grow and stretch, stretching and expanding into an infinitely sized room. She'd be lost forever in such a place. Time would have no meaning down here and neither would space, apparently. Grasshands knew that's what she couldn't stand. Sylvia needed Deena. Her plan revolved around Deena's head. Sylvia leapt out of her seat and grabbed Deena's mummy by the wrists. It didn't move. Not at first.

But Sylvia felt the whole thing tug a bit. Try to separate from her. She pulled harder. Not too much. She didn't want to pull Deena's arms from the sockets. She'd be lost inside this nightmare forever, with no exit. Infinitely floating inside the motherfog's belly. *No thank you.*

Sylvia stared at the empty ocular orbits of Deena's head. Into the physical manifestation of Grasshands, the childhood manifestation of her own wonder and love of the world. Sylvia, with her truest voice, her most honest and best tone, began to sing. In gentle quarter notes. Like a lullaby to a tender baby.

fa fa fa fa

She was singing herself to sleep. That's what she told herself.

Just this one last time. Sing yourself to bed, Syl.

fa fa fa fa

The motherfog didn't react. Not at first. But then it rumbled. Stirred. It quaked. Sylvia kept her eyes shut. She didn't want to give anything away. She sensed the worry around her. It infiltrated her blood, her bile, her bones, her brain.

Deena's mummy twitched and crackled like a nervous fire. The Christmas string lights sputtered and popped. Sylvia worked her grip up the forearms, the biceps, onto the shoulders where her fingers sank into rotting flesh. She stepped off her mosschair and across the gaping divide of the absurdly expanding room and sat on the mummy's lap. She straddled Grasshands.

She moved her fingers behind the head. She forced it with all her strength into her face. The whole time she sang a lilting lovesong.

fa fa fa fa fa fa fa fa fa

Sylvia sang herself into the mouth of Grasshands. Like she was resuscitating it with one note, forever. Maybe it didn't know what Sylvia was doing. What she planned. Maybe it did know but didn't care. Or maybe it had a death wish. It's hard to say.

It did struggle, though.

Grasshands pushed a mossy tongue-shape back into Sylvia's mouth. Like a chthonic ball gag. It tried to drown her out, tried to choke her, cut her off. Sylvia bit the tongue off and spat it out. Even when she spat the rotten part, she sang the spitting.

Fah!

Sylvia felt the release. The giving up. The motherfog withered from the inside out. The room shrank again to a one-person sized cave. Then it vomited her out the anus-mouth. A human fecal discharge from the intestines of doom. She collapsed onto the floor of the tunnel.

She heard, then saw, Ms. Gamelin charging at the motherfog with a flaring pike. She was yelling. Albert clenched the motherfog. He looked like a dog biting a loaf of bread in the middle.

Sylvia rolled out from underneath. The motherfog was flailing now. It looked like a cuboid brain with the ganglia whipping and darting. Desperate in its death throes.

Ms. Gamelin plunged the pike into the bowels of the thing and Albert let go.

The motherfog peeled away like an onion drying in a desert. Each layer rapidly curling and desiccating into a dusty husk. The husks wisped into the air and broke into gray hapless confetti, which was then absorbed back into the dirt of the tunnel. Sylvia knew that this metaphysical flaying would reveal the Shrinking Room. And in time, it did. The rotting, molding bones of Deena McKay choreographically tumbled from the last exposure and formed a monstrous shape. Some ancient creature. Difficult to look at for all its unsymmetrical formation. But it began to dance. And sing.

It wanted to have the final word.

Build soil, Sylvia. Build soil, it said.

Build soil, dear. Build soil.

The skull, deep in this new creature, tried to wink. But the bone fractured and fell apart and the rest of the haphazard improvisational creature shambled into a pile of forgotten remains.

Uncontrollably, Sylvia retched onto the pile. She had nothing in her stomach but water. And some fries. It all came up. Her eyes watered with the effort. She sweat. And she peed herself a bit.

It was like her body was once and for all done with this shit. Time to expel all toxins.

When the pulsating of her stomach was over, she wept. She didn't know where to put her grief. And what was the grief for? Herself? Albert? Natalia? Deena? The city of Caldecott, which surely would be waking up right now from a nightmare of epic proportions. They would have no answers. They wouldn't even have the right questions.

"Syl, look," Ms. Gamelin said from behind. She'd laid the weapon down at her feet. "The pike told me to put it down. I heard it in my head."

The singing pike was still going at it, crooning, but at a low volume. It refused to give up, she thought. It finally had gotten the hang of this stuff, and liked it. Now it would be hard to shut the goddamn thing up. But it wasn't to be.

The pike's light dimmed, then extinguished. From tip to handle it reverted back to its original make up—Sylvia's private possessions.

"No!" she said. She crawled over to it. Maybe if she touched it, the pike would stop changing.

Photos of her mother, her workout bra, three Game Boy cartridges, a Hootie and the Blowfish CD, a bag of collectible quarters, a box of tampons.

These things I give you.

The pike was gone. In its place: stuff.

Dumb possessions from a lost life she didn't want to live anymore.

Albert's breathing brought her attention back to the tunnel. It was shallow and wet. Ms. Gamelin was up near his torso as he lay against the wall.

"He's punctured a lung, I think," Ms. Gamelin said.

"How do you know?" Sylvia said.

"I saw it on a hospital drama."

Sylvia said nothing.

"Also, I punctured my lung once at summer camp when I was a girl. That's exactly what I sounded like. I'll never forget that sound."

Albert shifted. He almost knocked the women over.

"I appreciate your concern, Clara. But no hospital would even be able to diagnose me, let alone treat me properly. I'd need some kind of megafauna veterinarian. Which, last I checked, doesn't exist."

"The Army has to have some people who're willing to work on you," Sylvia said.

"Thank you, but no thank you."

They all rested there for a minute before anyone spoke. It was Ms. Gamelin.

"Does anyone else feel safe yet?"

Albert shook his head. He could barely speak.

Sylvia looked like a lost girl in a wood. She wondered if all the tickle spiders were gone. And if they weren't...?

Sylvia said to Albert, "You're going to go back and rip the roof off your house, aren't you?"

"Indeed. I am."

"Tell her I'm sorry I couldn't do more."

"Pssh," he said. "I'll tell her something else."

"Plethora moon bench?"

He nodded and laughed. It pained him, so he stopped. He winced. "That's right. Plethora moon bench."

"But do you mean it?" Sylvia said.

Albert stood up with a great awkward effort. He cocked his head at her, holding his side. Like she'd asked him to do basic arithmetic.

"You only say it if you mean it. That was our deal. So of course."

He began to limp back up the tunnel.

Sylvia yelled after him. "Tell me one more thing about Aristotle!"

Albert stopped but didn't turn around. He was thinking.

"Aristotle was wrong," he said. "Drama isn't cathartic. It doesn't purge the public of pity and fear. It only makes them itchy for more. Narrative is a drug. But it's also the cure. That's why Plato got the willies. But it's also why he was a crybaby." He paused. "Figure it out already, Plato!"

She wiped blood and creatureshit from her face.

"See you at work tomorrow!" she said.

"Yes, ma'am."

And then he was loping around the corner. His shadow—shrinking, shrinking, gone.

8.

Sylvia felt paralyzed. For the first time in a long time, though, it was from indecision rather than Grasshands or tickle spiders. Pure philosophical quandary. She was stymied by personal choices.

All the moss that lined the tunnel shrank and dried as they stood there. Sylvia noticed that it didn't totally disappear. That bothered her. Not enough to say anything about it. The smell of charred meat still hung in her nostrils. There was a ureic tang on her lips. Ms. Gamelin sorted through the unformed pike's new state. She kicked over the box of tampons.

"I don't think I can go outside," Sylvia said, finally.

Ms. Gamelin came to her and took her hands in her own.

"What do you mean? You have to go outside. I'm certainly not staying in this cesspit. I have a shower to take. Wine to drink. Cheese to eat." She checked her Casio. "Then again, according to this plastic toy of a watch, time hasn't passed at all since we've been down here. It's still 7:02 in the PM. Lucky for us. The whole night is ahead."

"Yay," Sylvia said. Her emotions were vaporized. She needed a long sit down. To ponder. To vegetate.

"What's going on? Spill it."

"I don't know how I'm going to face any of the people in town who had one of those goddamn spiders in their mouths for hours or days. Or anyone who lost a loved one to them or the moss."

"That's not your fault. It's also not the right time to start whipping yourself. Plenty of time to do that back at my place."

"If there's anything there."

"I doubt those spindly bastards took my hot water pipes."

Sylvia laughed. She looked up. "I'm sorry you got in this with me."

"I'm not. Serious. It's better than work. Higher stakes. Weirder shit, yes. But definitely not boring. What's really going on, Sylvia? What are you actually afraid of, at the end of the day?"

"Going back to work. Not knowing how to operate in a world where all of this happened."

"Well, you might not have a job for a while. I don't know if that library is suitable for patrons. Moreover, people may have cooled on visiting the library for a while."

"Maybe."

"There's always catering…"

Ms. Gamelin walked to the pile of stuff and picked some of it up.

"Here. Tell me about this," she said. She picked up a Game Boy cartridge. "What's the story behind this?"

"My mom bought that for me. It was like the last thing she got me before she died. I hated computer games and consoles. But she thought I'd love it. That I *should* love it. That I'd be the cool girl who played video games and shit. Never happened. My mom played my Game Boy more than I did. I just watched her. She was good."

"That's rather sweet."

"It was. Now it's just plastic."

"Hey. That's cynical. That's my shtick." Ms. Gamelin collected all the stuff and wrapped it in the workout bra. "I want to know more about this junk. Let's take it back to my place and you can fill me in on your life, okay?"

Sylvia said that sounded fine with her. She felt better. Ms. Gamelin had a way of making her not worried or irritable. A sense of ease and pleasure arose. It truly felt like no time at all passed while at the same time it was as if they'd been there for hours and hours. Maybe longer.

9.

They trekked back up the tunnel to the hole in the concrete slab. When they stood directly under it, they were disoriented. Blazing daylight shot down over them. The sky through the hole was a pastel orange-pink-yellow.

Sylvia put her hands together like a step for Ms. Gamelin to launch herself up. When she got near the top, Sylvia waited for Ms. Gamelin to reach down to help her up. But she didn't.

"Hey, down here."

No answer.

Sylvia swung herself over and got the other hand. Then a leg. She swung her whole body up and rolled onto the concrete. She stared up at the sun in the orange sky. It was sweltering out. Insects buzzed. The air was thick. So thick it was hard to breathe. Like walking into a sauna and doing deep breathing exercises. Her eyes took a minute to adjust to all the light.

"Clara Gamelin, where the hell are you? What the hell is going on out here?"

Sylvia blocked the overhead light with a hand to her brow. Ms. Gamelin stood a few yards away. She stood in front of a ridiculously tall woman. What used to be called an Amazonian, Sylvia thought. She studied them in school. But she'd not returned to the tract housing. There was no wooden skeleton of a house. No driveway. No construction.

There was no Christmas tree farm, either. There were no trees in the usual sense. Nothing coniferous. More like vast, enormous tropical plants. Ferns, palms. Massive spiny lobes like steroidal aloe vera and bestial succulents.

The tall woman side-stepped Ms. Gamelin and stood in front of Sylvia. Sylvia got up. The Amazonian wore a chartreuse raincoat of some material. And there was an elaborate headgear that held a thin sheer veil over her face. It was opaque enough to block all detail and most major features. But Sylvia could make out eyes, a nose, the flickering of a lip.

The woman extended a hand outward, palm side down. When she spoke, it sounded like she was straining to pronounce the English, even though she didn't sound foreign.

"My name is Abbess Ute of the Sisterhood of Elem Soborink. Welcome home, Clara Gamelin. Welcome home, Sylvia Hix."

CHAPTER FIFTEEN

1.

ABBESS UTE DIDN'T waste time explaining. She gave the women cool water from beaten metal cups and had them rest under a shadeplant.

The abbess's speech broke from the awkward strain she put on it at first. It was like a high school Spanish student slowly talking with a native speaker. The nervousness dropped after a minute.

"You are Clara Gamelin and Sylvia Hix. You both entered into that hole with Albert, the Giant of Appalachia, some three hundred years ago."

Ms. Gamelin began to protest.

The abbess raised a hand. It wasn't rude, but it was firm. Ms. Gamelin recognized her power and kept shut. It was a power earned. She could sense that.

"You defeated the creature variously known as the Mother of Spiders, the Night of Red Pillars, Grasshands."

Sylvia's brain buzzed at the last word. She swatted a massive, winged bug that landed on her forearm. It looked like it had landing gear.

"Two hundred years ago, Albert the Giant emerged from that hole. He told our ancestors the story of what happened. Then he found his way to the range of mountains that used to be called Smoky. There he lived his last days, continuing to grow to sizes that were unsustainable for this world.

"Next, you two have just emerged. We were told you would follow the giant. But we didn't know when. We always have someone from the Sisterhood of Elem Soborink wait by the hole in case you ever came out." The abbess seemed both sad, prideful, and elated. "I've maybe spent half my life standing by this hole."

Sylvia realized the enormity of the situation and began to cry. The abbess's veil fluttered. Ms. Gamelin reached over.

"Syl."

"Albert never got to see Natalia."

The reality of that also struck Ms. Gamelin. She was too deep in a state of shock to emote, though.

The abbess continued. "That is correct, Ms. Hix. Sadly, the Giant of Appalachia, may he rest in space, did not ever see his wife. She had been long dead when he emerged. Impossible."

Sylvia snorted at this last statement.

"Why don't we table that last word, huh, sister?"

The Abbess didn't register the sarcasm.

"We can locate the final resting place of the giant's wife, Natalia. The Sisterhood has saved many personal records across Caldecott, Indiana, and the general Midwestern Delta Region. A part of Albert is buried in a mausoleum on the site of the main library branch, if you should care to see it." She poised her body as if she was under review by Sylvia and Ms. Gamelin. "The branch will not break," she said.

Sylvia placed a hand over her mouth. "I want to see the library." She sipped her water. "Clara, what's your watch say now?"

"7:26 in the PM."

2.

Abbess Ute was conscientious of Sylvia and Ms. Gamelin's problem. The head gear and the veil seemed too much in the humidity, Sylvia thought. But that was the least of it.

"I've spoken too much now. I'll give you a moment. Would you care to ask questions?"

"So, when we went into that hole, we zoomed forward in time?"

"You know the answer to that, Clara," Sylvia said.

"Shut up. Miss, is this the future?"

Abbess Ute thought about it. Maybe it was a trick question? "It is. To you."

"And the year?" Sylvia said.

"The year is 2319."

"Fucking hell. How are we going to live, Abby?"

"That is not my nam—"

"How are we going to live?" Ms. Gamelin said, repeating the urgency.

"We were thoroughly prepared for your arrival by the Giant of Appalachia. Because of him, we have your shelter and amenities ready."

"Two-hundred-year-old amenities."

"Not true," Abbess Ute said. "Less than one hundred. Still, they are pleasant. You will be comfortable."

"Is there anything else in the world like what we just got done destroying down there?"

"There has never yet been anything as bad as what Clara Gamelin and Sylvia Hix destroyed on February 27, 2019. But aristotlemoss still grows in our areas. Bad moss. We cut back the moss in annual rituals. Here it is known as *sylving*."

"Oh, that's cute," Ms. Gamelin said.

"*Aristotlemoss*," Sylvia said.

Abbess Ute explained that when Albert emerged, he was reported to have eaten a reserved patch of moss he'd kept on him and had placed on the *Collected Works of Aristotle*. It turned out that he knew less about the philosopher than he thought. This caused a significant depression in him. Sylvia couldn't imagine that lasted very long.

"I got a question for you, sister," Ms. Gamelin said.

"Proceed."

"Is everyone else as humorless as you? Is the future unfunny? Do we have to wear those creepy veils? Are there flying cars?"

Abbess Ute paused.

Sylvia knew she could handle the future if Clara was there.

"If I am stiff and formal, it is because Clara Gamelin and Sylvia Hix are two of the most important figures in our thought, aside from the Giant of Appalachia. The future—now—is funny. Those who wear the veils do so out of respect for our fellow sisters. And yes, there are a few flying cars."

Neither of them could tell if the last part was a joke. Sylvia thought she could see an outline of a smirk behind the veil. They were offered more water. Time to rest.

The abbess cut off the question & answer session. The further away from the hole they came out of the better. Better that they made themselves comfortable and clean. Then they could have time to adjust and collect their thoughts.

Abbess Ute stood and walked into the swampland on a raised trail made of wooden planks.

All Sylvia could think of was how different any world she walked into was going to be. How foreign. She thought of what was 300 years before her leap. 2019 back to 1719. She knew that *Robinson Crusoe* was published that year. One of her favorite books as a girl. She read it in sixth-grade study hall. A man stranded on an island, forced to survive. She was stranded. But what was the island? The island was the future.

More bugs swarmed her for sweat and blood. They didn't pester the abbess. Ms. Gamelin swore as they tramped along the trail.

Looking up, Sylvia saw the moon. Even in daylight it was painted with patches, dark permanent areas—some brightly lit with electricity. She assumed it was where civilization had landed, started, and thrived. She'd always been staring at the moon of the future.

They crested a small hill just bursting with gorgeous, booming ferns. On the other side was the community. Concentric circles of earthen domes faced each other. In the center was a massive oven and firepit. The Abbess waited for them to catch up. She pointed toward the far side. "Those two with the yellow doors? Those are yours."

Theirs were the only two homes with yellow doors.

3.

Sylvia and Ms. Gamelin did the only thing they could do. They assimilated. Slowly. They joined the Sisterhood of Elem Soborink, which turned out wasn't a religious thing. They were humanists and spent most of their time helping the poor in the surrounding areas. Sylvia and Ms. Gamelin did not take the veil. They *did* take the smart chartreuse raincoats, though.

As was expected, much was made of their return. A large community dinner was held. Nothing extravagant. Simply a celebration of other humans. Everyone respected their distance. Some sidled up to shake hands or express their appreciation for what they did in what they called the Sanctuary. Otherwise known as, a hole in the ground.

Children flocked to look at them. The children were all uniformly pleasant looking and polite. To a shocking degree. Many of them had dark hair and olive skin. There was the occasional lighter-skinned person like them, but not many like themselves were found.

They spent a few days just living. Catching up. Putting down. Grieving. Abbess Ute said it would be normal. The Giant of Appalachia also grieved for his past.

Sylvia walked around the shifting geography of what used to be Caldecott, to see what still existed, if anything, of her past. She desired a reckoning. A totaling of her past into the present. Her slingshotting into the future wasn't a treasure to behold, she felt, but a stark brand of punishment. There was no escape. No relief. Only more pressure and a form of torture: the inability to recognize anything. And Albert, and now Ms. Gamelin also suffered the same torture. Almost every meaningful place from her past was either destroyed, bulldozed, grown over with invasive vines, burned down, or badly ruined. Her apartment building still stood, but the insides were uninhabitable. The area known as the Red Pillars didn't look the same at all. A vast earthen dome, much larger than any in the living area, was now there. A small hand-painted sign in meticulous script stated that every material object that had been a tickle spider was buried under this ground. It was both a gravesite and a memorial. Reviled and sacred all at once. The pillars were still visible and still remotely reddish. She placed a hand on one. The light wasn't different here. There was no terror, no fear. Just a concrete pillar. Nothing about the world now gave her a feeling of home, of Caldecott, of Indiana. She could've been in a South American jungle for all she knew. As if she was dreading it—because she was, she thought—she entered what was left of the library. Which was surprisingly more than she'd expected. Most of the outer walls held up, though nearly all the books were gone. Where to, she had no clue. Here she had some odd comfort. Here the callus of the future wore off and she had to deal with the raw flesh of the past. She sat down near where she used to check in materials and leaned against a box. The box skidded back and through a rotten canvas tarp down a hidden hole. The stairs leading to the basement. Sylvia shook her head. Of course. To travel all this way just to return to hell? No thanks. But she could see that the first floor had been punctured through years past and a giant shaft of afternoon light illumined the basement. That changed things. Downstairs to the right was a pile of rubble, but to the left was a giant concrete tomb that hadn't been there 300 years before. She knew immediately what it was. Albert's resting place. Or part of him, anyway. A small space between Albert's mausoleum and the wall was where she and Ms. Gamelin had just (had long ago) retrieved the D. H. Lawrence. She squeezed past Albert. "Excuse me," she said. Back in this cut-off part of the overflow stacks were still-intact books. Scattered and in various piles, the shelves long collapsed. Someone had found this trove and was attempting to organize. Someone with librarian instincts for order and taxonomy. It broke her heart. She tried not to grin at this. One pile of books was poetry. The Lawrence long gone, obviously. But Emily Dickinson was there. Sylvia had always found Dickinson intolerable. Insular, claustrophobic, self-involved. So she couldn't say why she picked up her complete poetry.

> *One need not be a Chamber – to be Haunted –*
> *One need not be a House –*
> *The Brain has Corridors – surpassing*
> *Material Place –*

Sylvia shut the book as if the poem was reading her. She pressed the book to her chest like a bomb. If she dropped it, she knew it would explode. She carefully exited the secret book room and slumped against Albert's mausoleum in the day's dying light. She finished the poem. Then another and another. She'd reconsider Dickinson; she'd take the book with her. It was her first new possession in the new world. Sylvia Hix owned precisely one thing. Maybe she'd be able to find a way to live her life as a poem. Barring that, she'd keep them close.

When a few weeks settled, the abbess asked to speak with Sylvia and Ms. Gamelin.

"Again, we welcome your arrival and feel lucky to be here with you. Still, everyone in our community must have a position. We would like to know what you'd want to do here. With us."

The abbess sat at Sylvia's table. She'd brewed water for black tea., which they could now grow abundantly in the American Midwest.

Ms. Gamelin breathed deeply. "My skills were mostly administrative. I ran the library."

Abbess Ute nodded. In one sign of growing familiarity, the abbess had her legs crossed.

"We still have many historical records to sort and organize. I am not wholly pleased with the efforts my people have given. Would you like to start there?"

Ms. Gamelin accepted.

"And you, Sylvia?"

Sylvia thought. She closed her eyes and pictured all those kids. How could she help the children? What could she offer? What did she look like to them? Probably like a settler of the American colonies would to her. Strolling into her classroom, antique and distant.

"Living history," Sylvia said. "I'd like to teach the children about my time. And also let them teach me about this time."

Now Sylvia knew the abbess was smiling. She didn't need to see through the veil.

A historian from her own time. "A wonderful idea."

Sylvia visited Albert's mausoleum at the old library a few times a week. She talked to him. Gave him news. Read to him. Sylvia eventually asked Abbess Ute if they could have someone etch the phrase *The branch will not break* onto a stone and place it nearby. The abbess saw to it immediately. Sylvia began to sit on that rock when she spoke to Albert.

4.

Months crawled by. Comfort grew around them like loving limbs. Living in a swampy Midwestern share-and-share-alike community did them good. But where Sylvia predicted Ms. Gamelin would thrive—she didn't. She seemed to stay static.

Ms. Gamelin was distracted. She didn't follow conversations. She missed meetings or appointments. She would disappear in the midst of people. Or get suspicious around Sylvia and clam up. For a week, Ms. Gamelin didn't let Sylvia into her home. She said it was messy. Or that she had a cockroach problem. (Everyone had cockroaches. That was just part of the hot, sweaty future.)

It got to the point that Sylvia went to Abbess Ute to see if there was anything she could do.

"I'll look into it," was all the abbess said.

But the abbess did not look into it. She didn't do anything so far as Sylvia could tell. Sylvia began to worry. She woke up in a sweat, in a panic. On nights like that, when the insects shrieked and screamed through the night, and the wind was humid but sweet with woodsmoke, Sylvia opened her front door. She had a clear view of the fire that always burned in the center of the community.

In the dark, the stars were much more prominent. Salt spilled on velvet. (The sound of the word *salt* in her mind's voice made her cringe and recoil. She wondered how her mother knew how to keep things in and keep things out with salt. Sylvia knew she herself was kept out of her old life and boarded up in this new future.) Also up there was the human-settled moon. She lost herself in trying to focus on the residential glowing that existed there now. The life and work that went on up there. And to think how crazy she was for seeing that dark speck move across it. She was peering into that long-desired future she wanted, and now possessed fully.

She gave a glance to her friend's home. The yellow door was closed. The windows drawn. The only connection to her first and true world, slowly drifting away.

Nights like those, she never went back to sleep. She only lay on a jute rug next to her bed and stared at the ceiling, trying not to think.

5.

A week later, Sylvia was awakened by soft knocking at her door. It was Ms. Gamelin. She looked particularly clear-eyed and intense, as if a long and directive study of an arcane secret had finally reached its end. She'd cut her hair sometime in the past two days. And she seemed more youthful than ever. Sylvia knew what that was all about—lack of an office job.

"Clara, what's going on? What time is it?"

"7:02 in the PM."

That joke never got old.

Ms. Gamelin didn't ask to come in, and Sylvia didn't offer. They stood there at the threshold for a moment.

"Abbess Ute has requested that we leave with a group of men and women at dawn. There've been reports of an aristotlemoss overgrowth and laughter and spider-like creatures crawling into dog and cat mouths. Somewhere further down the Delta. They're saying it's a week's boat ride. Two weeks if we walk it."

Sylvia's heart raced. Her palms chilled. Fleeing to the future didn't change anything, did it? Shame on her, she thought, for thinking that safety existed in any permanent way.

"Do you want to go?" Ms. Gamelin said.

Sylvia stood there in her linen top and shorts. Barefoot. She needed to brush her teeth. She needed to re-pad her walking shoes. Bring tea. Her small but growing collection of knives.

"Sylvia? Yes or no?"

"Yes, of course. I'll go. Just let me get some things."

Ms. Gamelin reached in and took Sylvia's hand. Sylvia stopped.

From the side of the door, hidden, Ms. Gamelin brought out a pike. She offered it to Sylvia.

Sylvia was stunned. She took it into her hands. It was a resonant dark wood with a manic swirling grain. The blade was deeply inset into the shaft. It was longer than the old pike's blade, and curved. Hemp rope and a metal aglet kept it firmly in place.

"Where did you get this, Clara?"

"I had it made. I helped a bit. Took me a long damn time."

Sylvia felt the shell of the past few weeks and months crack and break apart.

"You thought I was being weird," Ms. Gamelin said.

"I thought you were going crazy or avoiding me. I thought—I don't know what I thought. Not this."

She hugged Ms. Gamelin. She hugged her a long time.

"And what about you? Nothing for you?"

"Don't be stupid, girly."

Ms. Gamelin went into her home and brought back a new machete.

No one told Sylvia that best friends first appear as monsters. Because now, right now it was technically years later—all those many, many far-flung years later—and Sylvia thought back to the spider she ate in the wood. She wondered if that was the start. The start of everything her life would become. Yes, it probably was. But so much had to be lived through that didn't add up or point toward now. She'd welcomed those oddities, those devastations, into her life. She would continue to welcome new oddities and new devastations into her life. She would try to reckon. She would try to cope.

Later that morning, a group of thirty or so people split up into three longboats and drifted downstream. Abbess Ute sat at the head of Sylvia's boat, quietly directing the ship. Her veil flowed in the breeze. Ms. Gamelin stepped into a different boat, shaking hands and trading names.

Sylvia told the women around her about the song she sang with her pike. How it worked. What had happened. Sylvia wondered if it would work with her new pike.

The abbess stopped her. That large hand of hers. The long fingers. Polite but firm.

"The Sisterhood of Elem Soborink tried that song, once. It doesn't work anymore," she said. "Besides, that was an old song, Sylvia Hix. Long dead. These people wrote a new one. A better one. They've written many. But theirs is the only one that works."

Sylvia asked to learn it. They taught it to her as they moved downstream.

She picked it up on the first pass.

It was beautiful. It was terrifying.

THE END

ACKNOWLEDGMENTS

I wrote this book after reading Neil Gaiman's *The Ocean at the End of the Lane*. I imagine that many horror writers owe something to him in some form. But that novel, in particular, seeded the core of this story. If you happen to know Neil, please give him a copy of this book in thanks. Unless I do it first.

The University City Library in University City, MO was the library I had in my head the whole time I was writing this. Some of the best hours in my life were spent reading and working there as a page. And the people who worked there are unforgettable.

Hat tip to early readers Laurel Hightower, Joe Koch, Michael Tichy, Dan Chaon, and Gordon B. White.

Christian Kiefer is literally the only person I've met who does what he says he'll do. XO, brother.

Richard Mirabella has encouraged this novel for years. As has Mike Bezemek.

Scarlett R. Algee put up with my emails.

And Ian Bonaparte helped shape the bones early on.

Thank you.

ABOUT THE AUTHOR

Kyle Winkler lives in Ohio with his family. Originally from southwest Indiana, he's lived all over the Midwest. He's the author of the cosmic horror novella *The Nothing That Is,* the weird story collection *OH PAIN*, and the novel *Boris Says the Words.* He still has his first library card from when he was seven years old. He's everywhere online as @bleakhousing.

Printed in the USA
CPSIA information can be obtained
at www.ICGtesting.com
LVHW022000300624
784334LV00005B/586